Boring, predictable, beige

Those words described her car, but they could just as easily describe her life, Eleanor Perkins thought as she inserted her key into her sedate, four-door sedan. For a moment she imagined a snappy red sports car in place of the sedan. She'd get behind the wheel, shake out the pins confining her hair in a bun, lower the top and roar through the streets, letting the wind play havoc with her locks.

As she turned the key, she heard a rustling in the bushes. Her heart leaped into her throat, and she froze. Then she rolled her eyes. "Don't be an idiot."

"You're not an idiot," a voice said in her ear. "I saw you hesitate before you walked over here. You should have paid attention to your instincts."

She jerked her head around. A man was standing far too close. He raised a gun slowly.

"What do you want?" *Stupid question. What do you think he wants?* "I'm not getting in the car. All the self-defense courses say—never get into a car."

If she hadn't been so terrified, she would have sworn a tiny grin flickered across his mouth. For just a fraction of a second his eyes twinkled. Then they hardened. "I won't hurt you as long as you do what I say. I need to get out of here and I need to do it now."

There was no way past him. *Be careful what you wish for,* she said silently. Right now she'd give anything to get back her boring life.

Dear Reader,

I've always loved stories that explore what happens when two people who seem to be polar opposites are thrown together. Mix in a series of stressful, even dangerous events, and those people are forced to face truths about themselves that may not always be comfortable or welcome. In *Two on the Run*, I had great fun making trouble for Michael and Ellie, then waiting to see how they handled it.

I hope you enjoy watching Ellie transform herself from a quiet, stuck-in-a-rut librarian into a confident woman who's not afraid to go after what she wants, and Michael change from a loner who refuses to trust anyone to a man completely in love with Ellie. When I finished *Two on the Run*, I wrote "The End" knowing that these two people had forged a bond that was strong enough to withstand any challenge. Michael and Ellie were a perfect match, and they would be together forever.

I love to hear from readers! You can e-mail me at margaretwatson1004@hotmail.com or visit my Web site, www.margaretwatson.com.

Sincerely,

Margaret Watson

Two on the Run
Margaret Watson

HARLEQUIN®

TORONTO • NEW YORK • LONDON
AMSTERDAM • PARIS • SYDNEY • HAMBURG
STOCKHOLM • ATHENS • TOKYO • MILAN • MADRID
PRAGUE • WARSAW • BUDAPEST • AUCKLAND

ISBN 0-373-71205-7

TWO ON THE RUN

Copyright © 2004 by Margaret Watson.

This edition published by arrangement with Harlequin Books S.A.

® and TM are trademarks of the publisher. Trademarks indicated with
® are registered in the United States Patent and Trademark Office, the
Canadian Trade Marks Office and in other countries.

www.eHarlequin.com

Printed in U.S.A.

For Bill. They're always for Bill.

CHAPTER ONE

AS SHE LOCKED THE DOOR of the Midland, Illinois, public library and stepped into the evening heat of the parking lot, Eleanor Perkins realized that once again she was the last to leave. All her colleagues had left long ago. But then, she told herself, they all had someone waiting for them at home. The only thing she had to look forward to was a quick dinner and the romance novel she'd begun reading the night before.

Clouds drifted across the moon, deepening the shadows that surrounded her car. A chill danced across her skin and slowed her steps, but she gave herself an impatient shake. "For heaven's sake, don't be a goose," she said out loud. "This is the library. What could happen here?"

Holding her keys firmly in her hand, she headed for her car, a sedate, four-door sedan. It was just like the rest of her life, she thought suddenly. Boring, predictable and beige. Far too beige.

For a moment she imagined a snappy red sports car in place of the sedan. She would get behind the wheel, shake out the pins confining her hair in a prim bun, lower the convertible top and roar through the streets of Midland, letting the wind comb wild fingers through her locks.

She shook her head. It would take more than a sports car to change her life. It would take a miracle. And she'd never believed in them.

As she inserted the key into the lock, she heard a rustling in the bushes beyond the car. Her heart leaped into her throat and she froze. Then she rolled her eyes. "Don't be an idiot."

"You're not an idiot," a voice said in her ear. "I saw you hesitate before you walked over here. You should have paid attention to your instincts."

She jerked her head around. A man was standing far too close to her. He crowded her against the door, and she opened her mouth to scream.

"Don't do that," he said in a low voice. Slowly he raised a gun. "Come around to the other side, and don't make any sudden moves."

"What do you want?" *Stupid question. What do you think he wants?*

"I want you to get in. Then I'm going to get in. And then we're going to drive away."

She stared at the gun in his hand. Moonlight glinted off the dark metal, making it appear huge and deadly. A spasm of fear shot through her, but she managed to shake her head. "I'm not getting into the car with you. That's what all the self-defense classes say— never get into a car."

Her heart beat frantically against her chest and her legs wobbled like soft Jell-O. But she forced herself to meet his eyes. "So you might as well shoot me right here."

If she hadn't been so terrified, she would have sworn a tiny grin flickered across his mouth. For a fraction of a second his eyes twinkled with humor, then they hardened again. "I don't have time to discuss your options. I don't want to hurt you," he said. "I *won't* hurt you as long as you do as I say. I need to get out of here, and I need to do it now. Move!"

She threw the keys toward him. "Take the car. Go wherever you need to. You don't have to take me with you."

He caught the keys without taking his eyes off her. Slowly he shook his head. "And let you call the police as soon as I'm out of sight? I don't think so."

"I won't call them. I promise."

"Right. And I bet you'd tell me that the check was in the mail, too." He froze for a moment as if listening to something, and she heard the distant wail of a police siren. Then he clenched his jaw and grabbed her arm. "Let's go. And we're going together."

He pulled her around to the other side of the car and she grabbed at the antenna, trying to prevent him from forcing her into the vehicle. Her purse smashed against the taillight and pieces of plastic spattered onto the asphalt. Her attacker peeled her hands away from the antenna and pushed her into the seat. She twisted to face him and managed to kick him in the thigh. He stiffened, sucking in his breath as if she'd hurt him.

Yes! She tried to lunge out the door.

He raised the gun again.

"Move over into the driver's seat."

His dark eyes were flat and cold, hard as granite. Any trace of humanity, including that hint of a smile, had disappeared from his expression. All that was left was cold resolve. And the gun that was now pointing steadily at her.

There was no way past him. And looking at his shadowed face, so hard and bleak, she had no doubt he would use the gun. "All right."

Watching him carefully, waiting for any momentary advantage, she slid onto the driver's seat and tensed as he eased himself into the car. He winced as he pulled the door shut behind him, then turned to point the gun at her again.

"Get going."

Her hands shook so badly that it took two tries before the engine turned over. Finally she looked at him. "Where do you want me to go?"

"Start driving west. I'll tell you where to turn." He shifted in the seat so he was facing her. "And don't speed or run any red lights or flash your headlights." His voice was icy and pitiless. "Don't pull any of those tricks they taught you in your self-defense class. I know every one of them."

"Can I ask where you're taking me?"

"You can ask anything you want. That doesn't mean I'll answer."

She looked down at the gas gauge. "I hope you're not planning on going too far, then."

"Why?" He leaned toward her.

She nodded toward the gauge, where the needle was hovering close to the large red *E*. "Because I'm almost out of gas."

She heard him swear under his breath, a short, ugly word.

"Don't you know you're supposed to fill your tank when it's three-quarters empty?"

"Sorry. If I had known I was going to be carjacked, I would have stopped to fill up on my way to work," she snapped.

Too late, she realized she'd let fear and temper get the better of her. She waited for him to explode in anger, to shove the gun into her side and tell her to shut up. To her surprise, instead of snarling at her he leaned back in his seat, and she saw that half grin hovering around the corners of his mouth again.

"You've got a mouth on you, don't you?"

It was the last response she had expected. But it was good, she told herself as she struggled to subdue her fear. She could bond with him. Wasn't a criminal less likely to harm a victim he'd bonded with?

"I'm a children's librarian," she told him primly. "I know the value of being firm. Children respond well to firmness."

She could have sworn he smothered a chuckle. "I'll keep that in mind."

She would remember that chuckle, she promised herself fiercely. Just as she would remember that glint of humor in his eyes. She would remember everything about him, from his hard, angular face to the breadth of his shoulders beneath his shirt to the lean, sinewy length of him.

And she'd identify him to the police when she got away from him. Her eyes skipped over him again. His dark hair was a little too long, and it looked as if he'd run his fingers through it several times tonight. He was a head taller than she was, which would make him a little over six feet. She thought his eyes were dark blue, but she couldn't be sure. And his face was imprinted onto her memory. That combination of toughness with a hint of tenderness would be hard to forget.

She would have no trouble identifying him in a mug shot.

The thought comforted her as she drove. Taut silence filled the car. Tension vibrated from her captor, sucking up the air and making her hands sweat. Energy poured from his body in waves as he alternated his gaze between her and the buildings flashing past the window. But at least he wasn't looming over her anymore. Although he kept the gun pointed at her, he leaned against the seat.

"Turn here," he said abruptly, gesturing with the weapon.

She obediently turned to the right, onto a street that wasn't nearly as well-lit. They were on the west side of Midland now, in a run-down industrial area. Empty buildings and cold smokestacks were all that remained of the once-thriving factories that had built the city. Now the area was as deserted and spooky as a ghost town. There wasn't a soul in sight to help her.

Even the derelicts who lived in this part of Midland knew better than to roam the streets after dark. Fear trembled through her again. What did he want in this part of town?

"I'm not going to hurt you," he repeated. He must have sensed her fear. "I need to get something before we leave."

"What do you mean, 'we'? I'm not going anywhere." She tried to sound confident, but she couldn't stop the quaver in her voice.

"Yes, you are." His glance flickered over their dreary surroundings once more. "This isn't a pleasure outing."

"Why do you have to take me with you? You just need the car."

"Like I said, I can't take the chance that you'll call the police." His voice had gone hard again.

"Then drop me off here. By the time I get to a phone, you'll be long gone."

"You think I'd leave you in this part of town?" His voice was incredulous. "Do you know how dangerous it is around here at this time of night?"

She stared at him, disbelieving. "Yeah, there are all kinds of bad things that could happen to me. A man with a gun might even try to carjack me."

"You never know." His voice held the suggestion of another chuckle.

They drove past more abandoned buildings, and he instructed her to turn a few times. After she made the last turn, they spotted a police car coming toward them. As it got closer, she felt his tension building, and he slid low in the seat. "Be careful," he warned in a low voice. "I'm watching you, and trust me, I've got nothing to lose." To emphasize his words, he prodded her with the gun.

Her hands trembled on the steering wheel, but she didn't flick on her high beams or stamp on the gas. She felt his gaze boring into her, felt the threatening presence of the gun. When the police car cruised slowly past, she looked in the rearview mirror. The officer hadn't even spared a glance back at her car.

"Has it gone yet?" he asked.

"It just turned a corner."

"You'd better be telling me the truth."

"Or what? You'll shoot me?" She wasn't sure how she managed to keep her voice calm.

He ignored her and turned to look over the seat. When he was satisfied that the squad car was out of sight, he sat up straight again. "Turn left here."

The maneuver would take them in the opposite direction from the cruiser. Reluctantly she turned and headed down another grim, dark street.

"Why me?" she asked. "Why did you take me?"

"Because you were there. And you were alone."

"My husband is expecting me home. What if he calls the police and tells them I'm missing?" she bluffed. "They'll be looking for this car very soon."

"Good try, but you're not married."

"How do you know?" She moved her left hand into the shadows to hide the fact that she wasn't wearing a ring.

"First of all, you're not wearing a wedding band. I looked before I grabbed you."

"That doesn't mean anything. Lots of married people don't wear rings."

"Maybe. But if you were hurrying to get home to your husband, why did you stay at the library an hour after it closed? There's no one waiting for you at home, not even a date. If there was, you wouldn't have stayed so late at work on a Friday night. I don't figure anyone is calling the police to report you missing tonight."

His words stung. Even a carjacker, a lowly criminal, knew how empty her life was. Was she so mousy, so plain and forgettable that a complete stranger knew no one would be waiting for her? "I guess you'll be surprised when the police stop this car, then."

"I guess I will be." His tone was mild, and she could tell he didn't believe her.

Her hands tightened on the steering wheel again, but this time with anger. She'd show him, by God. She'd get away from him and call the police, and the next time she saw him would be in a line-up at the police station.

"Stop here," he said, interrupting her fantasy.

She pulled over to the curb but didn't turn off the engine. She would wait for him to get out of the car, then she'd drive away.

"Turn off the engine," he said, steel in his voice. "And give me the keys."

She hesitated for a moment, but after glancing at the gun, twisted the key until the engine stopped.

Then she yanked it out of the column and threw it in his direction.

"What's your name?" he asked in a low voice.

"What difference does it make?" She turned to give him a defiant stare, and was startled when she saw understanding in his eyes.

"Look," he said, "if there were any other way of doing it, I wouldn't have grabbed you. But I had no choice. I want to know your name so I know what to call you. If I need to give you instructions, I don't want to have to yell 'Hey you.'"

"It's Eleanor," she finally said, her voice clipped. "Eleanor Perkins."

"Thanks, Eleanor. Now let's go."

"Wait a minute. What's your name? Or am I just supposed to call you 'scumbag'?"

He shook his head. "That's good, Eleanor. That's very good. But I hope you don't talk to those kids at the library that way. A mouth like that, you might scare them." To her surprise, a tiny grin flashed across his mouth, then disappeared. "You can call me Michael."

He pulled her out the door on the passenger side and eased the door closed behind her. She looked up to see that they were standing in front of another abandoned building.

Like the others, this one was completely dark and obviously empty. The thought of walking into that darkness made her shake so badly she could hardly stand.

"I'm not going in there."

"I don't remember giving you a choice. And we're sure as hell not going to stand on the street and discuss it," he said. "I need to fetch what I came for and get out of here."

He gripped her arm more tightly and started moving toward the building. The door hung crookedly on broken hinges and she stared in horror at the darkness beyond it. The impenetrable blackness shimmered as if alive.

Fear pressed down on her, crushing her chest. Her vision grayed and her head spun. Oblivious to his hands holding her, she turned and stumbled away from the door. "I'll wait in the car," she said, her voice high and thin.

He snorted. "Forget it. I may be a scumbag, but I'm not a stupid scumbag."

When he tugged on her arm, she wrenched away from him and ran blindly down the street. She had no idea where she was going and didn't care. She had to get away from the darkness.

It took only a few moments for him to catch her. He grabbed her upper arms and held on tightly, the calluses on his palms grazing her skin. "What the hell's the matter with you?" he asked, his voice a low snarl. "I told you I wasn't going to hurt you."

She couldn't answer. As he pulled her closer to the door, she struggled frantically against his grasp, lashing out blindly with her fists and feet.

"Hey, take it easy," he said. His grip gentled and confusion replaced the anger in his voice. "What's going on?"

When she continued to struggle, he wrapped his arms around her, pinning her against his body and immobilizing her hands. "Stop it, Eleanor. Listen to me! I'm not going to hurt you!"

She tried to push him away, but his body was solid and hard against her back, a wall of muscle and determination.

When she continued to fight, he merely tightened his hold on her. Finally, when she was squeezed intimately against him and suddenly very aware of every ridge and contour of his body, she stopped struggling.

The heavy summer air swirled around her, making her conscious of the heat radiating from Michael's body. His pungent male scent and the hardness of his lean muscles surrounded her. Sudden, acute awareness of his masculinity flooded her. The sensation was as uncomfortable and unwelcome as her previous terror.

"You can let me go now," she muttered.

"Not until you tell me what the hell is wrong with you."

She jerked free of his grasp, telling herself the unexpected feeling was just nerves. "You mean other than the fact that I've been kidnapped and manhandled?"

"Yeah. Other than that." He held her gaze steadily.

"I'm afraid of the dark, all right? Are you happy now?" she said, ashamed to admit to her childish fear. But she couldn't control it. As she stared at the

MARGARET WATSON   19

darkness, memories crowded in around her, enveloping her in a smothering blanket of terror.

"Damn it!" He let loose a string of curses in a low voice. "You can mouth off to a desperate man with a gun, but you can't walk into a dark building?"

"No."

He swore again, then sighed and ran his free hand through his hair. "Why did I have to pick a neurotic woman who's afraid of the dark?"

"I didn't ask you to pick me," she retorted, feeling her panic ease since he wasn't dragging her toward the door of the building.

"Yeah, well, I made a mistake," he muttered. "But there's nothing I can do about it now. You're just going to have to suck it up and come with me. We won't be in there for very long."

Before she could refuse, he'd grabbed her arm again and dragged her through the door into the inky blackness.

Easing the door shut, he stepped nearer to her. "I'm right here," he said in a low voice. "Stay close to me and you'll be fine. Here, take my hand."

Her heart pounded so loudly in her ears that she hardly heard him. But his hand brushed hers and she grabbed for it without thinking. She needed contact, needed to know she wasn't alone. His fingers twined with hers, and he held her hand in a firm but oddly gentle grasp. To stop her hand from shaking, she pressed her palm against his. He hesitated for a moment, then tightened his grasp. Her fear eased slightly.

"All right now?"

His words echoed loudly in the darkness and shattered the fragile spell between them. Once again she was trapped in a dark place with a man aiming a gun at her. Eleanor swallowed and tried to focus on the weak light filtering through the broken windows. "I'm fine," she lied.

"Then let's go. I have a flashlight close by. But you're going to have to take a few steps with me."

She tried to banish the fear and will her legs to move. It wasn't completely black inside the building, she told herself. After a moment, her eyes began adjusting, and she could make out ghostly shapes in front of her.

"That's the old shelving," Michael said in a low voice, as if he could read her mind. "This used to be a factory. It's been empty for several years."

"Why are we here?" she asked, forcing the words through chattering teeth. She wasn't sure which made her more afraid, the darkness or the possible reasons they were in this empty building.

"I told you, I have to get something." He stopped moving and turned to her. The whites of his eyes gleamed, his face nothing more than a shadow. "I meant it when I said I don't intend to hurt you. I know what you're thinking, but that's not why we're in this building."

"What do you have to get?" She didn't believe him, she told herself flatly. What could there possibly be in this empty building?

"You don't have to know that." He continued to watch her. "Can you keep moving?"

Somehow she nodded. "Yes." She couldn't bear to think about the alternative, which was standing still and listening to the blood thundering through her veins.

"Good." He gave her hand a squeeze. "I knew you were tough, Eleanor."

Her heart jumped in her chest with an odd flutter of pride. The next moment she told herself not to be an idiot. What did she care about words of praise from a carjacker? All she cared about was getting away from him as soon as possible.

Gathering her wits, she saw a large broken window on the other side of the building. If she could get to it she could escape from this space, and from him. And if she could get enough of a head start, she could find the spare key she kept in a magnetized box under her car. With a little luck, she could be away from this nightmare in a couple of minutes.

Could she run through her fear? Yes, she could. She had no choice. She closed her eyes for a moment, took a deep breath, then turned to look at him. "You don't have to hold on to me anymore. I'm not going to fall apart."

He turned to study her. "Are you sure?"

"Yes."

"All right." Tentatively, he let go of her hand.

She watched him steadily, and as soon as he turned his attention away from her, she shoved him as hard as she could.

He lost his balance and fell to the floor with a grunt

of pain. She hesitated for only a moment, then turned and began sprinting toward the window.

"Eleanor, stop!" His desperate whisper echoed off the walls. "Don't move! This place isn't safe!"

She didn't look back or slow down. She kept her gaze fixed on the yawning opening in front of her and tried not to think about the darkness pressing in on her from all sides.

"Eleanor, don't go any farther." She heard his footsteps behind her, but he was moving carefully. "Stop! The floor is rotten. I don't want you to fall through. You could get hurt."

Although he didn't raise his voice above a whisper, she could hear the urgency in it. She slowed down, staring at the floor, but could see nothing. Her stomach rolled and she searched desperately for the broken window and the reassuring glow from the streetlight.

"Stay there and I'll get the flashlight," he said behind her. "I don't dare come closer. We might both fall through."

She heard him retreating and she closed her eyes. This was her chance. She was almost there. Another thirty feet and she'd be at the window.

She took a step forward and heard an ominous cracking sound beneath her. She froze, but it didn't matter. Another sharp crack echoed, and suddenly the floor dropped away.

CHAPTER TWO

MICHAEL REILLY FELT the floor shudder before he heard the sharp crack of rotten wood splitting. He lunged in Eleanor's direction, knowing he would be too late.

The silence was even more deafening than the sound of the breaking timbers. "Eleanor?" he said in a harsh whisper. "Can you hear me?"

"I hear you." Her voice was surprisingly strong. "I didn't make it *that* far away from you."

He let out the breath he didn't realize he'd been holding. "Are you all right? Are you hurt?"

"No, I'm not all right. I'm stuck in the floor."

He exhaled in a rush when he heard her acerbic tone. Apparently she was more angry than injured. "Hold on a minute. I need to get the flashlight before I can get you out of there."

"Go ahead. Trust me, I'm not going anywhere."

"Are you sure you're okay?" he asked, oddly reluctant to walk away from her.

"Don't worry, I'll live. No thanks to you," she muttered.

Her words were a blow he hadn't expected, hitting him squarely in the chest. But after a long moment he drew a hard breath. She didn't know those words were a grim reality, couldn't know that earlier tonight someone else hadn't lived, because of him.

He turned and ran up the stairs, stopping on the sixth step to remove the flashlight he'd stored behind the loose bricks of the wall. Then he hurried to the next floor. Keeping the light covered with his hand, he reached the stack of pallets that was his landmark. Groping behind them, he found the nylon strap of his backpack and pulled the bag out. In one movement he hefted it over his shoulders and headed back down the stairs.

It bounced against the wound on his back like a hot knife stabbing him with every step, but he ignored the pain. He'd be hurting a hell of a lot more if they found him. Once he and Eleanor were in the car, he could take off the pack. He could tend to his wound after they were out of Midland.

When he reached the first floor he aimed the flashlight at Eleanor, to reassure himself she was all right. She stood hip-deep in a hole in the floor. Her eyes were huge in the darkness, and he could practically taste her fear. But when the flashlight illuminated her face, she lifted her chin in a gesture of defiance.

The rush of relief was staggering and an unwelcome surprise. "I guess you can't be too badly hurt," he drawled, trying to hide his reaction.

"Why do you say that?"

"Because you're giving me a real mouthy look."

Her eyes flashed at him. "That look is amazement that you're not already locked up. What kind of a kidnapper lets his victim walk away from him? You have a lot to learn about committing crimes.''

''Since you're a librarian, maybe you can suggest some books for me to read.''

''The only book you're going to get is the one the police will throw at you when they catch you,'' she sniffed.

He smothered a laugh as he made his way across the creaking floor. Who knew the quiet, plain woman he'd snatched from the library would have such steel in her spine?

But his smile faded when he got closer to her. ''You were lucky as hell, Ellie,'' he muttered. ''Look at the holes in this floor.''

''My name isn't Ellie,'' she snapped.

He shined the light on her again. ''Why not? It suits you.''

She clamped her mouth shut, and he was delighted to see the temper spark in her eyes. If he provoked her enough, maybe she'd forget to be afraid of him.

But when he finally reached her, the last vestige of humor vanished. The edges of the boards she'd fallen through were jagged and sharp as knives. And she was steadying herself on the floor with hands that shook.

''Are you sure you're not hurt?'' he asked, instinctively reaching for her, but stopping before he touched her.

She nodded, her eyes huge and dark in the reflected light of the flashlight. He'd thought earlier they were blue, but now they were so dilated it was impossible to tell. "The boards scratched my legs, but that's it. I'm standing on whatever broke my fall."

He shone the flashlight down into the ragged hole in the wooden floor and his heart contracted in his chest. She was standing on one of the beams that held up the floor. If she had fallen a foot in either direction, she would have gone straight to the basement floor, a good twenty feet below.

"You're safe where you are," he said, tightening his grip on the flashlight. "Just don't move. I'll get you out of there in a minute."

"Wait," she said, laying her hand on his arm.

It was small and delicate and fluttered over his skin like the wings of a bird. She froze, then jerked away as if he'd bitten her. Desire surged through him with a blast of heat. He wanted her hands on him again, wanted to feel her touching him. He scowled and bit off a vicious curse.

"I have an idea," she said, gripping the ragged edge of a floorboard. "I don't want to go with you, and I know you don't want to take me. Just leave me here and go. By the time someone finds me in the morning, you'll be far away and I won't be able to tell the police where you've gone."

He rocked back on his heels and narrowed his eyes. "What are you talking about?"

"This solves both of our problems," she said. Her teeth were chattering, although she didn't seem to re- alize it. "I don't want to go with you, and you can't want to take me. Leave me here and take off."

"Leave you here, in this neighborhood? In an

abandoned building? With you standing on a beam twenty feet above a cement floor? In the dark?''

''I'll be fine.''

''The hell you will.'' He stared at her. ''You're out of your mind! I'm not leaving you here! Once I get you out of this hole, we're leaving. Together.''

''It'll be hours before anyone finds me. It won't matter by then what I tell the police. You'll have had plenty of time to get far away.'' She paused before continuing. ''I thought you were desperate to get away from Midland.''

''That's not the point,'' he said in a furious whisper. She was probably right. A real criminal wouldn't hesitate to leave her here. He had her car keys. All he had to do was walk out the door. It would be a lot easier than taking her with him.

He wasn't that desperate. There was no way he'd leave a woman in this abandoned warehouse, in this part of town. Especially since this particular woman was afraid of the dark.

''Look,'' he said, leaning closer. ''Leaving you here isn't an option. You're stuck with me, so get used to it.''

''Why?'' She frowned at him. ''You're running from something. You can't want to be slowed down by a hostage. Leaving me here is the logical thing to do.''

''Do you analyze everything?''

''Yes. Especially things that don't make any sense.''

''You think it makes sense to leave you here? You

might be hurt. You said your legs were scratched. God only knows what kind of infection you could pick up in this filthy hole. And who do you think is going to find you and rescue you in the morning? No one that you'd be interested in meeting, I can guarantee you that.''

She frowned. ''So you're not leaving me because you feel responsible for me? Because you're afraid I might get hurt?''

''You got it.''

''If you're such a thoughtful, caring guy, why did you kidnap me in the first place?''

''Never mind.'' He scowled at her. He was losing control of the situation. ''Here's the flashlight. You're going to have to hold it for me while I loosen those boards.''

He handed her the flashlight and showed her where to point it. She immediately pointed it in the direction of the windows. As he reached to snatch it away from her, he heard the sound of a car prowling slowly up the street.

''Damn it! What did you do that for?''

She glared at him. ''Do you expect me to do exactly what you tell me to do? I heard a car so I tried to attract some attention.''

''Quiet!''

He listened intently for a moment. It sounded as if the car slowed down, then speeded up again.

Letting out a string of curses, he laid the flashlight on the floor and aimed it toward the hole. Then he rocked back on his heels.

The wood was splintered and jagged, and he'd have to break pieces off before it was safe to pull her out. Taking off his shirt, he wrapped the fabric around his hand and grasped one of the sharp edges. Bracing himself, he pulled on the piece of wood until it broke off. He tossed it to the side and reached for another one, ignoring the burning pain in his back and the warm trickle of blood. He'd reopened the wound but it didn't matter. They had to get out of here.

"What's wrong?" she asked sharply.

"I think that might have been the police you heard driving by. We have to move."

"That's not what I meant. You're bleeding!"

He didn't even bother to look over his shoulder. "I'll take care of it later."

"Why are you bleeding?"

"It's a long story." He stopped pulling on the wood and swiped an arm across his forehead. "Do you want to discuss it now? Or would you rather get out of here in one piece?"

Even in the weak light from the flashlight he saw her flinch away from him.

"Damn it, Ellie, I'm not going to hurt you," he whispered in a harsh voice. "But if we don't pull you out of this hole and get the hell out of here, neither of our lives is going to be worth a nickel."

He felt her gaze on him but she didn't say a thing. Blood flowed down his back in a steady stream by the time he'd pulled off two more jagged splinters of wood. "Hold on to my arms," he said, standing up. "I'm going to lift you out."

He fitted his hands around her waist and tightened his grip. In spite of the wound in his back, he raised her easily out of the hole. She felt small and fragile in his grasp. An unexpected surge of protectiveness rushed through him. He was responsible for dragging her into his mess. Now, by God, he'd better get her out of it safely.

He lifted her against him and held her for a moment. "There isn't much to you, is there, Slim?" he murmured. He tightened his hold, and her breasts flattened against his chest. He was shocked to feel himself stir. In his haste to set her on the floor he almost dropped her.

"Are you all right?" His voice was husky and strained.

"I'm fine." She sounded subdued. He wondered if she'd felt the strange current that had passed between them.

"Then let's get out of here."

He slipped into his shirt and pulled the backpack into place again, ignoring the pain when it nudged his wound. Taking the flashlight, he aimed it on the floor as they made their way to the door.

They were almost there when he heard the sound of a car turning onto the street. He switched off the light, then glanced through a broken window. Cruising slowly down the street, coming closer and closer, was a Midland police car.

"Damn it!" He yanked on Eleanor's arm. "Get down! Now!"

She looked over at him, and he saw the indecision

on her face. He understood perfectly. There was a squad car outside the window, and she was in an abandoned factory with a man who'd kidnapped her.

She'd be a fool if she didn't try to get the cops' attention.

"I don't have time to explain," he said as he pulled her down beside him. "If they see you with me, they'll kill both of us. They won't wait to listen to explanations. Now get down."

When she hesitated, he pushed her to the floor and covered her body with his. He pulled his gun out of the waistband of his jeans and eased off the safety, then clamped his hand lightly over Eleanor's mouth.

To his surprise, she didn't try to scream, didn't try to push him away. She sucked in a sudden breath, then stayed perfectly still beneath him, her muscles tense and rigid.

The police car slowed in front of the building. Probably taking down the license plate from Eleanor's car, he thought grimly. So much for making sure she didn't get involved in his mess.

Suddenly the spotlight from the police car played across the building. It hovered above them, then traveled slowly down the length of the building. Seconds dragged by, each one agonizingly long. Finally the light disappeared and the squad car moved on. Michael waited until the sound of its engine faded into the distance. Then he slid off Eleanor and took her hand, helping her to her feet.

"Let's go. We don't have much time."

"What do you mean? The cruiser drove away."

"They'll be back."

"Because of my car?"

"That, and they probably saw your flashlight from the window. They must be waiting for reinforcements."

She pulled away from him. "What's going on?" she demanded, her face tightening with suspicion.

"I told you we don't have time to talk about it now." He grabbed her hand and pulled her toward the door. "Just get in the car and drive."

She hesitated for a moment, indecision in her eyes as she glanced at him. He could read her mind as clearly as if she'd spoken.

"Don't even think about it." As he tightened his grip on her hand, he could feel her gather herself, preparing to run. He held her gaze for a long heartbeat, then she turned away and climbed into the car.

As she pulled away from the curb, he saw headlights behind them. It was the police cruiser. Apparently it had just circled the block.

"Don't look back," he warned sharply. Tugging at his seat belt to lengthen it, he moved closer to her. "Keep driving. Don't go over the speed limit or do anything to attract attention."

He hesitated before bending closer, then cursed himself for a fool. He didn't have time to worry about the niceties. Her life, as well as his, could depend on what he did in the next few minutes.

Taking a deep breath, he skimmed a kiss over her cheek, then nuzzled her neck.

When she jerked away from him, he caught her

chin in his hand. Her skin was warm and incredibly smooth against his fingers.

"Don't," he said. "Act like you're enjoying it. I have to give them some reason why we were in that building."

She looked at him out of the corner of her eye. Beneath the sharp-as-glass glare in her eyes, he saw a bewildered vulnerability that intrigued him.

"Pretend you like me," he muttered, holding her chin so she couldn't move away from him. A drop of sweat formed above her ear and slowly slid down her cheek. He watched it, fascinated, then bent closer and caught it on his tongue.

His heart pounded as he inhaled her scent, something sharp and citrusy. It suited her, he thought. As he brushed his face against hers, unable to resist the contact, he was mesmerized by the creamy softness of her cheek.

She shivered, and he murmured in her ear, "We're acting here, Eleanor. Make it look good. Slow down, turn your head and give me a kiss."

She hesitated, and he said more sharply, "It's not just my life that depends on this. Yours does, too. They have to think we're a couple who've been making out in that empty building."

"Like they'd believe anyone would go in there voluntarily?" But she turned her head, barely touching his mouth with hers.

Sensation rocketed through him. Heat pooled in his groin and he cursed himself. There couldn't possibly be a worse time for his hormones to go on alert.

"What should I do now?" she murmured.

Touch me, he wanted to tell her. But he pulled away slightly. "Turn left here. We'll get to a busier area."

The police rode their tail but made no attempt to halt them. Michael slipped an arm around Eleanor and felt her tremble. "They haven't stopped us yet, so they must think we got carried away by our passion and that's why we were in that building." He leaned toward her and kissed her once more.

She shivered again when his lips brushed her neck. Then she swallowed, and he felt the ripple of movement beneath his mouth. "I could get used to this," he murmured into her ear.

She stiffened as he eased away from her. "Don't bother," she said coldly, but her voice trembled. "I don't make a habit of kissing criminals."

She glanced at him and he saw fury in her eyes.

"Look," he said quietly. "I'm sorry. I shouldn't have kissed you, but I didn't have a choice. I had to make the cops less suspicious of us."

"So now you're apologizing to me?"

"I'm not a complete barbarian," he said, his voice gruff. Her astonished, wary gaze roused disturbing sensations. Her eyes tugged on something deep inside him, finding a part of him that had been buried for years. He couldn't look away.

The moment lengthened and tightened. Anticipation quivered in the now-silent car, until she jerked her gaze back to the street in front of them.

"*Barbarian* is exactly the right word," she said. A

slight tremble belied the tartness in her voice. "I'm not going to trust you just because you suddenly remember the manners your parents taught you."

The heat inside him vanished in a flash. "I knew you were a smart woman. You'd be a fool to trust me. Don't ever count on the lessons I learned from my parents."

When she looked his way, he saw doubt and fear in her eyes again. "Who are you?" she whispered. "What's going on?"

"Keep your attention on the road," he ordered as the car veered toward the sidewalk. "I need to get the hell out of Midland."

He noticed her fingers tighten on the steering wheel. He knew that if she lifted her hand it would be shaking.

Silently cursing himself for allowing her to distract him, he reached along the back of the seat and twined his own fingers in her hair, pulling strands from her messy, crooked bun.

She reached up and slapped his hand away. "What do you think you're doing?"

"You have to look the part if we want the cops to think we've been fooling around."

"Do you expect me to believe the cops would notice something like that?"

"Absolutely they would. Cops notice everything."

"Spoken like a man who has spent a lot of time with them," she said with a sniff, and he had to restrain a reluctant smile.

"You don't back down, do you, Ellie?"

"I'm not about to dissolve into a puddle of tears, if that's what you mean."

He leaned back in the seat again and watched her. Eleanor Perkins was certainly unique. He didn't think he'd ever met a woman quite like her. She'd stood up to him from the very beginning. And it wasn't as though she wasn't afraid—he'd tasted her fear, seen it in her eyes, in her trembling hands.

Now she was involved in his sordid mess through no fault of her own. He'd hoped to have her home quickly, without telling her his name or anything about him. But it was too late. The police had her name and address. By tomorrow, they'd know she was missing. If they ever put two and two together and connected him to her disappearance...

"Pull over here," he said abruptly as the police car moved closer.

The car rolled to a stop beneath a broken streetlight. He slid next to her, pulled her into his arms and fastened his mouth to hers.

She stiffened immediately and tried to push him away. "The cops are watching," he muttered against her lips. "Unless you have a death wish, make this look good."

He felt her resistance, but slowly she allowed him to pull her closer. When he wrapped his arm around her and buried his fingers in her hair, she tensed again. But as he massaged her scalp, he felt her relaxing against him. Finally, with an odd little murmur, she slipped her arms around him. She held him awkwardly, but she was holding him.

It was all for show, he told himself. They were only acting. But he noticed the taste of coffee in her mouth and the softness of her lips. He drank in the tiny sound in her throat as he touched his tongue to hers, and he felt the way she clutched his shoulders.

What the hell was he doing? This was a woman he had kidnapped at gunpoint. They weren't on a date. He had no business kissing her like he meant it.

He jerked away as if he'd been burned. As he stared at her in the darkness, her ragged panting echoed the thundering of his heart.

The police cruised slowly past, but he hardly noticed. Time stretched and grew taut as Eleanor's wide eyes gazed into his, inches away. Her breath feathered against his mouth and he tightened his fingers in her hair. The thick strands felt cool and heavy against his suddenly hot skin.

Out of the corner of his eye he saw brake lights flash, and he tightened his grip on her. But then the squad car moved on and finally turned the corner.

As he eased away to put some distance between them, Michael took a deep, shuddering breath. ''I guess we convinced them we were for real,'' he said.

''I never knew I had such a talent for acting,'' she said coolly. But the quaver in her voice spoiled the effect.

''You did a damn good job.'' He swallowed hard. ''Let's get out of here.''

''No. I'm not going with you.'' Her voice was firm, but he saw a mixture of fear, awareness and humiliation in her eyes. ''Take me back to the library.''

"This isn't an optional trip," he said, leaning toward her, hoping he looked menacing. "Get moving."

But instead of putting the car in gear, she opened the door, jumped out and ran.

CHAPTER THREE

AS ELEANOR SPRINTED DOWN the dark, deserted street, she could hear the sound of his footsteps pounding closer and closer. Apparently the wound on his back wasn't slowing him down. But even if she couldn't outrun him, she had to try. She couldn't bear to be in the car with him for another moment.

Not after the way she'd reacted to his kiss.

He had just been acting. He'd had to convince the passing police that they were lovers in the throes of passion. But for a long, mortifying moment she had forgotten they were pretending. She had lost herself in his kiss, forgetting it wasn't real. And she was sure he'd realized it.

Could she be more pathetic? Now her kidnapper knew she was desperate enough, and pitiful enough, to be attracted to a criminal. She couldn't face him again with that humiliating moment between them.

Suddenly an arm snaked around her waist and jerked her back against a solid chest. "What the hell do you think you're doing?" he rasped into her ear.

"Help!" she screamed. "Help! Police!" Her voice bounced off the vacant buildings and resonated in the darkness.

He clapped his palm over her mouth and lifted her off her feet. Kicking and struggling, she tried to pry his hand away and get free. But he was too big and too strong. He held her almost casually against the hard muscled planes of his body, as if she was so small that he didn't even notice her weight.

"Stop it, Eleanor!" His voice was a harsh whisper next to her ear. "If the police find us, they'll kill both of us. I told you that."

She yanked at his fingers again, trying to pull them from her mouth. His hand bit into her lips. "If I let go, will you promise not to scream?" he rasped.

When she jerked her head in the affirmative, he set her on the sidewalk and cautiously eased his hand away. But he kept his other arm wrapped around her waist.

She couldn't turn to face him. "Take me home," she begged, ashamed to hear her voice shaking. "I promise I won't call the police."

His arm tightened again. "You know, Ellie, I almost believe you. I think you're a woman who keeps her word. And that scares the hell out of me."

"Why?" she managed to ask.

"Because I can't afford to trust anyone." His breath whispered through her hair and his lips hovered near the crown of her head. She held her breath, wondering if he'd move closer. "Especially not a woman I've just kidnapped."

"You said the police would kill both of us. Why? I haven't done anything wrong."

"I promise I'll explain later." He stepped away

from her, but didn't let go of her arm. "We have to stick together," he said, and she heard weariness in his voice. "Neither of us has a choice."

His hand was oddly gentle on her arm, but she knew that was an illusion. If she made an attempt to pull away, his fingers would lock into an iron band.

There would be another chance to get away from him, she told herself. He would have to sleep sometime. He couldn't watch her every single minute. As soon as his back was turned, she would be gone.

But it wasn't going to happen right now. She slowed as they reached the car, and the pressure of his hand increased slightly. Just enough to let her know he was in charge.

"You drive," he said gruffly.

"Afraid I'll jump out the door if you're driving?" she asked.

"Yep. It's just the kind of damn fool stunt you'd pull."

Instead of being offended, she was oddly pleased at his words. She'd never been the kind of person who pulled damn fool stunts. But suddenly she could picture herself doing just that.

Settled behind the steering wheel, she sensed him watching her steadily. If she made a move toward the door, he would no doubt grab her before her fingers touched the handle.

"Where to?"

"Head over to Park Street," he said, naming one of Midland's busier highways. "There's a lot more traffic over there."

She eased the car away from the curb, and a few minutes later merged onto the busy street. She speeded up slightly, and he leaned closer.

"No speeding."

His words were sharp with warning, and she wondered what he would do if she ignored him. He wouldn't use the gun on her. She was certain of that. A man who would shoot a woman wouldn't have hesitated to leave her alone in the abandoned warehouse.

She pressed harder on the accelerator, tempted to find out. Then she slowed down. *Pick your battles,* she told herself.

He grunted with approval. "Stay at this speed."

Traffic thinned as they headed away from the business district, but quite a few cars still surrounded them. A flash of white caught her eye: a police car hidden in a small alley, its engine running. She gave the accelerator a small tap, hoping it would push them above the speed limit.

"Slow down," Michael said sharply. "I saw that police car, too." He leaned closer. "You'd better hope like hell he doesn't follow us."

She tried to ignore the flash of heat that shot through her with his face inches away from hers. Glancing into her rearview mirror, she felt her pulse skip a beat as she saw the cruiser pull out and slide into traffic behind them.

Michael noticed it, too, and swore under his breath. "I'm not kidding, Eleanor, this isn't the time to do something stupid."

She drove steadily, trying to keep the speedometer

needle just below the speed limit. Much as she wanted the police to stop them, Michael's warnings had made her nervous. Anxiety swelled in her chest as she waited to see where the squad car would go.

It wasn't going anywhere. It followed her closely for another block, then blasted its siren once. The bar on the top of the car erupted with flashing lights.

"They want me to stop." Her heart pounding, her mouth suddenly dry, she gripped the steering wheel desperately. She couldn't take her eyes off the lights behind them. "I have to pull over."

"Damn it!" He gave her a hard look, as if he suspected she'd done something to attract their attention. Then he sprawled on the seat, suddenly boneless. "I'm drunk and you're driving me home." His steady gaze bored into her. "I still have the gun, Eleanor. And I won't hesitate to use it." He slumped as if he'd passed out. Only his back was visible.

She pulled to the curb. Her hands, damp and cold, slipped on the steering wheel and her stomach heaved as she stared in the mirror at the squad car behind her. Michael might not shoot her, but apparently he wouldn't hesitate to shoot the police officer. This stranger's life now depended on her acting ability.

Sweat dripped down her neck and pooled between her breasts. Fear made her light-headed and she struggled to breathe. An eternity seemed to pass before a police officer got out of the car and approached her window.

Eleanor leaned forward, trying to block his view

into the car and deprive Michael of a target. "Yes, Officer?" she said.

He leaned closer, but instead of answering her, he looked past her at her passenger. His gaze lingered on Michael's limp form for several long moments, then the cop looked at her with expressionless eyes.

"Can I see your license and registration?"

She reached into the back seat, where Michael had thrown her purse. It took three tries to extract her driver's license from her wallet. Then she fumbled in the glove box until she found her registration papers. Her hand trembled as she handed them to the police officer.

"Can I ask what the problem is?" Her voice wobbled, and she didn't dare glance at Michael. He remained sprawled on the seat, apparently unconscious.

"You have a broken taillight."

Eleanor closed her eyes. She remembered hearing the sound of the taillight breaking as Michael tried to force her into the car. *How ironic,* she thought. After all the surreal events that had unfolded tonight, a broken piece of plastic was turning out to be the most dangerous.

The police officer studied her driver's license for a moment, then trained his flashlight on Michael. "And you were driving very carefully. It's been my experience that intoxicated drivers often drive under the speed limit." He transferred the light to Eleanor. "Have you been drinking?"

"No!" She stared at the man, shocked. It was the last thing she'd expected him to ask. "*I* haven't had anything to drink tonight.'' Her mouth was suddenly dry as sand.

The officer moved the light back to Michael. ''How about your friend? What's wrong with him?''

Eleanor took a deep breath. How would she feel if her date had gotten drunk and she'd had to drive him home? She'd be angry, she decided.

''He's definitely drunk.'' She put all the scorn she could summon into the words. ''I told him I'd be the designated driver, but I didn't think he would drink himself under the table. I had to ask two strangers to pour him into the car. Now I just want to dump him at his apartment.''

The police officer didn't appear to be paying any attention to her. His flashlight remained fixed on Michael, as if he was trying to study his face. Her stomach twisted sharply, and her damp hands slipped lower on the steering wheel. What was wrong with her? Why didn't she tell the cop that Michael had kidnapped her?

It was the gun, she told herself. The gun he was keeping carefully hidden, but was now pointing directly at the officer.

The flashlight moved slowly from Michael's head down his back, then suddenly halted. Moving only her eyes, she saw the black stain of blood surrounding the ragged gash on the back of Michael's shirt. Clearly, the police officer noticed it, too, because the flashlight remained frozen in place.

''Would you get out of the car?'' he finally said. His voice was hard and edged with tension.

"Why do I need to get out of the car for a broken taillight?"

He took the beam of light off Michael and trained it on her face, effectively blinding her. The man became nothing more than a dark shadow looming in the edges of her vision. "Just get out of the car, ma'am. Slowly. And keep your hands where I can see them." He moved a step away from the car and rested his hand on his gun.

What should she do? Eleanor thought frantically. If she got out of the car, Michael would have a clear shot at the officer. If she refused, would the cop pull out *his* gun? Was Michael telling her the truth? Would they both be killed?

Before she could make up her mind, Michael suddenly lunged in her direction. Out of the corner of her eye she saw the cop bring up his arm, as Michael shifted into Drive and stomped his foot on the gas pedal. The car shot forward.

The officer shouted as Michael's foot pushed the accelerator relentlessly to the floor. "Steer the car, for God's sake," he yelled in Eleanor's ear.

She veered into the line of traffic, bracing herself for an inevitable collision. Horns blared and tires screeched. A car swerved violently next to her, smashing her sideview mirror, shattering the glass. Somehow she managed to straighten the car and keep it from moving across the yellow lines.

"Good job," Michael said, easing his foot off the gas. Terrified, she automatically pressed the pedal to the floor. "Just keep going. Don't stop, no matter what happens."

The casing of the side mirror exploded into tiny pieces, and she glanced over to see how close the other car had gotten. To her surprise, there was no vehicle next to her.

"What happened?" she asked. "Where's the car I hit?"

"You didn't hit another car." Michael's voice was grim. "He's shooting at us."

"What?"

"Your mirror was hit by a bullet. No, don't look back," he said when she instinctively glanced in the mirror. "Just keep driving. Faster."

"Why are they shooting at us?" she asked. Her brain refused to work. "He said he stopped us because I had a broken taillight."

"The taillight has nothing to do with it," Michael said curtly. "Ruiz probably saw the blood on my back and recognized me."

"But he could have shot me, too!"

"He doesn't care, Ellie. He doesn't care who gets in the way."

"What did you do?" she whispered.

"Not now." He looked over his shoulder. "Turn here. Quickly."

Glancing in the rearview mirror again, she saw flashing lights behind her. A lot of flashing lights. Cruisers were several blocks away but drawing closer.

The sedan skidded around the corner on two wheels, tires screeching. It swerved as it straightened out, then Eleanor gained control and raced down the side street.

After a block Michael said, "Turn right."

She shot him a startled glance. "Don't you mean left? If we turn right, we'll be heading right back toward them."

"Turning left is what they expect us to do. They think we'll try to get out of Midland as fast as we can. So we're going to do just the opposite."

"All right." She swung the car around the corner, then pressed the accelerator again.

After she'd gone a couple of blocks, he twisted to look behind them again. "Okay, turn left again, then right two streets over."

The sounds of sirens got closer and closer, and her heart jumped wildly in her chest. When she'd made the two turns, he put his hand on her arm. "Stop here," he said, when they were in the middle of a block.

"Are you crazy?" she yelled. "We're just going to wait for them to catch up to us?"

"They're not going to catch up with us," he answered. The pressure on her arm increased for a fraction of a moment, almost as if he was reassuring her. "They're all heading in the opposite direction. So we're going to go back where we started."

"You're taking me back to the library?" She couldn't keep the surprise out of her voice.

"We're not going anywhere near the library," he said harshly. "As soon as they figure out who you are, the library will be swarming with cops. We're heading back into downtown Midland.''

"Is that safe?'' Her teeth were chattering, even though it was the middle of summer and the car wasn't air-conditioned.

"It's as safe as it's going to get for us.'' His tone was hard.

As she put the car in gear and pulled onto the empty street, she stared at the dark factories flying past. She felt oddly detached, as if she was observing two complete strangers acting out a script in front of her.

"Damn it, Ellie, snap out of it,'' he growled. "Don't fall apart on me now. We're almost there.''

"I'm not falling apart,'' she said, as she started down the deserted street.

"Yeah, you are. I can see your eyes glazing over.''

She glared at him through narrowed eyes. "Is this better?''

"Yeah, it is.'' He relaxed back into his seat. "I worry when you're not giving me grief.''

She opened her mouth to retaliate, then clenched her teeth together and stared out the windshield. He was right. She hadn't been paying attention. And he had known exactly what to do to get her to focus.

How did he know so much about her? she thought with a flicker of alarm. Was she that easy to read?

She didn't have time to gnaw at that question right now. "What do we do next?'' She was proud of how steady her voice sounded.

"Now we ditch your car. Somewhere it won't be found right away."

"What do we do then? How are we going to get out of Midland?" She froze. She had said "we" without even thinking.

"We'll get another car." He smiled grimly. "Don't worry, Ellie. The cops may outnumber us, but I have a few tricks up my sleeve."

"Learned, no doubt, from your years of trying to avoid them," she said tartly, trying to cover her uneasiness at the way she'd automatically aligned herself with him.

To her surprise, he didn't reply with a snappy comeback, as she'd expected. Instead he stared straight ahead. "Yes," he said, his voice was low. She noticed his jaw muscles working. His eyes were as hard and cold as a block of ice.

She wanted to tell him she didn't really think he'd spent years fleeing the police, but she couldn't force the words past her stiff lips. Although she was no longer afraid he would hurt her, she didn't know anything about him, she reminded herself. He really could be a desperate criminal on the run.

He continued to direct her through the streets of Midland, until she realized they were once again in the same area as the abandoned warehouse they'd stopped at earlier. "What are we doing here?" she asked uneasily.

"I don't want the police to find your car right away," he said. "Turn here."

She swung the car around the corner and saw a

row of dilapidated buildings. They looked like sight-less old men standing wearily in the night. The two-flats all had their shades and draperies drawn tightly against the night. There wasn't a soul on the street.

"I didn't know anyone lived in this area," she said.

"There are residential pockets here and there." He glanced up and down the street, but it was deserted. "Okay, pull into the alley."

The car bumped along the gravel-covered lane, dip-ping into the ruts. The alley was barely wide enough for a vehicle, and it was lined with garages as ne-glected as the two-flats. Streetlights with broken bulbs stood like dark sentinels over the decaying neighbor-hood.

"Stop here." He indicated a tall cyclone fence that enclosed what appeared to be a vacant lot. The fence had slats threaded through the links to hide the inte-rior from view. There was a large gate in the fence, locked with a sturdy-looking padlock.

Michael edged out of the car and used a key to open the gate. Swinging it wide on hinges that creaked, he motioned for her to drive through.

Vehicles of various sizes crowded the enclosed space, their shapes shadowy and mysterious in the dim light. After closing the gate behind them, Michael came to the driver's side and opened the door.

"Slide over," he said, easing in beside her. He drove toward what looked to be an impenetrable wall of metal, but turned out to be a narrow pathway twist-ing between the wrecks. Now that she was closer, she saw that all the vehicles were stripped to the bone.

Most had no doors or fenders, the hoods and trunks were gone, and there was little left of the interiors.

He steered the car into a spot between two mangled pickup trucks, then turned off the ignition. The sudden silence surprised her. It was hard to believe they were surrounded by the city of Midland.

''Where are we?'' she asked, uneasiness creeping over her again.

''This is a private junkyard. Belongs to a... business associate of mine.'' Michael's eyes were suddenly hard and bleak. ''No one will find your car and it'll be safe.''

She looked around, both fascinated and apprehensive. ''I wasn't worried about my car.'' The beige sedan, which she suddenly despised, was the least of her problems right now. ''I've never heard of a private junkyard. Where did all these cars come from?''

He paused for a moment, his expression flat and cold. ''Let's just say the owner is an entrepreneur. He sells them for scrap.''

Neither of them spoke again. Darkness and silence settled around them like a heavy cloak, and surprisingly enough, her fear began to dissipate. She might be alone with a stranger in a dangerous part of Midland, but she felt oddly safe. They were hidden behind towering piles of cars, the warm, heavy air of the Illinois summer night barely stirring. The place should have felt stuffy and confining, but instead was strangely intimate.

It was stupid to feel so comfortable, she reminded herself. ''Don't we need to get going?'' she asked.

"Not yet. I think we'll sit here awhile."

"What for?"

"I'm waiting until my gut tells me to leave."

"And how long will that be?"

"I'll let you know as soon as I figure it out." He eased back against the seat and she heard him suck in his breath.

Suddenly she remembered the blood on his back. "You're hurt," she said, frowning.

"Don't get your hopes up. It's not fatal."

"What happened?"

"A bullet got a little too close."

"You mean you've been shot?" She was horrified.

"It grazed me. Just needs to be cleaned and bandaged."

"You haven't taken care of it." Before she could think about what she was doing, she leaned toward him. "Let me see."

"No!" His voice was gruff. "I'll take care of it once we're someplace safe."

"Don't be so stubborn. At the rate we're going, that could be a while." She leaned closer and saw weariness in his face, lines of pain and exhaustion around his eyes. "As soon as we leave this junkyard, we'll get some first-aid supplies."

He shifted into a more comfortable position and gave her the ghost of a grin. "Are you always so bossy, Ellie?"

"Always," she said firmly. "Especially with someone who so clearly needs direction."

"I'm shaking in my shoes," he said mildly.

He didn't look at all intimidated. His face had relaxed and that faint grin flirted around his mouth again, as if he enjoyed sparring with her.

Warmth slowly unfurled inside of her, as if she'd taken a gulp of some potent brandy that heated as it flowed through her veins. She savored the feeling for a moment, then caught herself and scowled. That warmth could mean nothing but trouble.

"We can't sit here all night waiting for your gut to reach some decision," she said briskly. "You're hurt and the wound needs tending."

Michael gave her a faint smile that brightened the darkness, then he shifted painfully to sit upright. "Nag, nag, nag," he said, but his tone was mild. "All right, let's get going."

He eased open the car door, then stepped out into the night. Eleanor scrambled out her side, watching him with a frown. He seemed a lot weaker than when he'd forced her into the car at the library.

She refused to examine her fears about a man who had brutally kidnapped her just a few hours ago. He was hurt, and she was stuck with him now. The bullets the police fired at her had convinced her of that. She'd make sure Michael and she got to a safe place, then she'd take care of his wound. Only because she was curious to hear his story, she assured herself.

A few minutes later they stepped into the darkness of the alley. Without thinking, she reached for his hand as she tried to avoid the deep ruts in the gravel. He tensed when she slipped her hand into his, then his fingers tightened around hers. He steered her firmly over the uneven surface.

As they approached the mouth of the alley, he pulled her into the shadows. Angling his body in front of hers, he waited for what seemed like forever. One streetlight cast a small pool of light across the street. The rest of the lights were broken. The street itself was eerily deserted and silent. There were no cars, no people, not even an animal in sight.

"All right, let's go," he whispered. They moved away from the shelter of the garage and its shadows and started to cross the street. Before they'd gone more than a handful of steps, she caught a flash of light out of the corner of her eye.

Michael swore viciously and yanked her back toward the garage. They made it into the shadows before the car reached them, and Michael pressed her against the warm wood of the garage, his chest crushed into her back.

Listening to the low growl of the car's engine as it crept closer, she felt a flutter of panic. What was she hoping for? Did she want the car to stop or keep going? Had the occupants seen them race back into the shadows? Was it someone looking for Michael?

As the sound of the engine got closer, she felt Michael tense, then he pushed her to the ground. But before he covered her body with his, she saw the distinctive black logo of the Midland police force on the side of the car and the bar of lights on top of it.

Seconds ticked by too slowly as the car cruised slowly past their hiding place. She trembled violently as she waited for the cruiser to stop, braced herself for the hail of bullets that would surely follow. An image of the disintegrating side mirror of her car played over and over in her mind. The police had been shooting at her. Had been trying to kill her.

But the car continued down the street without hesitating. When the sound of the engine finally faded away, she drew air deep into her suddenly aching lungs. She'd been holding her breath without even realizing it.

"Let's go."

Michael rose slowly and painfully from the ground, then started moving in the direction from which the car had come. She stumbled after him, glancing over her shoulder, expecting the police car to reappear any moment.

"Don't worry, he's gone."

"How can you be sure?" she whispered.

"Because if he'd seen us, he would have stopped. He won't be back for another hour or so." Michael hesitated on the curb, his gaze sweeping the area. Then he urged her to the other side.

"Maybe he's waiting for us around the corner," she muttered.

"He's not. He's on patrol. If he had noticed anything suspicious, he would have stopped. Since he didn't, he must be continuing his rounds."

"I guess when you're a criminal, it pays to know police routines," she said. Fear again laced her voice.

"Yeah, it does." Michael pulled her into the shadows of the next alley, then looked down at her. "But that's not why I know what the police are going to do next.''

''Then how do you know?''

''Because I'm a police officer.''

CHAPTER FOUR

"WHAT?" Eleanor stared at him, unable to believe her ears.

Without a word, he pulled a battered wallet out of his back pocket and let it fall open. The faint light glittered off a badge for a few seconds before he snapped it shut and began to slide it back into his pocket.

"Let me see that."

Silently he handed it to her. The rich scent of leather surrounded her as she held the square object in her hands. The wallet was warm from his body. Trying to ignore the sensory assault, she examined the badge, then the picture identification that accompanied it. There was no doubt. Michael Reilly was a detective in the Midland Police Department.

"What's going on?" she blurted. "It's time you told me everything. Why did you say the police would kill you? And me, as well, if they found me with you?"

"Because it's the truth." His face was shuttered now.

"Why would they kill one of their own officers?"

"Because of what I know about some of them. And

they'll kill you because of what I might have told you." She heard the pain and exhaustion in his voice. It was as if he had been wearing a mask since he'd kidnapped her and was finally letting it slip.

"What are you going to do?"

"I have to get out of Midland. Hell, I should probably get out of the Midwest." The shadows in the alley hid the right side of his face. "I need to talk to the FBI."

"There's an office in St. Louis. That's less than a hundred miles away. Why didn't you just get into your own car and drive there?"

"Believe me, that wasn't an option." He closed his eyes, as if trying to block out a scene he wanted to forget.

"And that's why you kidnapped me? So that I would drive you to the FBI office?"

He nodded. "I couldn't just steal a car, because the owners would report it stolen and the police would be looking for it. I needed a car that no one would report missing for at least a few hours, to give me a head start."

"Why did you pick me?"

"It's like I told you. You were in the wrong place at the wrong time." His voice was flat. "I saw your car in the parking lot and figured that it belonged to the custodian. But when you came out, I knew my luck had changed. You were perfect. You were working late on a Friday night. Chances were there was no one waiting for you at home."

"You were right." She couldn't keep the wistfulness out of her voice.

Propping himself against the wooden wall of another garage, he studied her. "Why is that, Ellie?" he asked gently. "Why isn't there someone waiting for you?"

She berated herself for letting him see so much about her. "I work long hours. And I don't meet a lot of eligible men working in the children's section of the library."

He touched the top of her head, then pushed her glasses back up her nose. The small gestures felt more intimate than a caress. "And you don't go out of your way to attract them, either, do you?" he murmured.

She shrugged his arm away and looked at the ground, trying not to let him see how much his words hurt. "My social life is not your concern."

After a moment he said, "You're right. I'm more concerned about your life, period. As in saving it."

He touched her cheek once, his fingers as gentle as a misty rain. "What are we going to do with you?"

She wanted to say, "Take me with you." She ached to say, "I'll help you." The impulse shocked her. She wasn't an impulsive woman. She didn't give in to wild cravings. She made careful, reasoned decisions. Looking away from him, staring down the dark alley, she said, "Take me home, I suppose. You know I won't call the police. Not now."

"Why not?" he asked, his voice barely above a whisper. "I kidnapped you."

"You also tried to protect me. You pulled me out

of that hole in the warehouse floor, even though I told you to leave me. You covered my body with yours when the police came by.'' Her face heated at the memory of lying on the unyielding floor, his hard body blanketing her. "You haven't hurt me, Michael. And I don't believe you're a criminal.''

"Thank you," he said quietly. "That means a lot to me. But you know I can't take you home. It's not safe. Let me take you to a friend or a relative outside of Midland.''

"I don't have any relatives.'' The realization brought a lump to her throat. Her life was in danger, and there was no one she could turn to. No family who would mourn if she died. "My parents are both dead, and I don't want to endanger my friends.''

"Then I'm sorry, but it looks like you're coming with me.'' A strained smile crept over his face, a pale shadow of the teasing grin he'd flashed earlier. He brushed one finger over her cheek. "Look at it as an unexpected vacation.''

Her nerves jolted at his touch and she wanted to lean into him. But before she could make a fool of herself he drew his hand away. "There's nothing to be sorry about,'' she managed to say. Her cheek was still tingling. "Maybe I can help you.''

At that his mouth tightened. "Forget it. I'll find someplace to leave you once we're out of town. The last person who tried to help me ended up dead.''

"What did happen, Michael?'' she whispered. Something awful had occurred earlier tonight. The knowledge was reflected in his bleak eyes.

"I'll spare you the details. All you need to know is that there are a number of detectives and patrol officers on the Midland police force who'd like to see me dead." He paused and his eyes darkened. "Tonight they figured out that I know about their criminal activities, and that I probably have proof. If they don't stop me, they'll go to prison. So they'll try to stop me at any cost."

He pushed away from the wall, wincing with pain. When he tried to take a step, he staggered, and she reached out to steady him. His arm was hard and corded with muscle, and his skin felt dry and hot. She tightened her grip on him.

"So that's your entire plan? Get out of Midland somehow and take this proof of yours to the FBI?" She spoke more sharply than she'd intended, disconcerted by the sensations he aroused in her.

"That's it."

"You must have had a backup plan in case things went wrong."

"I'm not big on planning, Slim. I'm more of an impulse kind of guy. I rely on my intuition." A faint smile flickered across his mouth.

That grin affected her more than she liked. "Maybe you should have thought things through more carefully," she said sardonically. "Maybe that's why we're hiding in an alley in this part of Midland and you're running from your fellow police officers right now."

"Intuition is the only reason I'm still here." The smile faded from his mouth. "It kept me from dashing out to my car tonight. If I had, I'd be cooling on a slab in the morgue right now."

He closed his eyes again, but opened them almost immediately. "I'm getting a bad feeling from these questions of yours. Are you one of those people who has to plan everything in excruciating detail?"

"There's nothing wrong with that," she retorted.

"I wouldn't know. That's not how I operate."

"Well, someone had better start thinking ahead if you want to get out of this situation."

"You go ahead. If I don't like what you come up with, we'll do something else." He shot her another wicked grin. "We'll call it the plan to be named later."

A strange ripple of electricity moved through her every time he smiled at her. Clearly she'd had too much adrenaline coursing through her blood tonight, and it had overloaded her circuits. That was the only explanation for the feelings he was rousing in her.

He wasn't the kind of man who would be interested in her. If he met her on the street or in the library, he wouldn't give Eleanor Perkins a second look. Heck, he wouldn't give her a first look. She knew that. She was making far too much of his charm. Obviously, he didn't mean for her to take it personally. After all, she was the exact opposite of exciting, impulsive Michael Reilly.

And she could add good-looking to the list. His eyes were a vivid, bright blue, and his dark hair, in need of a trim, gave him a rakish, devil-may-care look. And when he grinned at her, a dimple creased his right cheek and a devil danced in his eyes.

She knew what he saw when he looked at her. She was ordinary in every way. The word *mousy* could have been invented for her hair. Thick and straight, it refused to hold a curl, and she despaired of ever doing anything with it other than piling it into a bun on the top of her head. Her eyes were an ordinary blue. But it didn't really matter, because they were hidden behind her glasses.

No, there was nothing about her to appeal to someone like Michael Reilly. The man exuded sex appeal. God knows he'd already made her heart beat faster.

''Are you always so levelheaded and practical, Ellie?'' he asked softly.

He was staring at her as if he hadn't really seen her before now, and it made her uncomfortable. ''Shouldn't we start moving?'' she asked. ''Or do you intend to skulk in this alley all night?''

That faint hint of a grin crossed his mouth again, and he pushed away from the wall. ''You're a slave driver, woman,'' he said.

Then he peered around the corner of the garage toward the street, and suddenly there was nothing casual or devil-may-care about Michael. ''Let's go,'' he said without looking at her. ''We need to get out of here before that patrol officer comes back.''

MICHAEL GRITTED HIS TEETH as he stepped away from the protection of the dark alley. His wound had been bleeding steadily, and for a moment the world spun in sickening circles. Blindly he reached out for the support of the garage again. But Eleanor slipped her small hand into his.

"Hang on to me," she said briskly. "You're a little dizzy."

He couldn't help chuckling. "You're something else, Ellie. Who would have guessed a few hours ago that you'd be bossing around a hardened criminal?"

"I'm bossing around a complete idiot who thinks he can ignore a bullet wound." She sounded as if it was a personal affront. "We're not going anywhere until we take care of that injury."

"You terrify me, Slim."

They staggered a few steps, then she asked in a small voice, "Why do you call me that?"

"Because you are, I guess." He remembered how she'd felt when he'd lifted her out of the hole in the floor at the warehouse. "You're tiny and delicate and, well, slim."

"No one's ever called me delicate before." He heard surprise and shyness in her voice.

"Then I guess nobody's looked at you lately."

"Or you're too used to flirting." The warmth had disappeared from her voice. "You can turn it off anytime now. I'm not susceptible."

No, she probably didn't think she was. But he'd seen a side of Eleanor Perkins that intrigued him. And attracted him, if he was honest with himself. She was brave and she was smart. And she was resourceful. She might not be beautiful, but he doubted that one of the drop-dead gorgeous women he was used to dating would have done as well in these circumstances.

A grin flitted across his mouth. God help any real criminal who tried to kidnap Ellie. Before she was finished with him, he'd probably run screaming in the other direction.

But the vulnerability deep in her eyes intrigued Michael. And the delicate softness of her skin stirred an unwelcome weakness inside him.

Now where the hell had that come from?

Disgusted with himself and the direction of his thoughts, he tried to walk a little faster. He staggered again and draped his arm over Eleanor's shoulder to brace himself. She stiffened momentarily, then shifted closer so he could rest his weight against her. She seemed to know instinctively what he needed.

"We're going to have to stop soon."

He heard the concern in her tone, and something moved in his chest. He had kidnapped her just hours ago, but now she was worried about him. He had bullied and terrified her, and all she could think about was how to take care of him.

"There's a flophouse hotel a couple of blocks from here," he said roughly. "We'll stay there."

"Can you make it that far?" She glanced up at him, and he saw the worry in her eyes.

"I'll have to, won't I?"

She watched him for a moment before she nodded. "I guess you will."

She shifted again so that she was supporting more of his weight. He hated feeling so helpless, hated knowing that he would be worse than useless if the police found them. Hated being terrified that Ellie was in danger and it was his fault.

"Let's rest a minute," she said.

He shook his head. "Can't."

They struggled along in the shadows for what felt like an eternity. Every step sent fingers of fire digging into his back, a new trickle of blood down his skin.

They turned another corner and he began counting the steps, forcing himself to put one foot in front of the other. "Are we almost there?" Ellie asked, panting.

"I'm too heavy," he said immediately, trying to lift his weight off her shoulder. "I can walk on my own."

"You're an idiot, Reilly," she said, tightening her arm around him. She didn't even look at him. "I don't think you can go much farther."

"I'll be fine."

He'd make it to that hotel if he had to crawl there. He wasn't about to leave Ellie vulnerable on the streets of Midland.

"Stop," she suddenly ordered, and he stumbled to a halt.

"What?" he breathed, praying it wasn't another police car.

"There's one of those all-night convenience stores. I'm going to get some first-aid supplies."

"Damn it, Ellie," he exclaimed. "We don't have time."

"Then we'll make time." She glanced up at him.

"Do you want to be able to leave Midland tomorrow? Or would you rather be lying in a gutter somewhere, too weak to move from loss of blood?"

"I think you've read too many mysteries," he muttered, but he didn't resist when she steered him toward an alley across the street from the brightly lit store.

"Don't move. I'll be back as soon as I can."

"Take your time. Don't act rushed. We don't want the clerk to remember you."

She disappeared into the store and out of his sight. Tension twisted more and more tightly inside him as he waited for her to emerge. He'd put his life in her hands. She could be on the telephone with the Midland police right now, telling them exactly where to find him.

But he didn't think she was. Eleanor was a woman of her word. He'd figured that out a while ago. And she'd told him she wouldn't call the cops.

Minutes ticked by with agonizing slowness. Finally, in spite of his certainty about her, a wisp of doubt crept into his head. Had she changed her mind? *Was* she calling for help?

Then the door opened and she was hurrying across the street. "Sorry I took so long," she said. "I hope you weren't worried."

"I was worried as hell," he rasped. "What happened in that damn store?"

"The night clerk was chatty." She slid her arm around Michael and eased him out of the alley. He refused to think about how right she felt against him.

"She was lonely and wanted to talk. You said not to hurry, and I figured she would be more suspicious if I rushed off." Eleanor glanced up at him. "I didn't want her to remember what I bought."

"I didn't mean you should exchange life stories with the clerk," he said through gritted teeth. "The longer you talked to her, the more time she had to remember your face."

Anxiety speared through him, along with an odd shame that he'd doubted her. "You should have gone in there, bought what you needed, and gotten out."

"I'm sorry," she snapped at him. "I guess I missed that lesson in criminal school."

She kicked at a garbage can and it toppled over, the hollow sound echoing down the street.

"Oh, now, that's mature," he said, but his heart lightened. He'd been right to trust her.

"And you would know mature if it hit you in the face?"

He grinned into the darkness when he saw the scowl on her face. "That's my Ellie. Always with the quick comeback."

She glanced up at him and he saw the fury in her eyes. "The more I get to know you, Reilly, the less surprised I am that somebody wants to kill you. You probably laughed at your fellow detectives once too often."

"I'm not laughing at you." He tightened his grip on her shoulder. "I'm relieved as hell that you're all right."

"I didn't know what to do other than talk to her,"

she muttered, not looking at him. "At least I held a magazine close to my face so she couldn't see me very well."

"Good job." He squeezed her shoulder again. "I guess I snapped at you because I was worried."

"Were you worried that I had changed my mind about helping you? Were you afraid that I had called the police?"

He was ashamed of his momentary lapse of faith. "I was worried, period," he finally said. But he'd hesitated a moment too long. Disappointment and hurt flickered over her face.

"I don't like not being in control," he muttered. It was the truth. Memories from his childhood threatened to surface, pictures of a terrified young boy cowering in front of his father. Michael pushed them away. Right now he had to concentrate on staying alive. And keeping Ellie alive.

Her face relaxed as she looked up at him. "I'm sorry," she said softly. "I should have realized that. Control is very important for police officers, isn't it?"

He choked back a laugh. It was the last thing he'd expected her to say. But then, every other word out of her mouth surprised him. "And you know this because of all the contact you've had with the police?"

"I do a lot of reading." She spoke in the prim tone he'd already named her librarian voice.

"That'll tell you a lot about the world."

"You'd be surprised." She glanced back at him, triumph in her eyes. At least she wasn't still angry.

"I'll bet I would." He closed his eyes as he stumbled over a curb, then quickly steadied himself. He would be damned if he let Ellie see how weak he was.

"We need to stop, Michael."

Hearing her say his name caused a quiver deep in his gut. Ruthlessly, he pushed it away. "The hotel I'm heading for is just around the corner."

"Do you want to rest?" she asked.

"Can't." Once again the irony of the situation struck him. Less than three hours ago he'd kidnapped her at gunpoint. Now she was helping him hide, and worrying about his wound.

A few moments later, her arm tensed around his waist. "Is that it?"

"Yeah," he managed to reply. The Hotel St. Jacques wasn't nearly as grand as its name. Half the neon letters in the sign were burned out, and the exterior had a sad, neglected air, as if the building had absorbed all the hopelessness and desperation of its surroundings.

"What now?" Ellie asked in a low voice.

He pulled his wallet from his pocket and fished out a couple of bills. "You're going to have to pay for the room up front. In cash. If you act nonchalant, the clerk will barely notice you. Make it quick and leave immediately. Don't share your life story with him."

"All right." Her hand trembled slightly on his waist and a trace of fear flashed in her eyes. Then she straightened. "I can do that."

"You can do anything you want to do." That was no less than the truth, he realized. Eleanor Perkins was one hell of a woman. He tightened his grip on her shoulder for a moment, then let his arm drop away. "I'll wait here."

Eleanor crossed the street and disappeared into the hotel. She was back out the door in less than two minutes. "You were right. He barely looked at me," she reported, flushed with victory. "He was reading a magazine and pushed the key across the counter without even looking."

They walked across the street and into the hotel, and again the night clerk didn't look up. Michael saw the nearly naked woman on the cover of the magazine and realized why. He wondered with an odd jolt of protectiveness if Ellie had realized what the clerk was reading.

Before he could ask, she wrapped her arm more firmly around him and steered him toward the stairs. They had taken only a couple of steps before Ellie stopped.

"Give me this," she said, and she snatched the backpack from his shoulders.

"Wait a minute." Anxiety flashed through him as he watched her sling the pack over her arm. He didn't want the evidence out of his hands. "I can keep that."

"Don't be ridiculous," she answered briskly. "You don't need to have this dead weight bouncing against your wound."

Michael glanced at the pack, which was swinging against her side. He was too weak to fight her for it. "You are one bossy woman," he muttered.

"You're right. And I especially like to pick on injured men who can't fight back."

In spite of the searing pain in his back, in spite of his fear for Ellie, he smiled. "Now why doesn't that surprise me?"

He was still smiling when they stopped in front of a door. Ellie fumbled with the key, then the door swung open with a groan. He reached inside and flicked on the light switch, then pulled her with him as he stumbled into the room and shut the door behind them.

The room was gray. The threadbare rug had faded to a muddy gray, the walls had long ago lost whatever color they'd originally been, and even the knobby bedspread on the double bed had faded from its original white to a dingy, depressing hue.

Eleanor stood rooted to the floor, her gaze traveling around the room. Finally it rested on the piece of furniture that dominated the room, the bed.

The only bed.

CHAPTER FIVE

"THAT'S A SMALL BED. And there's only one."

"Of course there is."

"I thought there would be two."

"Ellie, most of the people who use these rooms have no use for a second bed."

She turned to look at him. "You mean...you mean only prostitutes use this hotel?"

"Got it in one," he replied.

"That means the man at the desk thought I was a prostitute when I paid for the room."

"Bingo."

Her eyebrows snapped together and he waited for the storm to gather in her eyes. But instead of the outburst he expected, a calculating expression stole over her face. "So that's why he didn't really look at me." She gave Michael a satisfied smirk. "He'll never be able to identify us."

"Exactly."

She looked around the room again, this time with interest in her eyes. "I always wondered what a brothel would look like."

He suppressed his laughter, wincing as a sheet of liquid fire scorched his back. "I don't believe I've ever heard that word used to describe this place. I take it you got that term from one of those books you read.''

''It's interesting, whatever you want to call it.'' She looked at him again. ''Are there a lot of places like this in Midland?''

A wave of exhaustion swept over him. ''Way too many.'' He swayed on his feet and reached for the wall. ''Don't worry about the bed situation, Slim. I'll sleep on the floor.''

She dropped the backpack and moved closer to him, her expression full of regret. ''I'm being stupid,'' she said. ''Blabbering about prostitutes and worrying about the fact that there's only one bed instead of taking care of that wound of yours. Let me see it.''

''I can take care of it. Just give me the disinfectant.''

''Don't be silly. I'll clean it up for you. Lie down on the bed.''

In spite of his pain and exhaustion, his body reacted instantly to her words. ''You're in your bossy mode again, aren't you?'' He frowned at her to hide his reaction.

''Yes. And I can be very stern if I have to be.'' She stood with her hands on her hips, and he wanted to kiss her.

''Oh, goody,'' he said, unable to keep the grin off his face. ''I love it when you talk mean to me. If I don't behave, are you going to give me a spanking?''

Her cheeks burned but a smile fluttered around her

mouth. "You're darn right I am. Now lie down on the bed." Her soft blue-gray eyes twinkled and laugh lines crinkled around them. The smile transformed her face.

"Yes, ma'am. When a lady tells me to lie down on the bed, I always obey."

Eleanor watched as Michael eased himself onto the bedspread. She stifled a gasp of horror when she saw the back of his shirt, stiff and soaked through with blood. "You didn't tell me you were wounded so badly," she whispered.

"It's not exactly the kind of thing a kidnapper tells his victim." He turned his head to look at her and tried to smile, but she saw the pain in his eyes. "What should I have said? Go ahead and take a whack at me because I'm wounded?"

She ignored his sarcasm. "You've lost a lot of blood," she murmured. She couldn't stop herself from touching his shirt lightly.

"Tell me about it." He'd turned his face away from her and the comforter muffled his voice.

"I'm afraid your shirt is stuck to the wound." Her stomach curled at the thought of pulling it away. "I don't want to hurt you."

"It's not stuck. Trust me. Just lift up the shirt."

She raised the material cautiously and tugged it away from the ugly wound. It pulled at his skin and her hands tightened. "This looks serious, Michael," she said, trying to keep the horror out of her voice. There was a deep gash through the skin and muscle of his lower back. The edges were ragged and still oozing blood.

He turned his head to look at her, and she saw the effort it took him to smile. "Just clean it up and slap a bandage on it, Slim."

"Is the bullet still in there?"

"Nope. It grazed me. Don't worry, I wouldn't make you dig a bullet out of my back. I just need to be patched up."

"I'll do the best I can."

He gave her a ghost of a grin. "From my limited experience, I'd say that your best will be pretty damn good."

He closed his eyes, but unexpected warmth stole through her at his words. Why did praise from him mean so much to her?

"I'll get the things I bought," she said hastily as she slid off the bed. She really was pathetic. She'd turned to mush just because an attractive man smiled at her. Heaven forbid if Michael realized she was attracted to him. She wasn't sure she'd be able to bear the humiliation. She'd met men like him before. Women swarmed all over them, attracted to their charm and good looks. She would rather die than have him think she was one of those needy, pitiful women.

She fumbled in the bag from the convenience store and found the things she needed. "I got a bottle of peroxide," she said. "It's going to sting a little."

"Just don't enjoy this too much, Slim." He opened his eyes to give her a half smile.

"If I wanted to enjoy it, I would have used alcohol," she retorted.

He winced. "Ouch. You're all heart."

"You'd better believe it."

As she poured the peroxide onto a gauze pad, she squared her shoulders. She hesitated for only a moment before she gently touched the gauze to the ugly furrow in his back. He didn't move.

"Did I hurt you?" she asked.

"No. Go ahead and do your worst."

Reassured, she cleaned the raw wound, then used more peroxide to wash the blood from his skin. When everything looked clean and dry, she squirted some antibacterial ointment into the wound, covered it with more gauze squares, then taped them in place.

"There," she said. "All set."

He eased himself off the bed inch by painful inch. "Thanks, Ellie," he said, but his face was leached of color.

"You told me I wasn't hurting you." She stared at him, appalled.

He gave her a weary look. "Would you have finished the job if I was yelling and squirming?"

"Probably not," she admitted.

"Don't worry about me. I'm tough." He gave her a brief smile that held no humor at all. "And it'll feel better in the morning."

"You need some aspirin," she said, reaching into the bag from the convenience store and handing him four tablets. "Then lie down and get some sleep." She didn't look at him as she moved around, collecting the things she'd used for his back. "I'll sleep on the floor."

"I don't think that's a good idea."

She glanced over at him. "I'm certainly not going to let *you* sleep on the floor."

"Neither one of us should sleep there." She watched him struggle to give her another half smile. "The germs on that rug would probably kill us by morning."

She looked down at the worn, dull rug, which was gritty with dirt. In spite of herself, she shuddered at the thought of sleeping there. "You're probably right."

"There's plenty of room for both of us in this bed." He gave her a weary smile. "Believe me, I'm not going to touch you."

Her first, instinctive reaction was disappointment. Horrified with herself, she stumbled backward until she came up against the wall. Then reality took over.

It didn't matter what her subconscious might want. She wasn't his type and she'd better remember that unless she wanted to make a total fool of herself.

"All right," she said, taking a deep breath and trying to look anywhere but at him. "We'll share the bed."

Michael turned away from her and shrugged out of his jeans. She told herself not to watch him undress, but she couldn't stop herself. He wore silk boxers with a leopard-skin print, and the sight of them made her mouth curl in an involuntary smile. They were exactly what she would have pictured him wearing.

If she'd allowed herself to think about him in his underwear.

Which, of course, she hadn't.

He winced when he pulled back the bedspread, and she hurried over to help him.

He eased onto his side and waved his hand over the exposed sheets. "Hop in, Slim."

Heat swept over her as she stared first at him, then at the light switch on the wall. She couldn't remember ever being so horribly self-conscious. What should she do now? Should she take off her slacks and blouse, then turn out the light? Or should she turn out the light first, then undress? She had no experience slipping into bed with a virtual stranger. And any tips she might have collected from her reading completely eluded her.

"It's okay, Ellie," he said, and for a moment she almost believed he knew what she was thinking. "Take off your clothes, then turn off the light. I promise I won't peek."

He closed his eyes, and she pulled off her blouse and slacks as fast as she could. After setting them on the chair, the only other piece of furniture in the room, she dashed across the rug and flicked off the light switch. Standing in the semidarkness in her bra and panties, she felt completely exposed and vulnerable—far more vulnerable than she'd felt when he first kidnapped her.

Trying to ignore the heat that flooded her skin, she hesitated for a moment at the edge of the bed. Finally, she slipped between the cool sheets.

"You can relax, Ellie. We're safe for now," Michael murmured in the darkness. "No one will look for us here."

He hadn't moved since she got into bed, and she lay beside him, rigid with tension. He turned over so that he was facing away from her. "Good night, Ellie."

"Good night," she managed to whisper.

She couldn't bring herself to move. For what seemed like hours she stared at the ceiling, listening to him breathe. He'd said there was plenty of room for both of them in the bed, but he was far too close. Heat from his body radiated against hers and his scent surrounded her. She smelled the faint tang of the antibiotic ointment. If she moved her hand just a few inches, she would be touching him.

His breathing grew regular and deep. He was asleep. Cautiously she turned onto her side, facing away from him. She could do this, she told herself. Obviously it didn't bother Michael to be sharing a bed. The least she could do was act equally mature.

Drawing deep breaths, she concentrated on forcing her muscles to relax. Remembering a yoga class she had once taken, she started with her head and worked her way down her body. But she was almost at her feet before she fell asleep.

SUNLIGHT SHIMMERED against her closed eyelids and Eleanor felt uncomfortably hot. She must have forgotten to turn the air-conditioner on when she got home from work, she thought drowsily. It felt as if she was curled up with a furnace.

The furnace moved and her eyes flew open. A pair of bright blue eyes watched her, their gaze hot and intent. There was a man in bed with her, she realized with a shock. And she was wrapped around him like ribbon on a present.

"Good morning, Ellie," Michael said, his voice gravelly and rough. "I hope you slept well."

He shifted again, and she realized with another shock that his arms were wrapped around her. When she tried to slide away, though, she found that her own were wrapped just as tightly around him.

Her face flamed and she struggled to free herself, but only succeeded in entwining her legs more thoroughly with his. Before she could pull her arms away, he freed one of his hands and gently brushed a few strands of hair off her face.

"Shh," he murmured. "It's all right. You're safe."

Safe was the last word she would use to describe what she felt, she thought wildly. *Safe* was comfortable and unexciting. Familiar. It was nothing like the sensations crashing through her body right now.

He moved against her and she felt the unmistakable bulge of his erection against her abdomen. When she froze, he grinned at her and pressed his hips more snugly against her.

"No, I don't have a gun in my pocket," he said, his voice a husky rasp of velvet over her nerves. "I guess that means I'm glad to see you."

She shifted her body without thinking, so that the

rock-hard length of him was cradled at the juncture of her thighs. The grin faded from his face and his arms tightened around her. "I guess that means you're glad to see me, too."

He bent closer, and she waited, trembling, for his lips to touch hers. But he didn't kiss her. Instead, he nibbled at her earlobe, sending tremors of pleasure shooting through her body. Then he leisurely trailed his mouth down her neck, leaving a burning path behind.

When he stopped and touched her skin with his tongue, she gasped. And when he nipped at her, his teeth gently scraping her skin, she moaned and moved restlessly against him, trying to get closer.

Every inch of her was alive, quivering with need for his touch. Tension built and throbbed inside her, spreading out until her limbs felt heavy and weak and her heart raced in her chest. All traces of her usual good sense vanished, disappearing like mist in the sunshine.

Never in her life had she experienced anything remotely approaching these sensations. Her few sexual encounters had been awkward, fumbling affairs that left her feeling faintly soiled. Those memories incinerated in the heat between her and Michael. Now she wanted every inch of him pressed intimately against every inch of her. Now she wanted something she couldn't even understand.

But Michael seemed to understand very well. He nipped at her collarbone, grazing it with his teeth. He moved an inch lower, closer to her breast, nipping at her again. She held her breath, waiting for the touch of his mouth against her breast.

He stopped at the edge of her bra, lingering for a moment in the valley between her breasts. As he licked her, almost lazily, he stroked her back, his hand moving in leisurely circles, lower and lower. When he reached her hips, he spread his hand wide and pressed her more intimately into him. She felt his heat and his hardness through the filmy, flimsy barrier of her underwear and his. The silky fabric only made it easier to glide against him.

When she moved again, needing to feel him closer, where all the pulsing tension centered, he groaned against her chest. His warm breath caressed her skin, making her shiver.

"Ellie," he whispered. "What are you doing to me?"

His hand stopped moving abruptly, and she felt him stiffen against her. "What the hell am I doing to you?"

He slid away from her awkwardly, backing off until he sat leaning against the wall. Scrubbing his face with his hands, he looked down at the bed, at the door of the room, then at the wall. Everywhere but at her.

"My God, I'm sorry," he said, and she heard the appalled shock in his voice. "I didn't mean for that to happen."

"So you said last night," she replied, pulling the dingy bedspread up to her shoulders.

"Last night I wasn't capable of anything but sleep. Apparently this morning I'm feeling a whole lot better.'' He scowled, finally looking at her. ''But that's no excuse. I never meant to touch you. And I promise you it won't happen again.''

''Fine,'' she said, hot with humiliation. ''I'll try to restrain my impulses to throw myself at you, too.''

For just a moment desire flashed in his eyes. Then he leaned back against the wall. ''No need to be sarcastic, Slim. I'm glad we understand each other.''

''I am, too.'' She pushed herself off the bed, clutching the bedspread and wrapping it around her. ''Now turn around so I can get dressed.''

''I won't peek.'' He turned away. ''Even though you peeked last night.'' His voice was a low, sexy drawl that seemed to wrap around her nerves like heavy velvet.

''Last night I was afraid you would fall and hurt yourself,'' she retorted hotly. ''I should have just let you collapse and lie on the floor all night.''

''Just what I would have expected you to say. That's one of the things I like about you. You're so predictable.'' One corner of his mouth curled up, but he kept his head turned away.

She threw the tangled bedspread onto the floor and pulled on her clothes, seething with anger. How did he know so much about her after only a few hours? And worse, why did it bother her so much?

Because she knew he was merely flirting, she told herself, fighting back the tears. In spite of what had just passed between them, he was the same charming, cocky man he'd been yesterday, and it hurt to realize it. It hurt to realize that when he said he hadn't meant to touch her, it had been no more than the truth.

As if he could read her thoughts, he murmured, "I really am sorry that happened." There was no hint of laughter in his voice now. "And don't go thinking it means something that it doesn't. I'm not the kind of guy you're used to, Ellie. I'm not a dependable, solid, white picket fence, forever kind of guy. I'm 'good times' Reilly. I'll break your heart if you give me half a chance."

"There's no danger of that," she answered coolly. "Because you're not my type, either."

It was ludicrous to pretend she even had a type. But she had no intention of telling him that. She'd suffered enough humiliation for one morning.

"I'm glad we have that straightened out." He spoke from behind her, and she whirled to find that he was too close to her. Her throat swelled and she wanted to back away. But she forced herself to look him in the eye.

"Me, too. I believe in laying my cards on the table."

His face softened as he looked at her, and she could almost imagine she saw regret in his eyes. Almost.

"I've noticed that, Slim. It's one of the first things I noticed about you."

Now wasn't that special? She scowled as she yanked his jeans off the chair and practically threw them at him. Most men noticed the way a woman looked. He'd noticed her opinionated, bossy personality.

She grabbed his shirt and held it out to him, but realized it was hard with his blood. Holding the shirt in her hands, staring down at the stiff fabric, made her forget about what had just happened between them. All the events of the night came crashing back.

"Aren't you going to give me my shirt?" he asked.

"You can't wear this." She turned to face him, the shirt clenched in her hands. "Do you have another one in your backpack?"

"Nope. I didn't exactly have time to pack a suitcase." He reached for the shirt. "This one will have to do."

"No." She moved it away from him. "They'll be looking for someone with blood on his shirt."

"And I won't stand out if I'm walking around bare-chested?"

"Don't be an idiot." She tossed the shirt on the bed. "I'm going back to that convenience store. I think they had a bin full of cheap shirts."

"No, Ellie. Don't."

"Why not? Are you afraid I'll turn you in?"

"Of course not," he said impatiently.

"Then why don't you want me to go? The store's right down the street—it'll only take a couple of minutes."

He looked away from her. "I don't want you out there alone," he said. "The city is going to be swarming with cops looking for both of us. Letting you walk the streets alone would be like letting a lamb stroll into a wolf's den."

"It would be more dangerous for you to go out there in that shirt," she pointed out.

"But at least I'd be with you." He scowled at her. "You have no idea what these guys are capable of."

"Yes, I do," she said gently. "I cleaned your wound last night."

Without waiting for an answer, she grabbed her purse and headed for the door. "I'll be right back."

Her false bravado slipped as she eased the door shut behind her. She leaned against the wall, almost sick with fear, picturing a bullet tearing into her flesh. Then she straightened her shoulders and reached for the rickety handrail.

She had no choice. Michael needed her help. If they were ever going to make it out of town, she would have to face whatever waited for her on the dangerous streets of Midland.

CHAPTER SIX

ELLIE'S FOOTSTEPS RECEDED as she headed down the stairs, and Michael strained to listen until the sound faded into an uneasy silence. Trying to ignore his worry, he eased himself back onto the bed.

The wound in his back didn't burn as it had the night before. Now it throbbed with a relentless dull, aching pain. The tape Ellie had applied pulled at his skin, making it itch, but he welcomed the distraction. That was better than focusing on the pain.

What was she doing now? She'd walked out the door without a qualm, with no idea how dangerous it was out there, he thought savagely. She couldn't even begin to imagine what his enemies could do.

Maybe she could, a small voice reminded him. After all, he had treated her pretty brutally last night. He'd manhandled her, kidnapped her, forced her into an unlit building when he knew she was terrified of the dark. He'd snatched away all control over her life.

A wave of regret swept through him, so intense that it shocked him. He wished he'd met her under other circumstances. He wished he'd met her when he wasn't running for his life—and when she wasn't his unwilling hostage.

It didn't matter, he told himself. He and Ellie were all wrong. She was precisely the kind of woman he avoided. A person only had to look at her to know she was a forever-after type of woman—and he wasn't a forever-after type of man.

But it sure hadn't felt wrong this morning. His body stirred as he remembered waking up with Ellie in his arms. Her sweet curves had fitted against him perfectly, pressing into him with an innocence that was far more arousing than experience had ever been.

"Get your mind out of the gutter," he muttered to himself, deliberately squashing the desire that leaped to life inside him. He pulled himself upright, swaying as he stood. The muscles of his back cramped painfully, but he forced himself to stay on his feet. The pain focused his attention on what was important. He had to be able to walk if he was going to get Ellie out of Midland.

And get her out he would. Nothing would stop him, he vowed. He'd make sure she was safe before he delivered his information to the FBI. It was the least he could do.

But where to take her? She'd said she had no relatives, and she didn't want to involve her friends. So it was up to him to find a safe haven for her.

There was only one person he would trust with her safety. Pulling out his cell phone, he pressed a button and listened to the phone ring.

After a terse conversation, he snapped the phone closed and began to hobble painfully around the tiny room. He braced one hand on the wall as he shuffled one foot in front of the other. His back screamed in protest, but he ignored it. He made himself concentrate on walking.

When his muscles loosened and he felt steadier on his feet, he glanced at his watch and realized that more than twenty minutes had passed. A cold river of fear washed over him, erasing everything else from his mind. What had happened? The store was only a couple of minutes away from the hotel. Had Ellie gotten lost? His gut tightened into a knot. Or had the police found her?

He slung the backpack over his shoulders and stumbled toward the door. Just as he wrenched it open, she appeared at the top of the stairs. Her hair was falling out of its bun and her lips were pressed tightly together, but she was back.

He wanted to snatch her into his arms and hold her until his heart slowed. He wanted to touch her, to make sure she was unharmed. Hell, he wanted to kiss her, to reassure himself that she was actually there with him.

''Where the hell have you been?'' he barked.

Her head shot up and she gave him a look that could have blistered paint. ''I stopped to read the newspaper and have a cappuccino. It took a while to find one, since this isn't exactly a Starbucks kind of neighborhood,'' she snapped back.

He relaxed against the wall. ''And here I was imagining that you'd been kidnapped or something,'' he drawled.

The sparks disappeared from her eyes. ''I'm

sorry," she said quietly. "I should have known you'd be worried."

"What happened?" He forced himself to keep his arms folded across his chest. He ached to reach for her and pull her close. The thought scared him almost as much as his earlier worries.

She sighed and walked into the room. He closed the door and turned to face her.

"I saw two police cars," she said, setting a bag down on the chair. "The first one was cruising by just as I walked out of the hotel. I jumped back in the door." Her forehead creased with worry. "I don't think they saw me."

"Then what?"

"I waited for about five minutes and didn't see them again. So I headed to the convenience store. I was about halfway there when I saw another police car."

"Are you sure it wasn't the same one?" Urgency punched into his chest and his heart speeded up.

"I don't know. I wasn't really paying attention to what the officers looked like."

"Officers? How many were in the car?"

"Two."

"In both cars?"

"Yes. They both had two people in the front seat." She frowned. "But only one wore a uniform."

He swore under his breath. "What did you do when you saw the second one?"

She pushed her glasses up her nose. "I kept my head down, as if I was looking for something. Before

I left the hotel I picked up a big bag that someone had left in the lobby. I filled it with crumpled newspapers and slung it over my shoulder. I figured that would make it harder to see my face.'' She struggled to smile at him. ''With the way I looked, I was pretty sure I could pass for a homeless person.''

He shook his head, amazed. ''Ellie, you are something else. Where did you learn a trick like that?''

Before she could answer, he held up one hand. ''No, don't tell me. You read it in a book, right?''

''Right,'' she said triumphantly. ''And it worked, too. The squad car never even slowed down when it passed me.''

''Then what?''

''Then I stayed in the store for as long as I could without making the clerk suspicious. I pretended I couldn't make up my mind about the shirt.'' She blushed and added, ''I also picked up a few other items I thought we could use.''

''Did you see anyone on your way back?''

She shook her head. ''Just a couple of cars. But they weren't police cars.''

He hoped. They'd have unmarked cars looking for him, too. But he didn't want to burst her bubble by telling her that. ''Okay, let's get out of here. If they spotted you coming out of this hotel, we don't have long.''

Her face paled. ''Do you really think they might have recognized me?''

He shrugged as he struggled into the blue chambray work shirt she handed him. ''Hard to tell. But we better assume they did. That's better than hanging around waiting for an ugly surprise.''

''Okay, let's go.'' She grabbed the bag, which wasn't empty, and turned toward the door, but he gave into temptation and took her arm.

''In a minute. First grab the garbage out of the trash can. We don't want to leave any evidence behind.'' For the space of a heartbeat he allowed his hand to linger on her arm. Her skin was warm and smooth, her muscles tense beneath his fingers. He tightened his grip and began to pull her toward him, then abruptly let her go. This was the wrong time and definitely the wrong woman.

She paused and stared at him for a moment, her eyes wide. The fear had retreated, replaced by a glimmer of awareness that made him jam his hands into his pockets. He was too close to grabbing her, too close to pulling her into his arms and just holding on.

''Come on, Ellie,'' he said, his voice deliberately harsh. ''We don't have all day.''

''You need to button your shirt,'' she finally said, her gaze fixed on his chest.

He looked down and swore again. What the hell was the matter with him? Was he so distracted by her that he couldn't even remember how to dress?

His fingers fumbled with the buttons, but she pushed his hands away. ''I'm sure your back is sore,'' she said. ''Let me do it.''

She didn't meet his gaze while her fingers brushed over his chest. They shook slightly as they pushed the buttons through the holes, but he forced himself to look away. Finally she was finished.

"You're respectable again," she said, forcing herself to smile.

"Not possible," he said, his tone harsh. "And you'd be smart to remember that."

A steely look replaced her smile. "Don't worry. It's not the kind of thing I'm likely to forget."

"Good," he muttered, wrenching the door open. He would be absolutely nuts to get involved with Eleanor Perkins, he told himself. Even if they weren't running for their lives. She was exactly the kind of women he'd spent his life running away from.

But he watched her walk out the room in front of him, and his hands ached to touch her. His body ached to feel her wrapped around him again. And all he could think about was the way her skin had tasted, sweet and fresh and innocent.

He scowled and pulled the door shut behind him with a little too much force. Far too innocent for a man like him.

She headed down the stairs without hesitating. But before they reached the lobby, she stopped and looked at him. Uncertainty filled her face. "What now?" she whispered.

The desk clerk was writing in a notebook, his face furrowed with concentration. "We just walk out," Michael whispered back. A devil inside him prompted him to add, "If he looks up, act like we've just shared a night of unbridled passion."

Her face turned red, and he could see a sharp retort

hovering on her lips. But she glanced at the clerk
again and pressed her lips together. Michael was
vaguely disappointed that she'd restrained herself
from giving him the quick comeback she clearly
wanted to throw at him.

Her head held high, she swept toward the door. He
wanted to call her back and remind her that few prostitutes had attitude like that, but instead he followed
her outside.

Once on the street, he forced himself to concentrate
on their surroundings. A couple of homeless men
trudged down the sidewalk and a few cars sped past.
But otherwise the neighborhood was deserted. No one
wanted to spend any time in this area.

"What are we going to do now?" Ellie asked quietly.

"Keep walking while I figure it out," he muttered.

She shot him an assessing look. "You still don't
have a plan?"

"I told you, I'm a seat-of-the-pants kind of guy.
We'll play it by ear."

"I hope you're not hard of hearing," she said under her breath.

"That's good, Ellie. That's very good." He
grasped her arm and steered her toward an alley. "I'm
impressed you can come up with smart answers this
early in the morning." He glanced down at her and
forced himself to give her a grin. "I had you pegged
as a night owl."

But instead of the retort he expected, she watched
him with warmth in her eyes. "You don't have to try

and distract me," she murmured. "I'm not stupid. I know how dangerous this is."

He stopped abruptly and pulled her around to face him. "You just keep on surprising me," he finally said. When she looked up at him, her eyes wide, his chest contracted. Her safety was in his hands, and he prayed he was up to the task. "I'll get you out of here. I promise," he said as he tucked a strand of hair behind her ear. She'd pulled it into a sloppy bun on the top of her head, but it was already falling down her back.

"I believe you," she answered. Their gazes met and locked, and as she stared at him, he saw absolute faith reflected in her eyes. The knowledge shook him to his core. He vowed that her faith in him wouldn't be misplaced.

"All right, this is what we'll do," he said rapidly, to cover the erratic thumping of his heart. "We're going to steal a car. We'll get out of Midland as fast as possible, then we'll figure out the next step."

"All right."

As easily as that, she placed her life in his hands. Humbled, he said, "Let's go."

They hurried down the alley, but before they reached the other end, he saw a glint of metal at the mouth of the lane, and Michael pulled her into the shadow of another rickety garage.

The flash of metal came from a police cruiser idling at the curb, its engine a low growl. It was clearly waiting. For them? Had the cops in the cruiser Ellie had seen earlier noticed her?

Michael stopped so suddenly that she stumbled. Cursing the pain and stiffness in his back, which slowed him down, he pivoted sharply, ignoring the tug on the wound. He began to run, yanking Ellie along with him, as the door of the squad car creaked open behind them.

"Hold on, Reilly," a man called in a low voice.

Michael froze at the sound, stunned into immobility. *Not you, too, Sam,* he thought to himself. Pain clawed at his gut and wound tightly around his heart. Slowly, reluctantly, he pulled his gun from the waistband of his jeans and turned to face the police officer.

"Put the gun away, you idiot." His partner, Sam Jenkins, shook his head as he approached them. Glancing back at the street, he crowded Michael and Ellie into the shadows, where they were barely hidden.

"What the hell is going on?" the cop asked, his voice an angry growl.

"Just get in the car and leave, Sam." Anger and bitter disillusionment swirled through Michael, but he refused to take his eyes off his partner. "And don't touch the gun."

"What kind of crap is this?" Sam said roughly. "They told me there was an APB out on you."

"Did they tell you why?"

"They claim you killed Montero."

"So what are you going to do about it?" Michael asked, holding the gun steadily on his partner.

"Not a damn thing until you put that gun away."

"No can do, Sam." Michael edged over a step so

he was standing in front of Ellie, his gaze switching between his partner and the other officer, who was now standing tense and rigid next to the squad car. It was the rookie he and Sam were training. "Take the kid and get out of here." Michael jerked his head at the cruiser, where the rookie watched with indecision.

"Not until you tell me what the hell is going on."

Michael's gaze hardened as he looked back at his partner. "My guess is you know what the hell is going on, which is why you're here. If you don't, there isn't time to explain."

Sam shook his head. Michael wanted to believe that the confusion in his partner's eyes was real, that the puzzlement on his face was genuine. But he couldn't take the chance. Ellie's life depended on it.

He felt her presence behind him. She was so close that he could taste her fear, so close that if he backed up another step she would be plastered against him. His resolve hardened as he stared at his partner.

"What's it going to be, Sam? Do we see who's fastest with a gun? Or are you going to get into the squad car and disappear?"

"I want to help you, man," Sam said in a low voice. "What do you need?"

It was so tempting to trust him. Sam had been his partner for the past three years. They'd covered each other's backsides more times than Michael could count. Never before had he hesitated to trust Sam, or worried that his partner wouldn't back him up.

But what were he and Hobart doing in this part of town?

"How did you find me, anyway?" Michael asked, his voice heavy with suspicion.

"I read the report from last night, after Ruiz stopped you. That was some fine driving, by the way."

He wouldn't be sucked in by the familiar banter. "What made you look for me here?"

"We've been cruising around this dump of a neighborhood since our shift started. Any sane man would have gone in the opposite direction last night. That's why I figured you'd end up here."

"That's cute, Sam," he said, his voice sour. "Real cute. But it's not good enough."

"What do you want from me?" Sam's low voice took on the ring of urgency, and he glanced back toward the squad car.

Did Sam really have him so well pegged? Or was there a more sinister explanation? Michael's resolve hardened. "Get lost, Sam. That's all I need from you right now."

His partner didn't budge. He lifted his chin in Ellie's direction. "Is she the woman who's missing? Did you really kidnap her?"

"Forget about her," Michael replied in a low, deadly voice. "If you want to help me, just get the hell out of here. And forget that you saw us."

His partner watched him with wary eyes, his hand hovering over his own gun. After a long moment, he sighed and deliberately shifted his fingers away. "You're in a hell of a mess, partner."

Michael gave a short, involuntary bark of laughter. "Now there's news."

"I hope you know what you're doing."

"As much as I ever do," Michael answered.

His reply brought a reluctant grin from Sam. "That's the Reilly I know and love."

Tension burned in the air and neither man looked away. Finally, Sam drew a deep breath, turned his back and walked toward the cruiser. Before he'd taken more than two steps, Michael called out, "And make sure Hobart keeps his mouth shut."

Sam glanced over his shoulder. "Don't worry about the kid. He'll do what I tell him to do."

Michael watched, his gun drawn, until his partner and Hobart got into the vehicle and disappeared around a corner. He waited for an eternity, scarcely daring to breathe, as he listened for the sound of a car engine doubling back.

Finally he turned to face Ellie. "Let's go."

She stared at him as if she'd never seen him before. No surprise there, he thought savagely. His face had to reflect how he felt, which was like a refugee from hell. As he waited, wondering if his partner would return, his soul withered into a hard kernel of pain.

"Come on, Ellie. Move it. They won't give us all day to get away." He put an edge of impatience in his voice. "They know where we are now. It's just a matter of time before this place is crawling with cops."

"Was that officer really your partner?" she asked, her voice troubled.

"Sure was. Couldn't you tell by the warm interplay between us?"

She took a step toward Michael and reached out as if to touch him. At the last moment she curled her fingers into her palm and let her hand drop to her side. "I'm so sorry," she whispered. "I can't even imagine how it would feel to be betrayed by someone I trusted."

"Yeah, well, it's been a lousy couple of days for trust. But we don't have time to stand around and analyze it. Let's go."

He stumbled back into the alley and grabbed for her hand, trying to bury the pain while he scrambled to figure out what to do. Ellie gripped his hand, then she let him go and stepped to his side. She wrapped her arm around his waist and pulled him close.

"Lean on me," she said, her voice urgent. "We'll move faster."

He draped his arm across her shoulders, but when he let some of his weight sag onto her, she stumbled on the uneven ruts of the alley.

"Damn it," he said, trying to draw away from her. "I'm too heavy for you."

She flashed him a steely look. "I'll tell you when you're too heavy for me. Don't go all macho on me, Reilly. We don't have time for that nonsense."

"Yes, ma'am," he managed to answer. He couldn't summon the strength for any more of a reply. The pain from his back was excruciating, and the ruts in the alley seemed ten feet deep.

They approached a two-flat that was clearly abandoned. Paint peeled from the walls, leaving gray wood exposed. The back porch hung off the structure, sagging to one side and tilting at a dangerous angle. All the windows were broken, leaving the building sightless and lonely.

But standing in the yard was exactly what they needed. A small, foreign economy car listed to the left, the side panels almost rusted through and the bumper dented in several spots.

"*There,*" he gasped, nodding at the car. "We'll take that one."

"That wreck?"

He ignored the disbelief in her voice. "That's the one." Painfully, he picked his way through the debris that cluttered the tall grass.

"Why that car? It doesn't even look like it will start."

"Precisely. Chances are no one will notice it missing for a while. That'll give us time to get out of town."

Wrenching open the stiff door caused the hinges to groan in protest and his back to shriek with pain. The car smelled faintly musty, as if the windows had been open during the last thunderstorm and the seats still weren't dry. He looked under the floor mat, but the owner hadn't been considerate enough to leave the keys.

Angling himself so he could look below the dash, he picked out the two wires he needed and touched them together. The engine sputtered to life, coughed a few times, then settled down to a steady, uneven rumble.

''Hop in,'' he said to Ellie, who stood hesitantly next to the car.

When he started to buckle the seat belt, though, she straightened as though she'd made a decision. ''Slide over and let me drive. They won't be looking for a woman by herself.''

She was right. But by allowing her to drive, would he be putting her at even greater risk? She'd be the prime target. And they'd shoot first and ask questions later.

As he hesitated, she bent closer. ''What's the matter, Reilly? Afraid I can't handle it?''

Damn it, he had no choice. Mustering all his strength, he gave her a faint grin. ''Not me. I saw you driving last night, Slim. I figure Midland's finest are still reeling from that car chase. Heck, there are probably still rubber fumes in the air.''

''Then move over.''

She tossed her bag into the back seat, then waited for him to unbuckle the seat belt. As soon as he edged over on the bench seat, she slid in behind the wheel. Fastening her hands around the steering wheel, she carefully backed out of the yard and bumped her way into the alley.

As they reached the street and the spot where Sam had been waiting for them, her knuckles whitened on the wheel.

There wasn't another car in sight. Michael took a deep breath, slid lower in his seat and prayed to a

God he wasn't sure even existed. "This is it, Slim. Go for it."

She shot him a worried glance, then eased the car onto the street. She was as stiff as if she expected to be hit with a volley of bullets any minute. Once again he cursed himself for getting her involved. But it didn't matter now. There was no way he could leave her behind.

"Which way?" she asked, licking her lips as if they were dry.

"Head back toward the city," he directed.

"Are you sure?"

"Believe me, I want to get you somewhere safe as much as you want to be there, but we can't leave Midland just yet. We have a stop to make first."

Her eyebrows snapped together and she focused on the second part of his statement. "What do you mean, we have to make a stop? I thought the idea was to get your information to the FBI as fast as possible."

"It is. But there are some things more important."

"What can possibly be more important than your life?" she asked impatiently.

"Two other innocent lives that may be in danger."

CHAPTER SEVEN

ELLIE TOOK HER EYES off the road to stare at Michael. Suspicion and doubt crept into her mind, dark and insidious. ''I thought you were the only one who knows about the corruption.''

''I hope to God I am. But the dirty cops may not think so.''

''What do you mean?''

Apparently he didn't hear her. Or he chose not to answer. Instead he stared straight ahead, lost in his thoughts.

''Stop if you see a newspaper box,'' he finally said, his voice hard. ''I need to know what the cops are saying.''

''There's one in that bag on the rear seat,'' she said. ''I grabbed it at the convenience store.''

Michael reached around and pulled the paper out of the plastic bag. He opened it with a snap, then sucked in his breath.

''What?'' she asked.

''It's just as bad as I thought it would be.''

''What does it say?''

As the car shuddered to a stop at a red light, he held the newspaper so she could see it. On the first page, toward the bottom, was a large picture of Michael. And above the picture the headline screamed Killer Cop on the Run.

She stared at the photos, her stomach cramping into a knot of fear, until Michael said sharply, "Go. The light's changed."

The car was drifting over the center line, and she wrenched the wheel around. "What do they mean?" she whispered. "Why are they calling you a killer? I thought you were just running away because you had evidence against them."

"They're saying I killed a man last night." His voice was flat as he read the article. "That I'm a rogue cop, unpredictable and dangerous."

"I don't believe that," she said immediately. "I don't believe you killed anyone, unless it was in self-defense."

"Thank you for that," he said quietly after a moment. "Thank you for believing in me."

"What happened last night?" She took a chance and darted a glance his way. He was hunched down against the car seat, his eyes closed, almost as if he was admitting defeat. "You didn't kill anyone, did you?" she asked sharply.

"Yes, I did."

She sucked in a shocked breath. His eyes opened and they were full of naked pain. "I didn't pull the trigger," he said. "But I might as well have. Someone was killed last night, and it was my fault."

"Tell me what happened," she demanded fiercely.

He tried to give her another of his grins and failed

miserably. "I told you I wasn't a guy you wanted to spend any time with," he murmured.

"Let me be the judge of that," she insisted.

He shrugged. "What the hell. You're already involved up to your neck. You might as well know the whole ugly story."

He looked down at his hands and didn't say anything for a long time. Finally he lifted his head and stared blindly out of the windshield, clearly reliving whatever had transpired the night before.

"I've been working on this corruption for some time," he began. "It took me a while to realize that something was going on, then even longer to gather the information I needed." He gave her a sardonic glance. "The cops involved weren't real open about what they were doing. And I had to be careful."

His face hardened, and he looked away. "I had a snitch," he said quietly. "A dealer who kept me current on various drug deals in Midland. I'd arrested him about a year ago, and he wasn't happy about it. His girlfriend had just had a kid and he claimed he wanted to go straight. Said he didn't want to end up in prison and not see his son grow up."

Michael's mouth tightened. "I wasn't sure if he was telling me the truth or just looking for a get-out-of-jail-free card, but we made a deal. I let him go and paid him for every tip he gave me. Six months ago he told me there were some Midland cops who were players in the local drug scene."

"What did you do?" she whispered.

"What anyone would have done. I told him I needed proof."

"And did he give it to you?"

Michael nodded, turning to look out the window again. "Oh, yeah. Pictures and all. A bunch of guys, too, at all levels of the force, all the way from lieutenants to patrol officers. So many that I knew more people had to be involved. People higher up in the food chain."

"So you kept the pictures."

He gave a curt nod. "That's what's in my backpack. All the pictures that Montero collected and all of my own findings. I realized I couldn't go to anyone in Midland about the problem—I had no idea how pervasive the corruption was. But I knew its tentacles had to go deep into the department. If they didn't have some powerful protection, these guys wouldn't have been able to operate. I was trying to find out how high the rot went."

"Until last night."

"Until last night," he agreed.

"What happened?"

"They got Montero," he said, his voice flat. "I'm not sure how it happened, but they must have caught him taking pictures. A few people knew he was my snitch, although I'd tried to keep it quiet. So they found my unmarked car and put him in the back seat. Then they shot him."

"How do you know that?" she whispered. Fear swept over her, chilling her to the bone.

"I saw them do it. And I couldn't stop it."

"Tell me." She longed to reach out and touch him, but he was too far away, in a place filled with anguished memories.

"I'd answered a call and was heading back to my car." He sliced a glance at her and his mouth thinned. "You can say what you want about my way of handling things, but if I hadn't listened to my intuition, I'd be as dead as Montero right now."

"Why?"

"I stopped in the alley between two buildings. Something just didn't feel right. And I saw six or seven guys standing around my car. One of them pulled a gun out of an ankle holster and said something to someone in the back seat. The cop moved away and I saw that it was Montero. Then they shot him.

"The cop who'd done the shooting tossed the gun onto the seat. Then they all just got into their squad cars and drove away."

"And you ran over to your vehicle."

"Close," he said, his voice grim. "I see you've figured it out."

"They had someone waiting for you?"

"Bingo. They knew that sooner or later I would show up. I guess the plan was they'd shoot me, then put the gun they'd used to kill Montero into my hand. They would have said that they caught me shooting the guy, tried to stop me, and I fired on them. That they had no choice but to take me down."

"That's how you got shot."

"Yeah. But I was a little more careful than they

expected. I waited for a few minutes, and sure enough, I saw the cop they'd left behind. I was trying to get behind him when he spotted me and fired. I managed to make it as far as the library, but I knew they would find me sooner or later. That's why I needed to grab you and your car. They wouldn't be looking for a civilian.''

''I'm so sorry,'' she whispered. ''You must feel like you've been betrayed by everyone you've ever trusted.''

''That's nothing new,'' he said, his voice hard and cold. ''My only regret is that this time I had to involve someone else.''

''What do you mean?''

''I mean that I hate like hell that I've put you in danger.''

''No, why did you say being betrayed was nothing new?''

He paused, leaving the silence pulsing with tension. ''Ancient history,'' he finally said, his voice distant and cold. ''Nothing to do with you.''

''You don't trust me, do you?''

His hesitation lasted just a moment too long. ''I trust you,'' he finally said. His words almost sounded grudging.

''Because you have no choice.'' She noticed that he didn't look over at her.

''I don't have a choice right now,'' he finally agreed. ''But once we're out of Midland, all bets are off. I'm sorry, Ellie. It's nothing personal. I can't afford to trust anyone. If I do, and I make a mistake, my information dies with me. And Montero will have died for no reason at all.''

''I understand,'' she said, staring out the windshield. And she did. She was just surprised that it hurt so much.

There was no reason why it should, she told herself. She had no relationship with Michael Reilly, other than that of hostage and kidnapper. She tried her best to ignore the memories of that morning, when they'd woken up in the same bed. She was certain Michael had already forgotten all about it. She was an inconvenience and he was in a hurry to get rid of her. When he left her behind it would be the last time she saw him. Unless she had to testify at a trial, she thought grimly.

''So where are we going now?'' She tried to steady her voice, horribly afraid that Michael would hear the hurt she felt.

''I have to check on Montero's girlfriend and kid. I need to make sure they're safe.'' His mouth compressed into a tight line. ''They might be in trouble if the cops think Gloria knows something.''

''Surely these cops wouldn't hurt a baby and a woman who isn't involved?'' Eleanor whispered, horrified.

''You're not involved in this mess, either. But they'd kill you without even thinking about it if they caught us.''

She pushed away her fear, unable to think about herself. ''But a baby? They'd kill a child?''

''They might leave the baby alone,'' he conceded.

"The kid is barely a year old. He couldn't testify against them."

"That sounds so cold." She shivered in spite of the heat pouring through the open windows.

"That's reality, Ellie," he said. "You're not in the library anymore. Life isn't like those books you read, where the good guys always win and everything works out in the end." His eyes were chips of ice in a face as unyielding as granite. "Kids and innocent women get killed and there's not a damn thing anyone can do to stop it." He took a deep breath. "I'm not sure I even want to try anymore."

The silence vibrated between them, thick and heavy. "This is where we have to be careful," he said after a few minutes, his voice still strained with tension. They were leaving the run-down industrial part of Midland behind. As they got closer to the center of the city there was more traffic and more people.

And a cruiser approaching them from the other direction.

"There's a police car," she said. At the same instant Michael began sliding down in the seat.

"I see it." His voice was grim and cold. "Make sure you're about two miles over the speed limit."

She checked her speedometer and pressed lightly on the accelerator. They passed the cops in a small burst of speed, and she watched in the rearview mirror as the squad car left them behind.

"They've turned a corner," she finally reported.

But he didn't sit up on the seat again. "You're going to see more of them before we get out of town.

Don't look at them, don't speed up or slow down when you see them. Just keep driving as if you don't have a care in the world."

"I'll try."

"I know."

She thought his voice warmed, but she didn't dare look down at him. Another police car approached, and her heart pounded as if it wanted to jump out of her chest.

She forced herself to keep her eyes on the road instead of looking at the cruiser. Time expanded and slowed down until if felt as if she were standing still, certain the cops would look over and identify her at any moment.

When the police car was safely past, she drew in an unsteady breath. Her hands squeezed the steering wheel so tightly that they began to cramp. When she wiggled her fingers, Michael glanced over at her.

"Turn left at the next street," he said gently. "You're doing just fine, Ellie."

She moistened her lips and tried to speak in a normal voice. "Where exactly are we going?" Her voice came out shaky and weak.

"Not much farther. We're only a few blocks away."

He directed her around a few more corners until they drove down a quiet side street lined with apartment buildings. Although they were old, most of them looked cared for. Several people walked down the sidewalks, and cars lined the curb.

"Park here," he said when they approached an open spot between two vehicles.

She eased the car into place, then looked at him. "How do I turn it off?"

"You don't. We may need to leave in a hurry."

They sat in the car, listening to the engine chug, as seconds stretched into minutes. Michael raised his head just enough to scan the area, and finally he sat up. "I don't see a thing. I'll be right back."

"Aren't I going with you?"

He glanced at her, his hand on the door, and his face softened. "You have to stay in the car. We can't leave it running in this neighborhood or we'll be stranded without wheels when we come out. You'll be fine. Pretend like you're reading one of those books of yours and don't look anyone in the eye. I don't see any cops nearby."

Before she could ask him anything more he opened the door and eased himself out. Moving stiffly, he hurried into the alley between two buildings and disappeared.

The car chugged steadily as the minutes ticked by. What would happen if the police were waiting at Gloria's apartment? Michael could be walking into a trap.

Admiration fluttered through her. He had to know it was a possibility. But he'd chosen to come here, anyway. He'd chosen to make sure an innocent woman and child were safe.

She looked in the direction he'd disappeared, but didn't hear or see anything out of the ordinary. Heat shimmered off the vinyl upholstery, and muggy summer air surrounded her. But as she waited for Michael to return, she shivered with fear.

MICHAEL WAITED in the shadow of a two-flat while he surveyed the back of Gloria's building. Heat rose from the concrete and swirled around him, the smoggy heat of summer in the city. He ignored the sweat that trickled down his back, ignored the stinging pain when it washed over his wound. He focused all his attention on his surroundings.

Birds chirped and the voices of children playing rose from a yard several houses away. Somewhere a car door slammed and a mother called for her child. All normal sounds of a neighborhood.

He strained to hear anything different, anything out of the ordinary. But there was nothing unexpected. Sooner or later he was going to have to step into the open and walk up the back stairs of Gloria's building.

Bracing himself, half prepared for a hail of bullets, he walked through the alley and opened the gate to her backyard. He climbed up the stairs and knocked on her door, praying that she would answer.

"Detective Reilly." Her voice came from the shadows on the other side of the screen door, but she made no move to open it for him.

"I need to talk to you, Gloria," he said urgently. "Will you let me in?"

"You killed Rueben." Her voice was raw with tears and grief.

"It wasn't me," he said, pressing his palm against

the screen. "I didn't kill him. But I know who did. And you and Rueben, Jr., could be in danger."

She made no move to open the door. "Why should I believe you? The police came last night and told me what happened." She bent her face to the head of the baby draped over her shoulder.

"Do you have any idea what Rueben was doing for me?" Michael asked.

Slowly, reluctantly, she nodded. "He talked about it sometimes."

"The men who killed him were the men he was watching. They set it up to make it look like I killed him. And I'm afraid that they might come after you and Rueben, Jr., next."

"Why would they bother with us?"

"Because they're afraid of what Rueben might have told you," he said grimly. "You need to get out of Midland for a while."

"Is that why you're here? To tell me to leave?"

He drew in a deep breath, feeling anger, regret and grief churning in his stomach. "That's part of the reason. I'm sorry, Gloria. More sorry than I can tell you." He paused and looked at the child on her shoulder. "You and the baby were the most important things in the world to Rueben. All he ever talked about was his plans. He wanted to be there for you, for the baby. He wanted to watch his son grow up. And it's my fault that he can't."

The woman moved closer to the door. "It's not entirely your fault," she said. "Rueben chose to work with you." Her voice thickened. "It was a blow to my heart last night when the police told me you'd killed Rueben. He was so proud to be working with you. And he trusted you. I thought you'd betrayed him."

"I cared about him," Michael said quietly. "He was trying hard to make something of himself, to get away from the gang and make you proud of him. I wanted him to make it. I wouldn't have done anything to hurt him."

Gloria stared at him for a long moment, then fumbled with the door and pushed it open. "Come in, Detective Reilly."

Michael stepped into the kitchen. "Please believe me, Gloria. You have to leave town. I would take you with me, but it would be too dangerous for you. Is there someone who could help you?"

"I'll go to my mama," she said, and Michael sent up a prayer of thanks that she apparently believed him.

"Does your mama live in Midland?"

"Of course."

Michael fumbled in his pocket for his wallet and pulled out all the money in it. "You can't do that. Take this money. Go to St. Louis or Chicago. Anywhere you have family or friends you can stay with for a while."

"I can't take all your money." She looked at him, her gaze proud. "What will you do without cash?"

"Let me worry about that." He grabbed her hand and wrapped her fingers around the bills. "Just get your things together and leave, as soon as possible. And don't tell anyone where you're going.''

She glanced past him out the door, then looked him in the eye. "You took a chance by coming here."

"Rueben, Jr., already lost his father. I won't let him lose his mother, too."

She watched him steadily for a long moment, then nodded. "Rueben said you were a good man. He was right. Thank you, Detective."

"Call me Michael," he said, his voice rough. Her dignified words made the guilt even heavier inside him. "We'll talk again when this is all over."

"Be careful, Michael," she said softly. "Rueben said this city needs more police officers like you."

He slipped out the door and hurried down the steps without looking back. It would be a long time before he forgot the vulnerability of the dark-haired baby cradled in his mother's arms, or the grief etched on Gloria's face. And it would take even longer for his guilt to ease.

He slipped back into the lane then hesitated. An unwelcome thought crossed his mind. What if Ellie wasn't there? What if she'd simply driven away and left him stranded?

She wouldn't do that. He scowled to himself as he edged toward the front of the building. Why the hell wouldn't she do that? He'd taken her hostage and she finally had a chance to get away. She'd be crazy not to take it.

When he reached the end of the alley and saw the car sitting patiently at the curb, blue exhaust billowing into the air, something shifted deep inside him. Ellie believed him. And more important, she trusted him. Another tiny gate in his heart creaked open.

It terrified him.

The fact that she'd waited for him strengthened the bonds that were already growing between them. He'd fought his whole life against bonds, against feeling a connection with another person. The only person he'd let into his life was Charles Wilson. And fear that Ellie was worming her way past his barriers made Michael edgy and anxious.

He reached the car and pulled the door open. She looked up at him, her eyes lighting with relief. Scowling, he tried to ignore the answering joy in his own heart that she had waited for him.

He wanted to joke the feelings away, to ease the tension that suddenly brewed between them. ''What's the matter, Slim? Didn't you have anyplace better to go this morning?''

CHAPTER EIGHT

ELEANOR'S HEART SOARED as Michael slid into the car, only to crash again at his flippant words. What did she expect? she asked herself fiercely. Did she really think he was going to go all mushy and sentimental on her?

Not likely. His smart remark was probably as close as he would come to thanking her for waiting for him.

"I wouldn't miss this for the world," she replied, trying to keep her tone as flip as his. "There's nothing I like better than hanging around with the criminal element."

A brief flicker of regret passed across his face, then he settled lower in the seat. "Let's hit the road."

She wouldn't speculate on that regret, she told herself resolutely. That route led only to grief. Instead she tried to focus on their dilemma.

"Was your snitch's girlfriend there?"

"Yeah, she was."

Eleanor couldn't read anything in his shuttered face. She waited a moment, then said, "And?"

"And she's going to leave. I gave her money and told her to get out of town. I think she believed me when I told her she could be in trouble."

"She could have come with us."

He shook his head. "Too dangerous. Much better to split up."

Obviously he didn't want to discuss what had happened in the woman's apartment. And why was Eleanor surprised about that? Michael had made it more than clear he wasn't interested in sharing anything with her.

She watched the street signs flashing past, trying to ignore the pain welling up in her chest. She should have left when she had the chance, she told herself harshly. What kind of an idiot waits in the car for her kidnapper to come back?

The kind of idiot who believes him. And now she was just doing her civic duty. That's all that was going on. A ridiculous attraction to a kidnapper had nothing to do with it. She wasn't stupid enough to think anything could come of it.

"Where do you want to go now?" she asked, her tone abrupt.

He glanced at her, but didn't say anything. After a moment he looked away. "Stop here for gas, then head south out of town."

A few minutes later, they were on their way again.

"Can I ask where we're going?" she asked.

"We're aiming for a small town that's a couple of hours away. I'm going to leave you someplace you'll be safe. I don't want you involved in this mess any longer." His voice was sharp as he pressed his lips together. "And I don't need the hassle of worrying about you."

His words were like a slap, and she stared blindly out the windshield as she pressed down on the accelerator. "Fine," she said, her voice cool. "The sooner I'm away from you, the happier I'll be."

A beat of silence filled the car, then he sighed. "That's not what I meant, Ellie. I don't want to leave you behind. I want you with me. I need to make sure nothing happens to you. But I have to concentrate on what I'm doing. You're a distraction I can't afford."

"I'm a distraction?" She narrowed her eyes and allowed her temper to dispel the hurt his words had caused. "Was I a distraction when I got the supplies we needed to take care of your back? Was I a distraction this morning, when I bought you a shirt so you could be seen in public? I'm not some stupid piece of fluff who doesn't know her left hand from her right. I thought I'd helped you."

"You have helped me," he said, his voice quiet. "More than I had any right to expect." He shot her a quick glance, then looked away again. "And I think you know damn well what I mean by a distraction."

Her nerves jumped and her heart began thumping in an erratic rhythm. Surely he didn't mean that she, personally, was distracting him. In a male and female kind of way.

"You don't have to waste your charm on me," she said, tamping down the hope that was trying to take seed in her heart. "I already told you I believe you."

"Are you always this prickly?" he murmured without looking at her.

"I don't try to pretend to be someone I'm not,"

she said, staring out the windshield, her eyes fixed on the road in front of her. She fought the tears that threatened to fall. "I know exactly who I am."

"And that is?"

"An ordinary woman who lives an ordinary life." *Not someone a man like you would ever be interested in.*

"There's nothing ordinary about you, Ellie. Believe me." A hint of laughter was back in his voice.

"Thank you for the compliment," she said tightly. She knew what it meant. It meant the same thing as "she has a great personality."

"Where exactly are you taking me?" She hoped he would think the quiver in her voice was due to fear rather than her roiling emotions.

"I'm taking you to a friend's house," he said. "Someone I trust completely. He'll keep you safe."

"What if the police follow us?"

"No one's seen us in this car or they'd have tried to stop us by now. Once we get out of Midland we'll be safe."

She didn't want to ask, but she had to know. "What about your partner and the other officer? What if they waited to see what you would do? Maybe the police already know about this car."

He didn't answer right away. "I guess we'll find out, won't we?" he finally said.

His voice was steady, but she heard the pain beneath his words. She scrambled to find something to say to comfort him. "I don't think we need to worry about it. If your partner was involved, he wouldn't have let you go, would he?''

Michael shook his head slowly and stared out the window. ''He might have. The other guy in the car is a rookie and we're supposed to be training him. If Sam is dirty he wouldn't have wanted Hobart to know. So maybe that was why he let us go.''

''So you're not counting on his being one of the good guys?'' she asked in a quiet voice. ''In fact, you're not sure we're going to get out of town safely.''

He shifted in his seat to look at her, and she saw despair in his gaze. ''I'm not sure of anything right now,'' he answered.

''Poor Michael,'' she whispered. They were approaching the outskirts of town and she stepped a little harder on the gas pedal. ''Is there anyone you can trust?''

''I trust the man you're going to stay with.''

''That's it?''

''That's it.''

''I'm sorry,'' she said quietly.

''Don't be. That's the way I like it.'' His voice was hard and cold and his face looked as if it had been carved out of stone.

''That's no way to live,'' she protested.

''It's the only way to live,'' he retorted. ''You'll never be disappointed.''

She sneaked a quick look at him and saw the grim determination on his face. She was out of her depths, she realized with a spurt of fear.

The smart thing to do was stay at his friend's house. Maybe Michael was right. Maybe she shouldn't pay so much attention to the books she read. Maybe there wasn't always a happy ending. Her face flamed as she remembered the scene in the squalid hotel room that morning. She'd woken up wrapped around him like a vine on a tree.

She shook her head and pressed just a little harder on the accelerator. The last few straggling houses of Midland flashed past the car window, and a few moments later they were surrounded by fields of corn and soybeans. Almost safe.

"Are there any cars behind us?" Michael asked, interrupting her thoughts. He continued to slump in the passenger seat, out of the sight of passing drivers.

She glanced in the rearview mirror. "A few. No police cars, though."

"They wouldn't be that stupid," he said. "Any cars that have been following us for a while?"

"I don't know." She glanced in the mirror again. "I haven't been paying attention."

A wave of guilt swept through her. She'd been wrapped up in her own thoughts, feeling sorry for herself, when she should have been watching for cars tailing them. "There are four cars back there now," she said, glancing into the mirror again. "There's a minivan right behind us. Then there's an SUV, then a couple of sedans."

"Keep an eye on them." He shifted on the seat, his movements stiff and jerky. Another wave of guilt crashed over her.

"I forgot about your back. Does it hurt?"

"It's not important," he said, moving restlessly. "Getting you safely to Charles is all that matters."

They drove for several minutes in silence. The four vehicles were still behind them. She slowed the car, hoping that the others would pass them, but all the vehicles maintained their distance.

She stared in the rearview mirror. "Why won't they pass us?" she muttered to herself.

"What are you doing?" he asked, raising his head to glare at her.

"I'm slowing down so they'll try to pass us."

"Damn it!" he yelped. "Do you have a death wish?"

"Of course not. I'm simply trying to gather information."

"Stop trying to do my job," he snapped. "Pay attention to your driving and let me figure out what to do next."

"Oh, like you've done such a great job of that."

"I got us out of Midland, didn't I?"

"And there are four cars following us. Don't you want to know if any of them belong to the police?"

"Hell, no, I don't want to know if the police are behind us," Michael growled. "At least not right now. We're too exposed on this road. There's nowhere to turn and nowhere to hide. Unless you count the cornfields."

There was a long moment of silence. Then she said in a small voice, "I'm sorry. You're right. I hadn't thought that far ahead."

He gave her a tiny, weary grin. "I guess I'm good for something, then."

Memories of the two of them tangled together that morning flashed through her mind. Gritting her teeth, keeping her eyes fixed firmly on the road, she tried to banish the images. She had no intention of going down that road again.

"I guess you earn your keep," she managed to say. She was surprised at how light the words sounded.

"We're almost at Auburn," he said after a moment. "We'll try a few things there to see if any of those drivers are interested in us."

"All right." She looked in the mirror again, but none of the vehicles had turned off the road. All of them maintained their distance from each other. Of course, as Michael had pointed out, there was nowhere else to go on this road. The two-lane highway passed nothing more than an endless stream of fields and the occasional farmhouse. The roads that intersected led farther off the beaten path.

Just like Michael and Eleanor, the other vehicles were clearly headed for the next town.

OUT OF THE CORNER of his eye, Michael watched Ellie drive. She frowned in concentration, her forehead wrinkling every time she glanced in the rearview mirror. And she looked in the mirror a lot. Clearly, she was planning something.

A surge of tenderness welled up inside him, surprising him with its intensity. He forced himself to look away. He couldn't afford any damn distractions, not with half the Midland police force after them. And he certainly couldn't afford any tenderness when it came to Ellie. When they got to Charles's house in Pinckney, he was leaving her behind. It was the only sensible thing to do, and it was about time he did something sensible.

But the truth was he wanted her with him. He wanted it with an intensity that both shocked and alarmed him. He'd known Ellie for less than twenty-four hours. How could she have become so important to him in that short span of time?

He didn't know how it had happened. But looking out for Ellie's safety was now almost as important as his original mission. And that was not acceptable.

He would allow nothing to distract him from his job. He owed it to the citizens of Midland. He owed it to all the decent, honest police officers in the city who did their jobs and didn't take dirty money.

And he owed it to Montero, who wouldn't get to see his son grow up, after all.

''We're almost at Auburn,'' he said abruptly. ''There's a fast-food restaurant a few blocks into town. Pull into the drive-thru. That will give us a chance to see what they do.''

''All right.''

Ellie sounded subdued. He wasn't sure he'd ever heard her sound subdued before. ''Are you all right?''

''I'm fine.'' She looked at him. ''Why do you ask?''

He didn't care for the cautious, guarded woman who stared back at him. ''You haven't tried to argue with me for at least fifteen minutes. I'm afraid you're getting sick or something.''

Light flared briefly in her eyes, then she looked back at the road. ''I'm fine,'' she said, her voice carefully neutral.

He watched her, trying to analyze what was bothering her. He hardly noticed when they reached the tiny town of Auburn. Houses and small stores flashing past the car snapped him back to attention.

''Here's the restaurant,'' he said, pointing toward a lighted sign. ''Let's see what happens.''

She slowed down and steered the car into the drive-thru lane. Then she stared out the window with him, waiting to see what the other vehicles would do.

One by one, they drove past the restaurant. None of them turned in, and none slowed down. Closing his eyes, Michael said a prayer of thanks. Grabbing the backpack, he pulled out the money he'd hidden there in case of an emergency. ''Let's eat.''

Fifteen minutes later they were back on the road, sipping cups of coffee as they drove through the town of Auburn. Ellie's hands relaxed on the steering wheel. Her hair had come completely loose from her bun and trailed down her back like thick skeins of silk. And her mouth was pursed in concentration.

He wanted to move closer, he realized. He wanted to touch her skin again, to see if it was really as smooth as he remembered.

As he watched, mesmerized by his building fantasy of Ellie in his arms, her knuckles turned white on the steering wheel and she whipped her head around to watch an auto repair garage fly past.

"What?" he asked, jolted out of his reverie, turning in his seat to look behind him.

"It's probably nothing," she said, gazing again into the rearview mirror. "But one of the cars in the parking lot of that garage looked a lot like one of the cars that was following us out of Midland."

He muttered a harsh curse as the garage disappeared into the distance. "Are you sure?"

"I'm sure it looked like one of the cars behind us. I'm not sure it's the same car."

"Keep going," he said, watching the road behind them. The air in the car became thick and stifling as he stared out the back window. Ellie held herself stiffly as she drove.

Finally, after at least five minutes, he turned around in his seat. "They didn't follow us," he said.

"Are you sure?" She looked in the mirror again, worry plainly etched on her face.

"I'm sure. There's not a car or a truck behind us, and the road is pretty straight right here. I'd see them if they were there."

"Okay."

She swallowed once, and he caught himself watching the ripple of muscle in her neck, wondering how it would feel against his mouth. Muttering a curse under his breath, he tore his gaze away before he could make a fool of himself.

"We're going to Pinckney," he said, his voice too

harsh. "It's another eighty miles or so. Do you want me to drive for a while?"

She frowned at him. "Of course not. You need to rest your back. You're going to be doing plenty of driving today after you get rid of me."

Her words hit him like a blow to the gut. "I'm not 'getting rid of' you," he said, louder than necessary. "I'm trying to keep you safe."

"That's what I meant."

She gave him an innocent look that made his chest flutter. A reluctant, appreciative half smile touched his mouth. His Ellie was quick.

And she wasn't his Ellie. Scowling, he swiveled and looked out the window. She wasn't his anything. As soon as they got to Pinckney, she'd be out of his life. In a few weeks, when he looked back on the last twenty-four hours, he'd have trouble even remembering what she looked like.

Like hell he would.

The sloppy bun that barely managed to contain her rich chestnut hair, the soft blue-gray of her eyes, the sleek, satiny smoothness of her skin, all would stay with him for a long, long time. Not to mention that triumphant look she got in her eyes when she managed to best him. No, he wouldn't be forgetting Eleanor Perkins anytime soon.

It was only because he'd taken her hostage, he tried to convince himself. You don't forget a woman you've kidnapped at gunpoint. He didn't need Ellie. He didn't need anyone, especially not an annoying woman who had managed to get under his skin almost as soon as he'd met her.

He especially didn't need a woman who had felt so right curled into him when he woke up this morning. No, the fact that Ellie felt as if she'd been made for him, as if she was the missing piece of a puzzle that had finally found its home, didn't mean a thing. It was nothing but nerves and adrenaline.

He was sure Ellie would say the same thing if he asked her.

Which he didn't intend to do.

"Tell me about the man you're taking me to." She interrupted his thoughts, and he was grateful for the distraction.

"His name is Charles Wilson. Betty is his wife."

"Are they relatives of yours?" she asked, her voice polite and distant.

He hated that distance. She was talking to him as if he was a complete stranger with whom she was making polite conversation. He wanted to grab her and shake her.

"Are Charles and Betty Wilson your relatives?" she repeated.

"No," he said, his voice short. "They're friends."

"I see."

The polite, artificial tone of voice was one she would use at a cocktail party, to discourage some bore who was telling her the story of his life.

Michael's temper rose. Struggling to subdue the feelings she roused in him, he turned to face her. "I don't think you do. You know I don't trust many people.''

''So you told me,'' she murmured.

''I couldn't afford to trust anyone. When I was growing up…'' He swallowed once and turned to look out the window, appalled at what he'd almost revealed. He never told anyone about his childhood.

''Charles and I go way back,'' he finally said. ''He'll keep you safe.''

She darted a glance at him, her eyes cool and distant. ''I never doubted that I'd be safe. I trust you, Michael.''

The subtle rebuke was like a slap in the face. ''Damn it, Ellie, I trust you, too.''

''Right. And that's why you're dumping me at your friend's house.''

''That's not a matter of trust. It's a matter of life and death.'' His raised voice filled the car.

''Maybe I don't want to be kept safe,'' she said. ''Maybe I don't want to be protected and coddled. Maybe I want to help you.''

As if she realized too late what she had said, her eyes widened and she bit her lip, then stared fixedly out the windshield. A hint of red swept up her neck into her cheeks. Ellie wasn't used to blurting out her feelings without thinking.

Unleashing her wild side was apparently another sin she could lay at his feet.

He wanted to yell at her, to tell her it was more important to save her life. That he wouldn't be able to live with himself if she got hurt because of him. But he bit his tongue and tried to steady himself.

"I appreciate the thought, but you have to see how dangerous that would be. You could get killed."

"Just like I could have gotten killed last night when a man with a gun kidnapped me," she retorted.

"I'm not discussing this, Ellie. You're staying with Charles. End of discussion."

"Fine," she said stiffly. "You can drop me off there."

"And you're going to stay there until it's safe to leave."

She glared at him, but he thought her eyes looked bruised and hurt beneath the temper. "Once you drop me off you have no control over what I do. I'll stay there if I please. And I'll leave if I want to."

He swiped a hand through his hair. "If I had known you would be such a pain in the ass I would have run right past the library last night."

"I guess it's too bad for both of us, then, that you stopped when you did."

He waited through a beat of silence. Then he sighed.

"I'm sorry, Ellie. I didn't mean that and you know it. I was damn lucky when I picked you last night. I wouldn't have made it this far without your help."

"So how are you going to make it farther by yourself?"

He started to grin. He couldn't help himself. He should have expected her to pounce on the first sign of weakness from him. "That's good," he said. "I knew you were quick. But the answer is still no."

"You'll be sorry."

"Probably," he said. And he realized that he would be sorry to see the last of Ellie. Way too sorry. "But I'm not going to be selfish," he said, trying to sound noble. "Your safety is more important than my happiness."

Her lips quivered as she tried to suppress a grin. "Nice recovery, Reilly. But I don't believe for a second that you're into self-sacrifice."

She was wrong, he realized with a hint of panic. He would sacrifice a lot for her. Much more than he was willing to think about. And far more than he could afford.

"I need to get some sleep," he said abruptly. "Wake me up if you see anything that doesn't look right."

"Fine," she answered, her voice cool again.

He had no intention of sleeping. But he needed to put some distance between them. He was flying far too close to the flames.

He sank down into the lumpy seat and turned his head away, pretending to sleep. The side mirror hung from the car at a crazy angle, and he stared into it. Ellie couldn't see a damn thing out of it, but it was perfectly placed for him to keep an eye on the road behind them.

While he watched, he counted the miles until they reached Pinckney. Charles would know what to do. He might be able to make Ellie see reason.

God knows he'd had plenty of practice dealing with stubborn hotheads when Michael was growing up. If Charles Wilson could handle a young Michael, he should be able to cope with Ellie Perkins.

And Michael knew Ellie would fiercely resist if she thought anyone was managing her.

He smothered a small grin. Maybe he was figuring out how to handle Ellie all by himself.

CHAPTER NINE

THE WHEELS OF THE CAR hummed monotonously against the pavement as mile after mile of corn and soybeans flashed past the window. Ellie shifted on the seat and glanced at Michael one more time. He appeared to be asleep, slumped against the back of the seat.

It was just as well, she told herself. He needed rest to allow his back to heal. And she needed time to compose herself before she faced him again.

She couldn't believe she had told him she wanted to go with him and help him. It had to be the dumbest thing she'd ever done in her life. She should be thanking God he was willing to drop her off in Pinckney.

She had no business thinking of Michael Reilly as anything more than her kidnapper. She certainly shouldn't be reliving those moments in bed with him this morning.

But she couldn't get the images out of her head. She'd never felt so sensual or so desirable. She shivered at the memory of Michael's hand on her body, the slow sweep of his fingers down her side and back. And her skin tingled with the memory of his mouth, trailing sparks wherever he tasted her.

Clearly, she was out of her mind. The experience of being kidnapped must have made something come unhinged in her head. It was the only explanation for these aching, yearning sensations that churned inside her.

"We're almost at Pinckney," Michael said, interrupting the steady droning of the car. "Pull over here and change places with me."

"Are you sure you can drive?" She studied him briefly. His eyes weren't as feverish as they'd been that morning, and his color wasn't as gray. But lines of pain and exhaustion still bracketed his eyes.

"I'm sure," he said. "It's about time I pulled my own weight."

It didn't take a genius to read his determination. So instead of arguing, she steered the car onto the shoulder of the road, next to a field of corn that was at least six feet tall, and slid out of the driver's seat.

Hot, humid air slapped her in the face as she headed around the passenger side of the car. While they'd been driving there was at least a breeze from the window. Now the air was still and heavy, pressing down on her like a wet wool blanket.

Michael struggled to pull himself out of the car, and she offered him her hand. He scowled at her, but finally reached out and grasped it.

He eased himself out slowly and stiffly until he stood next to her. "Thanks," he muttered, dropping her hand as if it were on fire.

As he started to move toward the driver's side, he

stumbled on the uneven ground. She leaped forward and caught him before he could fall.

For a moment they stood pressed together, touching from chest to thigh. The muscles and planes of his body burned into her, causing a hot flush of awareness to sweep through her. When his arms tightened and pulled her closer, her heart leaped in her chest and began thumping erratically.

''Michael,'' a voice whispered, pleading. It was her own, she realized with astonishment. And from the heat that flashed in Michael's eyes, he had no trouble figuring out what she wanted.

He brought one hand up to her face and brushed away the hair that had fallen into her eyes. ''Ellie,'' he murmured, his voice thick and heavy with need. ''Just one kiss. That's all I want.''

He slid his fingers through her hair and muttered her name again as he pressed closer to her. The hard length of his erection burned into her through all their layers of clothes. He closed his eyes and groaned, taking her mouth with his.

It wasn't the kind of kiss she was used to, polite and well-mannered and restrained. It was hot and hard and desperate, as if he were a man dying of thirst and she was his only source of water.

Heat and fire and throbbing need swept through her, obliterating any memories of other men and other kisses. Her knees weakened and she would have fallen if he hadn't tightened his arms around her. When he backed her up against the car, she moaned into his mouth, and he pressed even more intimately against her.

His tongue caressed hers, tasting and teasing, his slow, sensuous movements matching the thrust of his hips. A heavy ache centered low in her abdomen and she moved restlessly against him.

"Ellie," he muttered, sweeping his hand down her back, urging her hips closer to him. "My God, Ellie. Touch me."

She'd clasped her hands around his neck, but as his breath whispered against her neck she realized she hungered to explore him. She tested the muscles of his upper back, finding them hard and tense as bands of iron. Slowly she slid her hands around to his chest, where she found the tiny nubs of his male nipples poking against the thin fabric of his shirt.

He sucked in his breath as she explored, testing the tiny peaks with her fingertips. When she squeezed once, he thrust his hips against her in a jerky movement.

"My God. Stop," he whispered as she brushed her fingertips over him again, enthralled by his response. He grabbed her hands and pulled them back around his neck. "I'm going to embarrass myself if you do that again." He nuzzled her neck, then tugged lightly at her earlobe with his teeth. "It's my turn now."

His mouth trailed down her neck, leaving hot flames of need in its wake. When he reached the V of her blouse he paused, and she squirmed against him with frustration. Her breasts throbbed and tingled, swelling with need. She held her breath, silently pleading with him to move lower.

But he moved back to her mouth instead, taking it in a storm of desire. She could only hold on, swept away by her longing for him, shattered by her body's response. She was completely and utterly in his power, and she gloried in the surrender.

When he yanked her blouse out of the waistband of her slacks she felt his hand trembling. Her heart caught in her throat as he slid his palm over her abdomen.

"You're so smooth," he whispered into her mouth. "So soft. Are you this soft everywhere?" He nuzzled her neck. "Can I touch you and find out?"

His fingers danced along her skin and his words sounded velvety and rich. His hand crept toward her breast but he moved much too slowly. She moaned, pressing herself into his fingers, and felt him smile against her flesh.

"I take it that's a yes?"

She couldn't have spoken if her life depended on it. All she could do was hold her breath, waiting, waiting for him to move closer. Heat and wetness throbbed between her thighs, and she shifted so his leg slipped between hers.

When he finally touched her breast, she felt his hand through the filmy fabric of her bra. "This has to go," he whispered, reaching for the clasp. And suddenly her breasts were free. He sucked in his breath as he cupped one in his hand.

His finger circled her, coming closer and closer to

her nipple but moving infinitely slowly, as if he could learn everything there was to know about her from the tips of his fingers. "You're even softer than I imagined," he whispered, licking at the corner of her mouth. "But our survey still has a long way to go. Are you ready for the next step?"

She whimpered deep in her throat; speaking was impossible. Slowly, as if he was holding his breath, he rubbed one finger lightly across her nipple. She gave a little cry and shuddered against him.

He groaned her name and shoved her blouse up to her shoulders. When he fastened his mouth to her nipple, pleasure so intense it verged on pain rocketed through her. She arched back with a shocked cry and wrapped her arms and legs around him, conscious of nothing but her need for him.

His sharp intake of breath and involuntary flinch were like a splash of cold water on her overheated skin. Her eyes flew open and she saw the pain from his wound reflected in his eyes.

"Your back," she whispered, shocked and horrified. "Michael, I'm so sorry." She dropped her arms and legs and tried to scoot backward, only to find the car blocking her way.

"Shh," he said, trailing one finger down her throat and pulling her toward him again. "There's nothing to be sorry about."

She stared at him, appalled. "Yes there is! I just jumped on you like…like a cat in heat. I forgot all about your back."

Laughter lit his eyes. "And you think that's something to apologize for?"

"I hurt you!"

"Oh, yeah. You did. But it's not my back that hurts. It's another part of my anatomy altogether." He pressed his hips against her suggestively. "Want to kiss it and make it better?"

A laughing devil danced in his eyes. When she simply stared at him, dismayed at what she'd done, he pulled her hands to his mouth and pressed his lips against first one palm, then the other.

"I guess that's a no," he sighed, rolling his hips against her again and stealing her breath. "At least for now. I suppose this isn't the time or the place. But I reserve the right to ask for a rain check."

Her head spun and she watched him, speechless. How could he joke about what had just happened? She was shaken and disoriented. The foundations of her world had been shifted and realigned, and nothing would ever be the same again. In a few short minutes, Michael had shown her a universe of sensation and feelings she'd never even imagined.

And now he stood in front of her, his chest brushing against her oversensitive breasts, his erection gliding against her in a way designed to drive her out of her mind, and he had the nerve to smile at her as if what had happened between them was as ordinary as a hot day in July.

"I don't know what came over me," she muttered, and he laughed out loud.

"I'd love to explain it to you, but it's not the kind

of thing I like to do in public.'' He bent over and brushed his mouth lightly over hers. ''I'll take a rain check on that, too.''

He stood much too close for another moment, pressing her against the hot metal of the car, then closed his eyes and backed away. Giving her just enough room to slide around him, he waited until she got into the passenger side, then walked around and slid into the driver's seat.

Eleanor watched as he steered the car down the still-deserted road, his jaw set and his eyes once again focused on his mission. She was in trouble. Big trouble.

In less than twenty-four hours, she had let Michael Reilly become far too important to her.

It was a lesson she apparently needed to learn: be careful what you wish for. She had wished for excitement and adventure in her life, and now she had it. But the excitement came with a price. And that price might very well include her heart.

Pressing her lips together, she stared out the window at the endless rows of corn. At least she'd discovered one thing, she told herself. She wasn't undersexed, or cold, or too stiff. She still throbbed with heat and need. It had merely taken the right man to show her what passion and desire meant.

The problem was, this was exactly the wrong time. And Michael was exactly the wrong man.

MICHAEL KEPT THE CAR between the white lines on the road and tried to steal glances at Ellie. But she

kept her face turned away, staring out the window at
the endless cornfields. He'd had no idea that vegeta-
bles could be so fascinating.

Then a horrible thought struck him. What if she
was crying?

My God! She wouldn't do that to him, would she?
He glanced at her again and noticed her stiff, straight
back and clenched fists.

No, Ellie wouldn't be sitting there crying. She'd
more likely be fuming and sparking with anger.

But he'd made a terrible mistake. He'd let her
know he wanted her. And he'd tasted her response,
felt it to the bottom of his soul. She wanted him, too.

Could there be a more frightening discovery? They
were on the run, with both his life and hers in danger.
And all he could think about was making love. To a
woman he wanted more than he'd ever wanted anyone in his life.

He swore steadily under his breath, calling himself
every name he could think of. It didn't help. He still
ached for her. And it still terrified him.

They were almost at Pinckney, he saw with relief.
A few more miles and he could leave her with
Charles. Then he could try to forget about her.

They were all wrong for each other. Hell, they'd
probably kill each other within days if they actually
tried to get together. Her planning, analytic, careful
ways would play havoc with his intuitive, free-for-all
style. And settling down was the last thing on his
mind.

The houses on the edge of Pinckney came into

view and he almost sighed with relief. Only a few more minutes and he could begin to forget about her.

She turned to him with that polite look on her face and said, "Has your friend always lived here?"

It was cocktail-party talk again, and Michael wanted to shake her. They'd gone way beyond polite. But maybe it was a good thing. It would make driving away a lot easier.

"No," he said, his tone short. "He's from Midland originally. He and his wife moved out here so Betty could have a garden."

"Did you meet him while you were a cop?"

"No." He didn't want to tell her anything more about Charles, but he owed her at least a fragment of the truth. It was the least he could do before leaving her with a stranger.

"I knew him when I was growing up. He was the police chief."

She frowned. "I thought you didn't trust anyone on the Midland police force."

"Charles is retired. Has been for several years." Michael risked a glance over at her. "I trust him completely. He'll keep you safe."

"You already told me that, and I already told you I believed you."

Her voice was cool, and he wanted to smash through the ice, to find the heat that had swamped him just minutes ago. But he didn't dare. In a few minutes he had to say goodbye and not look back. So he merely nodded. "I just wanted to reassure you."

"Thank you."

She looked away again and his jaw tightened. It shouldn't be this way between him and Ellie. He wanted the banter. He wanted the triumphant look in her eyes when she thought she'd gotten the better of him. Hell, he wanted the heat and the fire that raged through him whenever he touched her.

It was a good thing he couldn't have it, he told himself savagely. Because if he could, he might make the biggest mistake of his life.

"Charles is on the other side of town. He lives on a lake and spends his time fishing." Michael risked another glance at her. "If you spend any time with him at all, he'll have you out in his boat, putting worms on a hook."

"Really?" She turned toward him, anticipation lighting her face. "I've always wanted to learn how to fish."

Damn it, she was one surprise after another. Instead of the wrinkled nose and distasteful expression he'd expected, she actually looked interested. Would Ellie ever stop surprising him?

Not in a hundred years, a small voice answered.

And that scared him more than anything else.

"Charles will adore you if you want to learn how to fish. He'll be able to relive—"

Michael stopped abruptly. He had no intention of sharing pieces of his childhood with Ellie. He wasn't about to tell her how Charles had taught him to fish. Every tiny piece of himself that he gave to her was one more he'd have to reclaim when he drove away.

And he was afraid she already held far too much of him.

"What will he be able to relive?" she asked, her voice once again that of a polite stranger.

"Nothing." Michael scowled. "I was just trying to make conversation."

"Don't bother for my sake." Her voice went from polite to frigid. "I'm perfectly capable of taking care of myself."

"That's sure as hell the truth," he muttered.

"What did you say?"

"Never mind. It wasn't important."

"Fine."

"We're almost there," he said after a few more strained minutes of silence. "Their house is just around the next curve."

"Did you call ahead so they're expecting us?" She spoke while staring out the window, as if she couldn't bear to look at him.

"Yeah. I called this morning, while you were out getting the shirt. But I told him we'd be here closer to the evening. I wasn't sure how long it would take."

"Good," she murmured. "I wouldn't want to surprise them."

He could have told her that Charles wouldn't be surprised by anything Michael did, but he kept his mouth shut. There was no point. He was going to be saying goodbye to her in a few minutes.

He was already putting mental distance between them, and he felt a sharp pang of regret. But it couldn't be any other way.

"There's the driveway to the house."

Charles's home was set back from the road, shaded by a handful of towering oak trees. Lilac bushes lined the road, revealing only glimpses of the white-painted house. Michael slowed down, then turned into the driveway. But as he rounded the last curve in the drive and the house came into view, a flash of light from his right side caught his eye.

Easing to a crawl, he peered into the bushes, and what he saw made his stomach roll and his heart protest. He slammed on the brakes.

Ellie was jerked against her seat belt. She turned to look at him and he knew he'd see a question in her eyes. But he couldn't move his head to meet her gaze, couldn't respond to her question. He'd turned to stone, and any small movement would make him crumble into dust.

"What's wrong?"

He couldn't answer. All he could do was stare at the car half-concealed in the bushes in front of Charles's house, and feel his heart shrivel in his chest.

CHAPTER TEN

"WHAT IS IT, Michael?" He heard the thread of fear in her voice, felt her touch his arm. "What's wrong?"

Instead of answering he jammed the car into Reverse and shot out of the driveway. They skidded and swerved as he shifted into Drive and pressed the accelerator. The flimsy foreign car shuddered as the engine sputtered and coughed, then took off with a lurch.

He didn't speak to Ellie as they sped through Pinckney. With anger and despair churning through him, he swore in a steady monotone, the harsh words filling the car as he furiously blinked his eyes. He refused to cry. He clenched the steering wheel more tightly and pressed harder on the accelerator.

"Why don't you stop and let me drive?"

Ellie's voice was gentle, inviting him to confide in her. But he ignored her and stared out the windshield as the last house in Pinckney flashed past.

"I'm fine."

"All right." She settled back in the seat, not looking at him, not speaking. But she rested one hand lightly on his arm.

The small weight of her hand burned into him. He

felt the imprint of every finger, the warmth of her palm. And he was shocked to realize it comforted him.

Her touch didn't take away the gaping, aching hole inside him. Nothing could do that. But it softened the edges of the black despair that had filled him at the sight of the car next to Charles's driveway.

Michael wanted to pull to the side of the road, he realized in horror, and drag her into his arms. He wanted to bury his head in the cool fall of her hair and let the touch of her hands soothe away the pain and anger.

He shook off her hand and clenched his teeth. He wouldn't allow himself to do that. Not in a million years. The last person he'd trusted had just betrayed him in the worst possible way.

"Who did that car belong to, Michael?"

He glanced over at her. Her eyes were filled with compassion and sympathy, blue-gray pools of understanding.

He deliberately looked away. "It was a Midland police car. An unmarked."

"How can you be sure?"

"I recognized the dent in the trunk." His voice was grim. "I put it there myself three months ago."

"That doesn't mean Charles is involved," she said evenly. "There could be a lot of reasons why someone from Midland went to see him."

"When I'm on the run with information that could put away a substantial part of the force? When the people on the force who know me know that Charles

The Harlequin Reader Service® — Here's how it works:

Accepting your 2 free books and mystery gift places you under no obligation to buy anything. You may keep the books and gift and return the shipping statement marked "cancel." If you do not cancel, about a month later we'll send you 6 additional books and bill you just $4.47 each in the U.S., or $4.99 each in Canada, plus 25¢ shipping & handling per book and applicable taxes if any.* That's the complete price and — compared to cover prices of $5.25 each in the U.S. and $6.25 each in Canada — it's quite a bargain! You may cancel at any time, but if you choose to continue, every month we'll send you 6 more books, which you may either purchase at the discount price or return to us and cancel your subscription.

*Terms and prices subject to change without notice. Sales tax applicable in N.Y. Canadian residents will be charged applicable provincial taxes and GST. Credit or debit balances in a customer's account(s) may be offset by any other outstanding balance owed by or to the customer.

Play the Lucky Hearts Game

and get...

2 FREE BOOKS
and a **FREE MYSTERY GIFT**...

yes! **YOURS to KEEP!**

I have scratched off the silver card. Please send me my *2 FREE BOOKS* and *FREE mystery GIFT*. I understand that I am under no obligation to purchase any books as explained on the back of this card.

Scratch Here!

then look below to see what your cards get you... 2 Free Books & a Free Mystery Gift!

336 HDL DZ5X   135 HDL DZ6E

FIRST NAME

LAST NAME

ADDRESS

APT.#

CITY

STATE/PROV.

ZIP/POSTAL CODE

(H-SR-05/04)

Twenty-one gets you
2 FREE BOOKS
and a **FREE MYSTERY GIFT!**

Twenty gets you
2 FREE BOOKS!

Nineteen gets you
1 FREE BOOK!

TRY AGAIN!

is the first person I'd run to?'' He curled his lip in derision. ''Not likely.''

''Just because a Midland police car was near his house doesn't mean Charles is involved. Maybe they were merely looking for information.''

''I doubt it. I called Charles this morning when you were out. I told him there was something rotten going on in the force and I would be out to see him later. He wouldn't have let anyone from Midland in the house.''

''Maybe he didn't have a choice. Maybe he's in trouble.''

He shook his head ''Charles might be old enough to be retired, but he's not stupid and he's not feeble. He wouldn't have opened the door to anyone from Midland.''

''You can't jump to the conclusion that he's involved,'' she said sharply. ''How long have you known him?''

''Twenty years,'' he muttered.

''Don't you think that's long enough to know what kind of man he is?''

''I thought it was.''

''Then why are you assuming the worst?''

Because I always do. The words trembled on his lips but he caught himself before speaking them. He wasn't about to invite Ellie to psychoanalyze him.

''What choice do I have?'' He heard the rage and pain in his voice and focused on them. It was that or surrender to the despair hovering in his heart. ''If I make the wrong assumption, you'll be dead, I'll be dead and so will any chance of justice for Rueben.''

''And what about Charles? Aren't you worried about him? Maybe you should call him.''

''Charles can take care of himself. I'll call him when we're farther away. I don't want to let him or anyone in that house know how close we are.''

''You have to trust someone, Michael.''

''I do. I trust myself.'' He glanced at her reluctantly. ''And you, I guess.''

''See? You're not alone.'' The compassion in her eyes deepened.

''How can I forget it? I may trust you, but you're a liability,'' he said harshly, unable to meet her eyes. ''I can't concentrate on what I have to do because I have to worry about both of us.''

He expected her to erupt with anger, or at least retreat in a hurt silence, but she surprised him once again by laying her hand on his arm. ''It'll be all right. I won't get in your way,'' she said. ''I promise.''

''It won't be all right,'' he raged, her calm voice and instinctive understanding just deepening his pain. He wanted her to rage back at him, to snap at him with a quick answer and a quicker glib retort. The last thing he wanted was her understanding. It rubbed like sandpaper against the wound in his heart.

''You're getting in my way just by being here. All the time I have to spend worrying about you is time I can't spend trying to figure out how to get this information where it needs to be!''

"We'll figure it out together," she said, her voice still that soothing, maddening murmur. "If you're sure Charles is all right, your only job right now is to concentrate on driving."

What if Charles wasn't all right? He eased his foot off the accelerator, worry now replacing his anger. What if Ellie was right? Was something wrong at Charles's house? Had someone from Midland driven out there and forced his way inside?

"Charles is tough," Michael said, staring out the windshield. "He's the fittest sixty-eight-year-old I've ever known. And he's no fool. If he wasn't working with that scum from Midland, he wouldn't have let them into his house."

"Maybe they didn't ask," Ellie said.

He looked at her sharply, unaware that he'd spoken out loud. "Charles was a cop for over forty years. And he didn't get to be chief of police because he was stupid."

"I'm not arguing with you." She hesitated, then said in a softer voice, "I'm just wondering why you're assuming he's guilty. You've known him for a long time. I would have thought you'd give him the benefit of the doubt." Her voice got stronger. "If it was my friend, I'd assume something was wrong."

"That's the difference between us." He gave her a look that dared her to deny it. "I'm a realist. I know what the world is really like. All you know are those damn books you read. I've already told you, in the real world there's no such thing as a happy ending."

"You're wrong, Michael. Dead wrong." She

shifted in her seat. "But you're going to have to learn that for yourself. I just hope your friend Charles isn't suffering because of your blind stubbornness."

"Charles is fine," he growled. "We have to worry about ourselves."

But she'd planted a seed of doubt that he couldn't ignore, no matter how hard he tried. Was he a fool for hoping, in a perverse way, that she was right? Probably. Experience had taught him, over and over again, that the only person he could count on was himself. He couldn't allow hope to poison his mind. He couldn't take that chance.

"Maybe we should go back and check, just to be sure," she said after a moment.

Wavering, he slowed down and pulled onto the shoulder of the road. "We might be walking into a trap."

She held his gaze as the car rolled to a stop. "If we are, you'll figure it out," she said softly. "You trusted Charles before you saw that car in his driveway. What's changed since then?" She waited a second, and when he didn't answer, she continued, "Not everyone in the world is deceitful and treacherous."

He ran his hand through his hair. "Who appointed you as my conscience?"

"Forget it. Don't pay any attention to me. Just keep driving. Turn your back on Charles and head to Chicago or St. Louis or wherever you're going. Who cares what might be happening with him? Your job is far more important than one old man." He'd been trying to provoke her and finally she snapped. Thank

God. Her anger was a lot more comfortable than her sympathy.

Scowling, Michael started the car and did a quick three-point turn on the narrow road. "You're forgetting the old woman who lives with Charles," he said, the sarcasm in his voice souring the air in the car. "Don't you want to point out that she's probably sick? Or maybe hurt? There must be more guilt you can dredge up somewhere."

"I don't need to," Ellie retorted. "There's more than enough to go around right now."

He pressed harder on the accelerator. Her words had heightened his concern, but he wasn't about to give her the satisfaction of saying so. "No wonder you're not married. Who could live with such a nagging, bossy woman?"

Shocked silence filled the car. Appalled by what he had just said, he slammed on the brakes again.

"My God, Ellie, I didn't mean that."

She met his gaze, her eyes stony, her back ramrod straight. "No need to apologize, Michael. It's nothing I haven't heard before."

"You know it's not true. I was just pissed off at you because you were making me feel things I didn't want to feel." He wanted to reach out to her, to take back the ugly remark, but there was no way to erase his hateful words. So he curled his hands into fists and stared out the windshield instead.

She leaned closer, her eyes flashing. "Maybe you need to feel those things. Maybe you're not going to be a worthwhile human being until you do."

"You wouldn't be the first person to tell me I'm not a worthwhile human being."

She didn't respond to his lame, weak joke. Instead, she stared at him with what looked suspiciously like pity. "I feel sorry for you, Michael. You're so busy protecting yourself that you have no idea what people are offering you. It must be sad to go through life with such a handicap."

"You don't know what the hell you're talking about." Infuriated at her insight, Michael pulled the car back onto the road and took off, so forcefully the engine nearly groaned in protest. "I'm perfectly happy with my life the way it is."

"That's what's so sad. You don't even know what you're missing."

"And you're the expert? Where did you get all your experience? From those books you're always quoting?"

"I may not have much of a life, but at least I know what I'm lacking." She was practically shouting at him. "You don't have a clue."

He didn't want to hear more from her because a part of him was afraid she was right. "Look, I'm going back to Charles's house, okay? What more do you want?" he snarled.

"Nothing," she said, turning away from him. "There's nothing more I want from you."

But that wasn't the truth, Ellie acknowledged to herself. She wanted much more from Michael.

Much more than he was capable of giving her.

His cruel words echoed in her brain, repeating relentlessly like a tape of her worst nightmare. Maybe he was right, she forced herself to admit. Maybe she was too bossy. Maybe she was too opinionated. But she wasn't about to make herself into something she wasn't. She wasn't about to deny who she was in order to catch a man.

Because in the end, whatever that man got wouldn't be worth having.

And this wasn't the time to brood about it, she told herself. There were a lot of other things to worry about right now.

Such as if she was going to live long enough to worry about catching a man.

"Do you have a plan?" she asked, struggling to keep her voice level and polite.

"You're asking me? The man who doesn't know how to plan?"

Although his voice was strained, he was clearly trying to make a joke. She forced herself to look at him. If he was trying to make things better between them, she'd go along. "I thought maybe you'd reformed."

He shook his head with a wry smile. "You ought to know you can't reform a guy like me."

And she'd better remember that, she told herself sharply, if she had any hope of surviving Michael Reilly with her heart intact.

"What was it you called me yesterday?" he asked. "A barbarian? You know barbarians don't have any manners."

She was pretty sure it was the closest she would

get to an apology for the way he'd been acting. But it didn't matter, she told herself. He'd been hurt and upset and would have lashed out at anyone who'd been sitting beside him in the car.

"So what are we going to do? Jump out of the bushes at them and shout 'boo'?"

"You are definitely a piece of work," he said, but there was no heat in his words. "We'll stop when we're a couple of blocks away from the house and I'll call Charles on my cell phone."

"And then?"

He shrugged. "That's when we play it by ear. It depends on what Charles has to say."

The road hummed beneath the tires of the tiny car, and before long they had to slow down at the edge of Pinckney. But instead of the anticipation that had filled the air the last time they'd approached the town, now there was a sense of dread in the car.

She was afraid something had happened to Charles.

And Michael was afraid Charles had betrayed him.

Eleanor's heart beat relentlessly against her ribs as Michael steered the car into a busy parking lot and pulled out his cell phone. He punched in the numbers, then looked at her as the phone began to ring.

She sent up a prayer that he wouldn't be disappointed, that he wouldn't face another betrayal. It was becoming painfully clear that Michael had already suffered far too many betrayals in his life.

He tensed, then leaned toward her so she could hear both sides of the conversation. On the other end of the line a man's voice said, "Hello?"

"Charles? This is me," Michael said. "What the hell is going on?"

"Hello, Fred. I'm sorry you've had trouble getting through," the man said. "The phone seems to be fine now. There must have been a problem with the line."

Michael glanced over at her, his eyes suddenly hot with fury. "I understand. I'll be there as quickly as I can."

"No, I'm afraid I can't go fishing today. We have guests, friends we haven't seen for a long time. We have a lot of catching up to do."

"I'm only a few minutes away."

"Naw, I wouldn't do that. If you go out there by yourself in that big boat of yours, you'll scare the fish away."

Ellie saw the frustrated fury in Michael's eyes. "I'll send the state police. I'll tell them it's a hostage situation. Is Betty all right?"

"She sends her regards, too. Say, hi, Betty."

From what sounded like a great distance, a shaky female voice said, "Hi, Fred."

"Sorry we can't get together today. You come by later in the week. We'll take my boat out one morning and I'll show you how it's done."

"Hang in there, Charles. And call me as soon as you can." Michael's voice was grim.

"Don't worry. We'll get together soon."

From the steely tone of Charles's voice, Ellie had no doubt the retired chief could handle the situation. Michael snapped his cell phone closed and turned to her, his eyes raging and his mouth set in a hard line.

"You were right. The cops from Midland must be holding them hostage."

"Charles is awfully good at thinking on his feet."

Michael's eyes softened. "Yeah, he is." He hesitated for a moment, then said, "Thank you for forcing me to see there was a problem."

"I think you would have figured it out for yourself."

"Maybe not in time." His gaze touched hers briefly, then he looked past her out the window. "I'm sorry. I was a real ass."

"Not to mention an obnoxious jerk. But I'd like to think it was because of the pressure you're under."

He met her gaze again, and this time didn't look away. "I'm not sure I can claim that excuse. I think I might just be a jerk."

"Maybe so, but you do have a few redeeming qualities," she said, making her voice deliberately light. "I'm just having trouble thinking of them right now."

Instead of smiling, as she had hoped he would, he continued to stare at her. "Keep that in mind, Ellie. Don't go getting any wild ideas about me. Don't bother to try and reform me. I'm trouble all the way through."

She couldn't restrain a snort of laughter. "And that's about the most melodramatic line I've ever heard. I didn't know you had aspirations to the stage."

She drew a reluctant answering grin. "Maybe I was overstating a little bit. But it doesn't change the truth.

I'm not the kind of man who has anything to offer a woman like you.''

''I'll keep that in mind,'' she said evenly. ''In case I might ever be interested in anything you have to offer.''

She hoped her tone of voice implied that it was an unlikely event. Apparently she succeeded, because he looked taken aback for just a moment. Then he gave her a curt nod.

''I'm glad we're on the same page.''

''Absolutely.'' She nodded vigorously, but let her gaze slide away from his. ''So what's our next move?''

''We're heading over to Charles's house, of course.''

She whipped her head around to glare at him. ''He told you not to come. I heard him plainly. And you said you were going to send the state police.''

''I am going to call the state police.'' He picked up his phone again and punched in 911. ''But you didn't think I'd just drive away before I'm sure Charles is all right?''

She leaned back in her seat, watching him. ''Maybe you do have some redeeming qualities, after all.''

He flashed her a startled look, then recovered. ''Don't count on it.''

She heard the murmur of a voice on the other end of the phone, and Michael dragged his gaze away from her. Speaking slowly and clearly, he gave out Charles's address. He was afraid, he said, that there was a problem. He suspected an elderly man and woman were the victims of a home invasion and very likely being held hostage by the perpetrators.

Michael listened for a moment, then said he suspected a problem because he'd just talked to Charles Wilson on the phone. Charles had made it clear there were uninvited visitors in his home.

After a few moments Michael hung up and turned to her, his mouth a grim line. "I'm not sure they believed me, but at least they're going to check it out."

"Now what do we do?"

He drummed his fingers on the steering wheel. "We wait here," he finally said. She could see he hated the idea. "We have no choice. We can't take a chance on running into the Midland cops."

"So we'll wait here." Glancing around the strip mall, she said, "There's a fast-food place. Why don't we get something to eat?"

He stared at her as if she was out of her mind. "You want to eat?"

"I'm hungry," she lied. "And we don't have anything better to do."

"I sure as hell have something better to do!"

"What's that? Sit here and brood? Rush out to Charles's house and get in the way?"

He stared at her for another moment, then a rueful smile twisted his mouth. "You're managing me, aren't you?"

"I never manage anyone," she said primly. "I just make suggestions."

He snorted. "And the check is in the mail, right?"

She gave him a steady look. "Are we going to eat or am I going to expire from hunger?"

He actually laughed. "All right, I can take a hint as well as the next man." The smile disappeared from his face. "But you stay in the car. And stay out of sight."

"How about if we go into the restaurant separately? Wouldn't that be just as safe?"

"No, it wouldn't be. I don't want anyone to see you."

She sighed. "Do I have to spell it out for you?" she snapped. "I need to use the facilities."

"Why didn't you just say so?"

Happy that she'd managed to distract him from worrying about Charles, she fought to keep the smile off her face. "Because I was embarrassed."

He gave her a disbelieving look. "Like hell you were embarrassed. With a mouth like yours you've never been embarrassed in your life."

He couldn't be more wrong. But instead of answering him, she opened the door without looking at him and stepped onto the hot asphalt. "I'll meet you back in the car."

Ten minutes later he slid onto the seat next to her. "We've got a problem."

CHAPTER ELEVEN

SHE SHOT UPRIGHT, fear chasing down her spine. "What's wrong?"

"Take a look at that." He tossed a newspaper in her lap.

The headline screamed out at her: Rogue Cop Takes Librarian Hostage. Below the headline were pictures of her and Michael.

"This isn't good," she murmured.

"You got that right." He slammed the door and slouched over the steering wheel, scowling at her. "And where did they get that damn ugly picture of you, anyway?"

The photo was from her library ID. It was a particularly unflattering likeness that showed her hair pulled into a tight bun on the top of her head and her glasses sliding halfway down her nose. She frowned sternly into the camera as if the photographer were an unruly boy.

"I never take good pictures," she muttered.

"Whoever took that one should be shot. It doesn't even look like you."

She stared over at him, amazed at his words. She was afraid she looked very much like that picture. "Thank you," she finally managed to say.

"We've got to get out of central Illinois." He stared out of the window, clearly brooding. "Someone's sure as hell going to recognize us if we don't."

"Do you think the story has been in the Chicago and St. Louis newspapers?"

"Who knows?" He ran his fingers through his hair again. "Probably, if it's been a slow news day."

"So we're going to be recognized wherever we go."

"That about sums it up."

Fear snaked down her spine, as if a noose were tightening around her neck. The backpack on the seat behind them suddenly seemed to swell with a malignant presence.

"So I guess we'd better get to the FBI as soon as possible." She forced her voice to be steady and cool.

Michael looked over at her. "I made the right decision when I grabbed you," he said gruffly.

"What do you mean?"

"Anyone else would be hysterical by now. Or they'd be whining and blubbering. But you just say hey, the bad guys are after us so we need to get to the FBI right away." He shook his head. "I was damn lucky."

"Thank you. I think."

"You're welcome." He flashed her another killer grin. "Just don't spoil the image by mouthing off at me again."

"I'm afraid you're destined to be disappointed. You present such a tempting target."

His smile was fleeting. "That's what they all say."

Neither of them spoke for a while. Then Michael glanced at his watch for about the third time in the last two minutes. "What's taking so long?" he asked under his breath.

She didn't even want to speculate on the possible reasons. "Are there any more articles about you in the paper?"

He gave her an impatient look. "I'm not one of your kids in the library. You don't have to distract me."

"I have to distract myself." She took the paper from the seat next to him. "Let me see."

There was no other mention of them. But the pictures stared out at her from the front page. "No one recognizes people from their pictures in the newspaper," she said, trying to sound confident.

"You want to risk your life on that?"

"What options do we have?"

"We'll figure something out as soon as I hear from Charles."

Minutes crept past and the tension in the car swelled until it took up all the available space. The inside of the vehicle felt like a sauna, the temperature relentlessly climbing higher as the sun beat on the roof. Sweat trickled down Eleanor's chest and back.

Surely the state police should have arrived by now. Maybe there was a problem. She didn't dare look at Michael. She didn't want to let him see her worry, didn't want to see the fear in his eyes.

His cell phone trilled, startling her. He grabbed it and pried it open. "Yes?"

He listened for a moment, then closed his eyes. "Thank God. Are you sure you're both okay?"

The tension whooshed out of her like air out of a balloon. She leaned closer to catch what Charles was saying, and Michael turned the phone so she could hear more clearly.

"...fine. But that scum from Midland didn't like it one bit. They were trapped, though." Charles chuckled. "They didn't have a choice. When I told that state trooper they were just leaving, they had to walk out. If they hadn't left, the Smoky would have known something was wrong."

"Brilliant as usual, Charles."

"You were pretty good, yourself, to figure out there was a problem."

Michael glanced at Eleanor. "I had some help."

"You mean the woman is still with you?" Charles's voice became sharper. "The one you supposedly kidnapped?"

"I did kidnap her, but we got past that a long time ago."

Charles' voice took on a note of incredulity. "You mean she's there voluntarily now?"

"I think so." Michael glanced over at her and Ellie nodded vigorously. "But we've got a problem. I can't let her go back to Midland because the cops know who she is. I was going to leave her with you and Betty."

"Can't do that," Charles said immediately. "That scum will be back. This time we'll be ready, but she still shouldn't be here. Just in case."

"How did they get into the house, anyway?"

Ellie could almost see Charles growl through the phone. "Betty went outside to fill her bird feeders. The cops must have been here for a while, watching. As soon as she stepped away from the house they grabbed her. They were holding a gun to her head so I had to let them in."

"They'll pay for that," Michael said, his voice low and deadly. "Believe me, they'll pay."

"You worry about getting your information to the FBI. I'll take care of Betty."

"Any suggestions about where I can leave Ellie?"

"Don't leave her anywhere," Charles said immediately. "Any place that either you or I think of, those dirtbags will eventually think of, too."

"It's too dangerous to keep her with me."

"It's more dangerous to leave her behind," he said sharply. "I saw those men, looked into their eyes. They have nothing to lose. If they think she's a witness, they won't hesitate to kill her."

"What about you?"

"We'll be fine. They don't think I know anything worthwhile. They just wanted to use me to get to you. And I played dumb." He laughed abruptly. "Pretended I was confused, that I had no idea what was going on. I played right into those idiots' stereotypes of a senile old fart."

Michael grinned. "I'd like to have seen that."

"It was a masterful performance, if I do say so myself."

"I'll bet it was." Michael looked at Ellie. "We'd

better get going," he said. "I want this to end as soon as possible."

"I agree." There was no more laughter in Charles's voice. "Contact Fred Gorman at the FBI office in Chicago. I know him and trust him. I'll let him know you're coming."

"Got it," Michael agreed, scribbling the name down on a piece of newspaper. "I'll talk to you as soon as I have more information."

"Hold on a minute. Betty wants to talk to you."

"Thank you for sending the cavalry." Her voice was clear and strong. "Charles won't tell you, but it was touch and go there for a while. Those men were clearly desperate."

"You both be careful," Michael answered. "I'll let you know as soon as my information is delivered to the FBI."

"Believe me, the birds will be going hungry until then," she said, a rueful tone in her voice. "Charles warned me not to go outside, but I thought it would only take a moment to get to the feeders and back."

"I'll keep in touch," Michael said.

But before he could close the phone, Betty said, "There were two more things."

"What's that?"

"You were on television," she said, her voice somber. "Just before the Midland cops got here, they showed pictures of both of you. Said you were on the run and the woman was your hostage, that you were armed and dangerous, and that anyone who saw you should contact the Midland Police Department."

Michael swore violently under his breath. "Thanks, Betty. We'll be careful."

"Can you get some kind of disguise?" she asked, worry in her voice. "You know, the kind of thing you used to do when you were undercover?"

"Yeah," he said, glancing at Ellie. "We'll think of something. What was the second thing?"

"Charles will tell you."

"Are you here in Pinckney?" It was Charles's voice again.

"Yeah, less than five minutes away."

"They'll be looking for you. They heard your car in the driveway, and they've probably figured out it was you who called the police. You can bet they're still around."

"So what else is new?" Ellie heard the weariness in Michael's voice.

"There's an old farm road that isn't used much anymore. It's nothing more than a rutted dirt track, but I doubt if any of the Midland cops know about it. If you can get to the feed store without being seen, you'll be able to get past them."

Charles gave directions to the store and the road, then Michael said, "I'll talk to you soon. And thanks, Charles."

"No thanks necessary. I should be thanking you for saving our rear ends."

"No thanks necessary." Michael echoed Charles's words, but there was a softness in his voice that Ellie hadn't heard before. After a moment, he slowly closed his phone.

He stared down at it for a long time. Finally he looked up at her. "Thank you, Ellie," he said, so quietly she could barely hear him. "I don't want to think about what could have happened if you hadn't insisted I check on Charles."

"You would have done it on your own," she said immediately.

He shook his head. "Maybe eventually. And who knows what might have happened in the meantime?" He looked up at her, his eyes dark and full of pain. "I owe you."

"I'll just add it to your tab," she said, trying to lighten the mood.

He managed a small smile. "You do that." The car started with a whimper and he pulled out of the parking lot.

After a few moments on the main street, Michael turned onto a side street lined with quiet old houses shaded by large silver maples.

"How far is it to the feed store?" Ellie asked, looking over her shoulder.

"Just a few blocks. And we'll take side streets."

He hadn't seen her this nervous since he'd first snatched her, and he wanted to reach over and take her hand. Instead, he forced himself to grip the steering wheel and keep his eyes on his driving.

"We shouldn't have to go onto a main road again," Michael said, trying to sound reassuring. "And the cops can't search every street in Pinckney. They'll be watching the route in and out of town."

"How many Midland officers do you think are

here?'' She tried to make it sound like a casual question, but he could hear the fear in her voice.

''More than enough,'' he answered grimly. ''But, hey,'' he added, trying to take her mind off the danger, ''none of them have my secret weapon.''

''And what would that be?''

''You.''

She gave a snort. ''Then we're in worse shape than I thought. Can't you see I'm falling apart here?''

She tried hard to make it sound like a joke, but he was afraid it was true. ''Really?'' Raising his eyebrows, he gave her an exaggerated leer. ''Can I be the one to put the pieces back together?''

At least he was able to surprise a laugh out of her. ''That was good, Reilly. You're quick. But don't worry, I won't hold you to it.''

He wanted to be held to it, he realized. Even though—as he kept reminding himself—Eleanor Perkins was the absolute last woman on earth he should get involved with, he couldn't forget the way her body had felt pressed against him, or the way her mouth tasted.

Or the almost innocent wonder she'd displayed as her body reacted to his.

He shifted uncomfortably on the seat, cursing silently. He damn well better get his mind where it belonged.

''Do you remember what that car in Charles's yard looked like?'' he asked, his voice almost curt.

He felt her glance at him. But all she said was, ''Yes, I think so.''

"Then keep an eye open for it. And let me know if you see anything at all that makes you nervous."

"Okay."

Michael knew people dealt with stress better if they had a job to do. And he hoped that watching for the cops would keep Ellie occupied until they were out of Pinckney.

They were crossing a busier street, heading toward the feed store, when Ellie shot upright in the seat. "There, down the road about a block. Wasn't that the car in Charles's driveway?"

Michael looked in that direction, then hit the accelerator and steered the car toward the store. "Yeah," he said, rage welling up inside him like a dark, poisonous cloud. "That's them. Keep watching to see if they come after us."

He held his breath as he maneuvered around to the parking lot in the rear. Several pickup trucks idled alongside the loading dock, and a handful of other cars waited nearby. Once the building hid Eleanor and Michael from the street, he stopped and looked at her.

"Well?"

"They didn't move, at least not before we got behind the store." Her face was sheet-white and her eyes looked enormous. "What now?"

"Now we find this dirt road and get the hell out of Dodge."

He steered the car slowly past the parked cars and trucks, searching for Charles's escape route. "Where is that damn track?" he muttered, turning the car around. "Charles wouldn't have mentioned it if he wasn't sure it was here."

"How about that?" She pointed at what looked like nothing more than a rut between two rows of brush.

"Let's give it a try," he said. The opening in the vegetation was so narrow that he figured they'd be backing out in a few minutes.

The car bounced and swayed as he steered it into the narrow lane. Weeds scraped the car on both sides and overgrown scrub vegetation formed a canopy overtop, filtering the bright sunshine to in shady green. But the track continued.

"This must be it," he said, holding tightly to the steering wheel. The car jerked in one direction, then another as it struggled through the deep, ragged ruts in the dirt. "Charles wasn't kidding when he said this road wasn't used much anymore."

"No one is following us," Ellie said as she stared out the rear window.

"Good thing," he said grimly. "Because we sure wouldn't be able to outrun anyone."

They struggled along for several minutes until they emerged into bright daylight again. They crept up a slight incline and crossed a gravel road, then the track disappeared between six-foot-high rows of corn.

Green light enveloped them again, the air heavy with the pungent smell of dirt, humidity and growing plants. "Looks like we're taking the scenic route," he said, glancing in Ellie's direction.

She managed a tight smile. "If we can't see where we're going, no one else can, either."

"You're right." He held on to the steering wheel as the car bounced and swayed. "I just hope it isn't this scenic for very long. I don't think the suspension can take it."

"How far do we go on this trail?" she said, leaning forward.

"According to Charles, it loops around behind Pinckney for a couple of miles. Then it crosses the highway out of town. We drive through more corn for another mile or so, then meet up with the highway again. So if there's no one waiting for us at this first crossing, we should be okay."

"Good."

Her voice was a subdued murmur in the dim green light in the car. He glanced at her sharply again, but she stared out the window, her back unnaturally straight. It looked as if she was holding herself together with nothing more than grim determination.

"You're not wimping out on me, are you?" he asked, alarmed.

When she turned to face him, her gaze bored into him. "What exactly do you mean by that?"

"I mean you're not going to get hysterical, are you?"

"I have never gotten hysterical in my life."

He glanced at her again, at the outraged expression on her face and the indignation in her eyes. "Maybe that's your problem," he murmured. "Maybe it would loosen you up."

"I'm as loose as I intend to get," she replied coldly.

"There's nothing wrong with being afraid," he said after a moment. "Look at me. I'm scared witless."

"And you can do something about it. You're the one in control of the situation. I'm just along for the ride."

"Is that why you're so starched all the time? Because you're afraid of losing control?"

There was a long silence. Then she said, her voice tight, "I think we have more important things to do right now than psychoanalyze me."

"But not more interesting," he said.

"Maybe we should talk about your hang-ups instead." She turned to glare at him. "Why don't you trust anyone? Why won't you ever let anyone get inside your fences and help you?"

"Hell," he muttered. "All I was trying to do was take your mind off what was happening."

She settled back against the seat. "Well, you certainly did that," she said dryly. "I've completely forgotten that we're being chased by ruthless killers."

He scowled at her to conceal the grin that hovered around his mouth. "I can tell you one thing. You don't ever have to worry about being kidnapped by real bad guys. If someone actually managed to snatch you, that mouth of yours would scare him off in about fifteen minutes."

"It didn't seem to do any good with you."

"Yeah, but I'm not as quick as a lot of guys."

She rolled her eyes. "Right."

At least she didn't have that scared-rabbit look on her face now. That had frightened him more than anything else. If Ellie lost it, they were in big trouble.

"I think we're almost at the road," she said, peering through the corn. "It doesn't seem quite as shady up there."

"Okay." He touched the gun that he'd laid on the seat next to him. "We'll be ready."

She looked from the gun to his face. "Do you really think we'll need that?"

"No. But it doesn't hurt to be prepared."

They were approaching the highway. Just ahead, the corn stopped abruptly and a shimmering heat mirage rose off the black asphalt. He eased the car to a stop a few feet from the edge of the field.

"Stay here," he ordered as he slid out of the car. The scab on the wound in his back pulled painfully, reminding him of just how few options they really had.

As he reached the end of the row of corn, he lowered himself to the ground. Slithering across the last couple of feet of hard-packed dirt, he took a deep breath and finally eased his head out into the open.

"Damn it."

CHAPTER TWELVE

"WHAT?" she asked in a frantic whisper from right behind him.

He slid backward until the corn hid him again, then turned to her in a fury. "I told you to stay in the car."

"It sounded as if you might need help. What's wrong?"

"There's a car sitting on the shoulder of the highway, about a hundred yards back. It looks like our buddies from Charles's house."

She knelt on the ground next to him. "What are we going to do?"

"*You're* going to get back in the car." He frowned, mostly to hide the warmth that was spreading through him. She'd disobeyed his orders by getting out of the car, but she'd risked her own life to hurry to his aid. "Then I'm going to check it out."

"Why don't you let me do that?" she asked, whispering although there was no way the occupants of the car could hear them.

"Now why would I do that?"

"Because you're hurt. You shouldn't be crawling around on the ground. You're going to reopen that wound."

"And that would be worse than letting you wander around like an elephant in a china store?"

"I can be very quiet," she said fiercely.

He laughed. "Sweetheart, that will be the day. You wouldn't be able to resist telling those guys what they were doing wrong."

"So you're going to leave a trail of blood for them to follow?"

"That's very melodramatic, Eleanor. Is that a line from one of your books?"

She rolled her eyes. "Fine. Go ahead and be a tough guy. We still have plenty of peroxide and bandages."

She turned around and flounced to the car. At least she closed the door quietly. The grin he'd been trying to hide emerged as he turned back toward the road.

Someone had definitely been watching out for him when he'd snatched Ellie Perkins. She'd jumped in to save him when she thought he was in trouble, then tried to get him to wait in the car because she was concerned about his wound.

She was generous and caring—even to a man who had kidnapped her.

She was an alien. It was the only explanation. People like Ellie didn't really exist. He certainly had never met anyone like her before.

He watched the police car for a good twenty minutes. Only a few cars and pickups passed the cops, along with two large tractors. The beginning of a plan percolating in his head, he finally turned around and slipped back to the car.

Ellie still sat inside, but he could see her peering down the rows of corn. His heart tightened in his chest when he saw the worried expression on her face.

"Did you miss me?" he said, emerging from the corn.

"I was worried." Her blue-gray eyes filled with concern, she scanned him from head to toe as if to assure herself that he was okay. "I was afraid they'd seen you."

"They're too busy watching the road behind them."

"So what are we going to do?"

"A couple of big tractors went by while I was watching. We'll wait for another one to come along," he said, planning his strategy. "We'll watch what happens when it passes their car. I'm hoping that it will block their vision for a few moments. That's when we'll drive across the road."

He watched as she thought about his plan, noted the doubt in her eyes. But finally she nodded. "Okay. What do you want me to do?"

Clearly, she'd analyzed the alternatives and realized it was the only way. "We're both going to watch a few tractors go by. When we figure out the timing, we'll drive to the very edge of the field and wait for an opportunity."

After five or six farm vehicles rumbled past, he said, "We'll go on the next one." Taking his eyes off the road for a moment, he allowed his fingers to brush Ellie's arm. He needed to touch her, to ground himself. "I want you to get down on the floor as we cross the road. They're probably looking for a car with two people in it.''

He didn't want her to be in the line of fire, but he wasn't about to tell her that. She looked as if she was about to question him, but he heard another tractor approaching and leaned forward. ''Here we go.''

He watched its slow, awkward progress. ''All right. Get ready.''

She slid onto the floor and huddled under the dashboard. He flexed his hands on the steering wheel, calculating when to make his move. As soon as the tractor started to veer in front of the police car, he gunned the engine. The car struggled up the embankment, then shot across the road.

As they headed down the other side, the car swerved and bounced and Ellie's head hit the bottom of the dashboard. The track veered sharply to the right almost immediately and in moments they were safely hidden in the corn again.

There was no sound of a car approaching, but Michael gunned the accelerator anyway. They bounced along another narrow, rutted track, the car shuddering and moaning. The lane twisted and turned, and they were thrown first toward the roof, then into the door. Ellie smashed into Michael and grabbed for the seat. By the time he stopped the car, they were both white-faced and panting.

But they had put at least a hundred yards between themselves and the road.

''What now?'' she whispered.

''We wait. If they saw anything, they'll probably

drive down here to take a look, and we don't want them to hear the engine.''

The heavy, stifling air pressed around them. Sweat rolled down Michael's sides and chest. Ellie had beads of perspiration forming at her hairline. But they stayed motionless, sucking in the humid air, straining to listen.

The faint rumble of a car engine reached them. The vehicle should have been moving much more quickly on the country road, and anxiety speared through him. When the car stopped and the engine went quiet, he knew the Midland officers had found the track.

''Out of the car,'' he whispered, opening his door with a quiet click.

Ellie obeyed him without a word, easing the door closed behind her. She watched him with huge, frightened eyes. Clearly he didn't need to tell her they'd been found.

''I want you to hide in the corn. If you go in a few rows, they'll never see you. The stalks are too close together. Lie on the ground and keep your face down.''

''What are you going to do?'' she asked.

''I'm going to go the other way.''

He was going to wait for the two men to find the car. And if they did, he'd do whatever it took to protect Ellie.

She looked at him doubtfully, as if she suspected he wasn't telling her the truth. He had to resist the temptation to grab her and kiss her one more time.

Instead of reaching for her, he motioned toward the corn and then deliberately turned away.

But he watched her out of the corner of his eye. She didn't go nearly as far away as he'd ordered. After the second row she stopped and knelt in the soil.

He watched as she searched for something on the ground. After a few moments, apparently satisfied, she sat down between the closely planted rows.

Worry burned in his gut and he wanted to tell her to move farther back. But he heard the mutter of voices approaching and knew he couldn't risk speaking to her.

Instead of melting into the green vegetation, he crouched in front of the car. The approaching officers couldn't see him unless they got down and looked under the vehicle, and he would be close enough to Ellie to help if the rogue officers spotted her.

Their voices became more distinct as they got closer. In a few more moments they would turn the last corner and see the car. Michael tensed, waiting for the shout that would tell him it had been spotted.

"There's nothing here."

The man's voice was startlingly clear. The police were closer than he realized.

"We saw something cross the road when that damn tractor went past," a second voice insisted.

"It was probably another tractor." The first man sounded disgusted. "There's no way Reilly could have gotten past us. We're wasting our time out here. There's nothing around but corn, pickups and tractors.

And bugs." Michael heard the officer slapping at himself. "Damn bugs."

"What do you want to do?"

"I'm going back to the car. These bugs are annoying as hell. And look at these shoes. You know how much these shoes cost me? I just polished them this morning and they're covered with mud. You want to keep walking through this field, be my guest. I'm done."

Michael held his breath as one set of footsteps retreated. Finally the other man swore, letting loose a string of vicious curses. Then he, too, turned around and began walking toward the highway.

Michael didn't move until he heard the police car start up and head back down the highway. And then he waited for another fifteen minutes. Finally he peered around the car, half expecting to see one of the officers waiting for him.

But the only movement was from corn leaves rustling together as they swayed in the breeze. He stood and listened intently, making sure it was safe before he motioned to Ellie to rejoin him.

She ran toward him. "Are you all right?" she asked.

"Why wouldn't I be?"

"I saw you grab your back when you stood up. Turn around." She moved behind him, and he felt her fingertips skim across his wound. "At least it doesn't look like it's bleeding again."

"It's fine," he said, turning back. "Perfect, in fact." He scowled at her. "Which is more than I can say for you. Why didn't you do what I told you to do and go deep into that corn? If they had come another twenty feet, they would have spotted you."

"Just like they would have spotted you?" She lifted her chin. "I wanted to be close in case you needed help."

"And just what were you going to do? Nag them to death?"

"I was going to use this." She held up a rock about the size of two fists. "I figured I could bash at least one of them in the head."

His fear for her and the resulting anger drained away as he gazed at the defiant tilt of her head. She clutched the pitiful weapon in her hand as she stared back at him. But he saw the uncertainty in her eyes.

"My God, Ellie." He shook his head. "What am I supposed to say to that?"

"Nothing," she said, tossing the rock on the ground. "I suppose it was a stupid idea."

"Yeah," he said, unable to stop himself from reaching for her. "It was a damn stupid idea. But I'm finding that I like stupid."

He grasped her upper arms and pulled her close enough to see the dark flecks in her blue-gray eyes. "I don't deserve to have you help me."

"Probably not," she said, the uncertainty fading from her eyes. It was replaced by a glint of humor and an expression that started his blood heating. "But I figured it was my civic duty to make sure you get to the FBI."

"Your civic duty, huh?" He drew her closer until

only a whisper of air separated them. "I've always appreciated citizens who try to do their part."

"I've always tried to be involved in civil matters." Her voice was breathy and faint, as if she couldn't get enough air.

"One of us better be," he whispered, pulling her against him. "Because I'm not feeling very civilized right now."

He lowered his mouth to hers and felt her lips tremble beneath his. Then she opened her mouth and surrendered to him. Desire stabbed him, sharp and urgent. He needed to possess her. He needed to remind them both they were still alive.

Closing his eyes, he deepened the kiss and brought his hands up to frame her face. Tendrils of her hair slipped between his fingers, smooth and cool. He buried his fists in the thick mass and pressed his body against hers.

With a soft cry she struggled to free her hands from where they were trapped against his chest. Then she wound her arms around him and clung to him, holding on as if she never intended to let him go.

Don't do this, he warned himself harshly. There was no future for them. He wasn't the kind of man Ellie needed.

But she leaned closer and her breasts pressed into his chest, her nipples already stiff. She wanted him.

And he was hard and aching for her.

With an inarticulate growl, he lowered her to the hard ground and covered her body with his. He needed to be inside her, needed to feel her legs wrapped around him, needed to hear her cries of release fill the air.

He shoved her blouse up to her shoulders and pushed her bra after it. Her breasts fell into his hands, warm and smooth and soft. Her dusky pink nipples were hard and pebbled, and as he looked at her, she arched her back, offering herself to him with an inarticulate little cry.

"Ellie," he muttered, his tongue dipping into the hollow at the base of her throat. "What are you doing to me?"

He couldn't bear to take his time, couldn't wait to treat her gently and carefully. He moved lower and took her nipple into his mouth, unable to think of anything but his need for her. She stiffened beneath him with a shocked cry, then her head fell back and her fingers clutched at his shoulders.

Suddenly worried that he'd hurt her or scared her, he tried to raise his head. But she refused to let him go, holding his head to her breast. Her hips jerked against his, and she raised her legs and wrapped them around him.

He burned with the need to bury himself deep inside her. When her thighs tightened around him, he felt himself grow even harder. Taking his mouth from her breast, he trailed his lips down her belly, tasting and sucking, feeling her muscles quiver. Her legs fell open and he fumbled with the button on her slacks.

They were too snug; he couldn't strip them down her legs. Frantic to touch her, he slid his hand into the open waistband. When he cupped her through her panties she was hot and wet.

"Oh, Ellie." He tore at the fabric until he felt it rip. When he touched her, she jerked in his arms and cried out sharply.

Blood pounded in his head and desire raged through him. There was no thought, no hesitation. Nothing existed in the world but his need to be inside her, to possess her, to make her completely his. He moved away from her abruptly, but she reached for him.

"Don't stop," she begged. "Please. Don't stop."

"Don't worry, sweetheart. I'm not stopping anything."

Frantic now, he peeled his jeans down until they tangled around his feet. Lifting her hips with one hand, he stripped her slacks off with the other and tossed aside the torn panties.

With one thrust he was deep inside her. She gasped and went still for a moment, then moved tentatively beneath him. Groaning, he buried his face in her hair and cupped her hips in his hands, driving himself ever more deeply into her. When he began to move she rose up with a throaty cry, keeping her body plastered tightly against his, as if she couldn't bear to have any distance between them.

He felt her quiver, felt the tension coiling inside her. Suddenly she cried out, shattering beneath him. The first tremors of his own release moved through him and he thrust into her again and again, until there was nothing left.

They lay together, both of them trembling. After a moment he rolled over, carrying her with him so she sprawled on top of him. Ignoring the stab of his wound, he swept his hand down her back, lingering on the softness of her buttocks, letting her essence seep into all his pores.

She turned her head and brushed a tentative kiss across his neck. He felt her uncertainty, and reality returned in a rush. This wasn't some bimbo he'd picked up in a bar, someone who knew the score. This was Ellie, for God's sake. Ellie, whom he'd kidnapped less than twenty-four hours ago. Ellie, whose tentative kisses clearly showed her inexperience. Ellie, whom he'd vowed to protect with his life.

"My God, Ellie, I'm sorry," he said, trying to untangle himself from her.

She lifted her head and looked at him, her eyes dilated and smoky, her face flushed from his whiskers, her lips swollen from his kisses. He felt himself grow hard again.

"What are you sorry about?"

"This." He sat up next to her and looked at her lying on the ground, her slacks bunched around one ankle, her blouse shoved up to her shoulders. Her torn panties lay discarded in the dirt next to her. "And that," he muttered, reaching for her blouse and pulling it down to cover her breasts.

His fingers burned to feel their weight again, but he snatched his hands away. "Could I have been any more of a jerk?"

She sat up slowly, the passion fading from her face.

A faint blush of color tinged her cheeks. "What are you talking about?"

Her long legs were firm and supple and damp with sweat. Heat flashed through him. The memory of those legs sliding against him, tangling around him, made him ache for her. Before he could touch her again and turn a mistake into a disaster, he yanked his jeans up from around his ankles and turned away.

"This wasn't supposed to happen," he muttered.

She stood up behind him and he heard her fumbling with her slacks. When he was sure she was dressed again, he turned to face her.

"Go ahead," he said roughly. "Slap me. Or hit me. Or kick me. Do something."

"Why would I hit you?"

Her voice was cool and reserved. Her eyes were carefully shuttered. She was back in librarian mode. For a moment he wanted the other Ellie, the one who'd wrapped herself around him with complete abandon, whose cries of release still echoed in his ears.

He wouldn't allow himself to want her. He wouldn't allow himself to need her.

"I jumped your bones like an animal," he said roughly. He swept his hand in the direction of the corn. "We're in the middle of a cornfield, for God's sake."

"Did you notice me complaining?" Her eyes grew bright.

He hoped it was anger. He was afraid it was tears.

"Did you notice me telling you to stop?"

"I didn't give you a lot of chances," he said, terrified by his need to touch her, to wrap his arms around her and comfort her. He backed away another step.

She bent down to pick up her torn panties, and he was struck by another realization. "Hell," he said, horrified by the thought. "I didn't use any protection. Please tell me you're on the Pill."

"Don't worry about it." Her voice had no expression.

He'd needed her so much that he hadn't even thought about getting her pregnant. That had never happened before.

Panicked, he wanted to run, to get as far away as he could from his need for her. He wanted to run until Eleanor Perkins no longer filled his mind and his heart and his soul.

But that wasn't an option right now.

"Let's go," he said, his voice rough to hide his fear. "We're not safe yet."

CHAPTER THIRTEEN

ELLIE WATCHED MICHAEL back away from her, and felt her heart crumbling. He regretted making love to her. The truth was on his face and in his eyes. He thought it had been a huge mistake.

She looked down at the torn panties in her hand and curled her fingers into a fist around them. She didn't regret what had happened. How could she regret something that had made her feel more alive than she'd ever felt in her life?

"Get in the car," he said, his voice flat.

Without answering she opened the door of the car and slid onto the hot vinyl seat. It burned her skin through the fabric of her slacks, but she hardly noticed. She had barely pulled the door shut when he started the car with a jerk.

"You'll tell me if there are any...consequences."

If she was pregnant. She hadn't even thought about the possibility. Emotion squeezed her chest, but she wasn't sure if it was fear or hope. And that just proved she'd lost her mind.

"I'll tell you if I'm pregnant," she said, staring straight ahead.

She could feel him flinch. "And I don't have any

diseases,'' he muttered a few moments later. She could sense him looking at her, but refused to meet his gaze. ''In case you're wondering.''

''Thank you for telling me,'' she answered, struggling to keep her voice polite and distant. ''Neither do I.''

He snorted. ''That's one thing I'm not worried about.''

His words hit like a slap and tears burned behind her eyes as she stared out the window. She would not give him the satisfaction of crying, she told herself fiercely.

When she could speak without her voice quavering, she said, ''Just because I'm bossy and opinionated and...and frumpy doesn't mean that I've never slept with a man. Maybe you *should* worry about getting a disease from me.''

''That's not what I meant and you know it,'' he said hotly. ''I meant...oh, hell.''

''You meant what?''

''Never mind.''

The car jolted along the trail beneath the relentless sun. She bounced from side to side, smashing into the door, her head bumping the roof. The sun beat down mercilessly. Sweat dripped down her body.

After a particularly vicious swerve that sent her ribs cracking into the door, Michael jammed the brakes on the car and brought it to a bouncing halt.

''I meant that you're not the kind of woman who sleeps around, all right?'' His fingers gripped the steering wheel so tightly that his knuckles were white and he stared straight ahead out the windshield. "I wasn't putting you down, Ellie."

"Thank you," she said softly, watching a muscle twitch in his jaw. Some of the tightness in her chest began to ease. "I'm glad you clarified that."

"And I didn't mean I was sorry we had sex." Color tinged his cheeks. "I was sorry because I wasn't very thoughtful."

More of the ice in her chest began to break up. "Like I said, I don't recall complaining."

Finally he gazed over at her, a haunted look in his eyes. "Damn it, Ellie!" he exclaimed. "You should have complained. You're not a do-it-in-the-dirt kind of woman. You're the kind who deserves candles and soft music and clean sheets." He turned away. "You deserve a little romance," he muttered.

A tiny bubble of hope began to grow in her chest as the pain washed away. "We can have the romance next time," she said, lacing her fingers together to keep from touching him.

"There isn't going to be a next time." He glared at her, but she saw the flicker of desire in his eyes and it warmed her.

"And why is that?" she asked.

He stared at her for a moment, then sighed. "Ellie, I'm not the right guy for you. I told you before that I'm not a happily ever after person, and I meant it." He jerked his head back the way they'd come. "And if that little episode didn't convince you, I don't know what will."

She leaned against the seat, her heart pounding. "Maybe I don't want happily ever after, either."

He rolled his eyes. "Tell me another one. You have White Picket Fence written all over you."

"Maybe I used to feel that way," she said slowly. "But I've changed." She swiveled on the seat to face him. "A few days ago I wouldn't have believed that I'd go on the run with a man wanted for murder. I wouldn't have believed I would want to help him. But here I am." She looked away, uncomfortable baring her soul to him. She'd never shared such intimate thoughts with anyone. "I'm bored with my life. I'm bored with always doing the right thing, always being the responsible one."

She took a deep breath. "When you kidnapped me, I was terrified. But I realized pretty quickly that you weren't going to hurt me. And then I found that I was enjoying myself."

"Yeah, we've had a blast, haven't we," he said sourly.

"I said that wrong. Of course I'm not having a good time. I'm horrified by what's happened to you, and I'm appalled at the reason. But I'm here now, and complaining isn't going to help me. Or you. So we just have to keep moving forward." She grinned. "And to tell you the truth, this is the most excitement I've ever had in my life."

"Including wild sex with an inappropriate man."

Her smile faded. "You're not just a fling, Michael. I didn't make love with you for the thrill of it."

"And that's exactly my point," he said. "You

shouldn't have had sex with me at all. I know what women like you expect. I'll just end up breaking your heart."

"I won't let you do that." She stared at him, willing him to look at her. "'Women like me' might surprise you. I can take care of my own heart." She lifted her chin. "And I'll have wild sex if I want to."

Finally he turned his head. "It sounds like I've created a monster." But the tension in his face eased. "Okay, I'll trust you to take care of yourself. And if it's wild sex you're looking for, keep my name at the top of your list."

"It is," she said, then looked away. She'd already let her feelings for him get out of hand. But she'd rather die than admit it. So she would play it as loose as he did.

"I'm glad we have that straightened out," he said as he put the car back into gear.

"Me, too," she said, keeping her voice light.

"And you're not exactly frumpy," he said, but he didn't look at her.

"Not exactly?" she said, her voice dry. "Then what would you call it?"

"I'd call it conservative," he said after a long pause.

She smothered a laugh. "Conservative is one way of putting it, I guess." And that was going to change, she vowed. As soon as her life returned to normal. Or as normal as it could get after the revelations she'd had during the last two days.

He slanted her another glance. "I've never known

anyone else who could laugh at herself the way you can.''

She shrugged. ''You know what they say. The person who can laugh at herself will never lack for amusement.''

''I don't want to fight with you, Ellie,'' he said after another long pause.

''I don't want to fight with you, either.'' She wanted to be able to remember their time together without the bitterness of anger and harsh words.

''Good.'' He glanced at her out of the corner of his eye. ''But you can't fool me into thinking you're going to be Miss Meek-and-Mild.''

''Would you want me to be meek and mild?'' she asked curiously.

''Hell, no,'' he responded immediately. ''I'd be afraid you were sick or something.'' He paused for a second and she saw a hint of a grin hovering around his mouth. ''But awestruck and adoring would be kind of nice every once in a while.''

''Don't hold your breath, Reilly.'' She shifted in the seat, trying to subdue a smile. ''I don't do adoring.''

''That's what I was afraid of.''

They bounced along for a few more minutes until another gap appeared in the green jungle that surrounded them. Michael immediately jammed on the brakes.

''This must be the end of the trail.''

He stared at the blue sky ahead for a moment, then got out of the car. She immediately joined him.

"Now what?" she asked.

He glanced down at her. "I'm going to see what's waiting for us on the road. I want you to hide in the corn again."

"What if you need help?"

He turned and grabbed her upper arms. But instead of pressing into her, his fingertips slid down her skin in a way that felt almost caressing. "The point is to make sure you're safe, Ellie. Don't you understand that? If something goes wrong, if you think I need help, I want you to run even farther back into the field. I don't want you to get hurt."

A tiny ray of hope warmed her. She knew him well enough to know he wasn't going to say he cared about her. He couldn't say she had any importance for him. The only way he could express his feelings was by protecting her, by trying to make sure she didn't get hurt.

A tiny voice inside warned her not to delude herself. Maybe Michael Reilly was exactly who he said he was, a man who couldn't make a commitment and was content being that way. Maybe she was just setting herself up for heartache.

But she'd worry about that later. Right now, there was no way she'd watch him being captured or worse, and not try to do something about it. But he didn't need to know that.

"Fine. I'll stay in the corn."

"You'd better."

But he ruined the effect of his glower by pulling her toward him and kissing her, his mouth lingering on hers for a long moment. "I won't let anything happen to you. We're going to be fine."

He turned away and headed for the road, while she stood and stared after him. "Maybe we are," she said to herself.

Finally she hid in the corn, staying close enough to the track to watch him. He eased himself along a narrow row, then approached the highway slowly, crawling on his belly. When he got to the edge of the field, he didn't move for a long time.

She was beginning to worry that he'd seen something when he backed up and walked toward the car. She scrambled out of the corn and met him.

"What's going on?"

"Not a thing. There's no sign of the guys from Midland."

"Do you think they're still back where we saw them, waiting for us to drive past them on our way out of town?"

"Probably."

"That's not very smart."

He stopped walking and looked at her. Contempt filled his eyes and his mouth curled into a sneer. "That's why they're criminals. They're too lazy to do a job right. And they're too stupid to understand why it's important."

"So are we just going to drive out onto the road and keep going?"

"That's the plan. We'll get as far as we can today." He reached up and touched her hair. It had fallen out of its bun a long time ago and now was hopelessly tangled. "We still have to get us both a disguise before we reach the city."

The farther away they got from Pinckney, the more she relaxed. Some of the tension in Michael's shoulders eased, too. Maybe they would make it to the FBI, after all. And once Michael delivered his information, they would no longer be targets.

There would be no reason for the cops from Midland to continue pursuing them. The damage would be done.

And so would her reason for staying with Michael.

A vise gripped her chest and slowly tightened. She turned away and stared blindly out the window. What was wrong with her? Of course she wanted their pursuit to end. Of course she wanted them to be safe.

What she didn't want was Michael to walk away from her. And that's exactly what would happen when this was over. He'd told her that himself, more than once.

Most vehemently just about an hour ago, after the most shattering sexual experience she'd ever had.

Tears gathered in her eyes but she fiercely resisted shedding them. She would not cry, she vowed. She would not be that weak.

The restlessness she'd felt earlier came back, stronger than before. She wouldn't think about what would happen after this was over. Not now. She'd live in the present and not worry about tomorrow. She never had before, but she was ready to try. It was better than the way she'd been living, carefully planning every aspect of her existence, trying to control all the variables.

She hadn't really been living, she realized. She'd been surviving. She'd been doing damage control before it was needed.

Not anymore.

From now on, she was going to be Eleanor Perkins, risk-taker.

No. She was going to be Ellie Perkins, risk-taker.

"What's going on?"

Michael's voice interrupted her thoughts. "What do you mean?" she asked.

"You've been staring into that mirror for a long time. Is there something behind the car that needs to be watched?"

"Not at all. I've just been thinking," she replied, glancing over at him.

"About what?"

"Life in general," she said lightly. She wasn't ready to bare her soul again.

"God help us. Any revelations?"

The mock fear in his voice lightened her heart. He was at least making an effort to be agreeable.

"Just that I'm hungry." She kept her tone as airy as she could.

"We'll stop at the next town." He gave her a grin. "You're so demanding."

"I try to keep you on your toes."

They came to an intersection and he hesitated before turning left. The car shuddered its way back to the speed limit.

"This isn't the most direct route to Chicago. But I think it's safer."

"You mean they're less likely to look for us here."

"Yeah. I'm hoping they still think we're heading to St. Louis. That would be the logical place for us to go—much closer than Chicago. But if they've figured out we're going north, they wouldn't come down this road to follow us."

"That sounds like good thinking to me." It also sounded as if it meant they'd be together for a while longer.

She was pitiful. She'd rather be on the run than say goodbye to him.

And he'd made it clear he couldn't wait to be rid of her.

They were silent for the half hour it took to reach the small town, where they eventually stopped to eat dinner. When he pulled into a small diner on the side of the road, he drove the car around to the back of the building, where it couldn't be seen from the highway.

Ellie salivated at the smells coming from the restaurant. But she said, "Are you sure it's safe to stop here? We could keep going to a bigger town."

"This is fine. We're both hungry and we need to get out of the car for a while. We can't sit in the restaurant and take the chance that someone will recognize us, but we could eat back here." There was a grassy field behind the parking lot, and he nodded toward it. "We'll have a picnic."

He stood and watched the road for a few minutes.

When there were no cars coming in either direction, they headed into the tiny diner.

A few minutes later they walked out carrying disposable containers of food. Positioning themselves where they could watch the road without being seen, they began to eat.

The silence between them was peaceful. Then Michael turned to her.

"You said you were always the boring and respectable one. How come?"

Shame washed over her and she looked away. Then she defiantly looked back at him. "My family background isn't exactly normal."

"Join the crowd," he muttered.

She'd guessed as much, so she merely nodded.

"Are you going to tell me?" he asked after a moment.

She didn't want to do so. She wanted to keep her shame private and hidden. She didn't want him to know how she'd been manipulated. But he waited, watching her with understanding eyes, and she realized Michael wouldn't judge her.

"My father left before I was born," she said, staring down at the ground. "I guess my mother never got over it. She clung to me because I was all she had left." She risked a glance up at him, and he reached for her hand.

"She couldn't stand being alone. And she wanted someone to take care of her." She gave him a wry look. "I was the one and only candidate. When I did try to move away from home she had a breakdown."

Eleanor shrugged. "I took care of her, of course. I didn't have a choice. I was the responsible one, the one who made all the decisions." She tried to give him a smile and failed miserably. "I had to look after her."

He leaned forward, searching her face. "Is your mother the one who said you weren't attractive?"

She jerked away from him, shocked. "What do you mean?"

"Someone told you that," he said grimly. "And I'm guessing it was her."

Ellie looked down again as the remembered pain rolled through her. "She never said it in so many words. She just told me I'd have to rely on my brains to get by in the world."

"Selfish bitch," he said viciously.

"She was just a needy woman."

"And she stole your self-confidence."

At that Eleanor looked up and gave him a weak smile. "No one's ever accused me of a lack of self-confidence."

"I mean confidence in yourself as a woman." He leaned closer and grasped her chin in his fingers, forcing her to look at him. "You're a beautiful woman, Ellie. And if you'd stop hiding behind those baggy clothes and ugly glasses, everyone else in the world would see it, too."

"That's telling it like it is," she muttered.

"Are you going to sit there and pretend it's not the truth?"

After a long pause, she gave a jerky nod and looked

away. She felt raw and exposed and completely vulnerable. "You're right. She had me convinced that no one would ever find me attractive."

"She was full of crap."

Eleanor laughed in spite of herself. "Thank you."

"You're welcome. Now finish your dinner so we can get going."

"Yes, sir."

Was that it? Was it really as simple as that?

Maybe it was. Michael certainly seemed to find her attractive, if the episode in the cornfield was any indication. Maybe it had been her perception that was at fault, rather than reality. Had she thought herself unattractive only because her mother let her believe it? Her mother who'd had a definite agenda when it came to her only child?

Thoughtfully she took a bite of her food. It was certainly something to think about.

By the time they finished eating, shadows were lengthening and the sun hung low in the sky. It would be dark soon, she thought as they slid back into the car. The heat from the day had eased and there was an almost-cool breeze flowing through the car window.

"Next stop Chicago?" she asked cheerfully.

He shook his head. "We won't make it that far tonight. We're still four or five hours away. I thought we'd stop in Springfield. It's big enough that no one should notice two strangers. And there will be plenty of motels to choose from."

Her heart speeded up at the thought of spending

the night with him. But she couldn't help glancing behind them, looking for the headlights of a pursuing vehicle. "Aren't we still too close to Midland?"

"I'd like to be farther away, but they have no idea which direction we went after leaving Pinckney." His mouth compressed into a thin line. "They might even think we're still in town. The guys I saw in that car aren't going to admit we might have gotten past them."

"Will Charles and Betty be all right?" The thought of the older couple, alone and vulnerable in their isolated house, had been gnawing at her all day.

"They'll be fine. If I know Charles, he's got a warning system rigged up in case they come back, and he's waiting for them with a shotgun.

"But thanks for worrying about them." He touched her arm lightly and a shock of desire sparked across her skin. He drew his hand away quickly. Had he felt the connection, too?

"Wouldn't it be safer to travel in the dark? That way no one could spot us." She struggled to keep her voice even, to hide her reaction to his touch.

"It might be. But in the dark we couldn't see anyone, either."

His voice was huskier than usual. She longed to touch him, to find if that spark of desire was mutual, but she clenched her fists in her lap.

In an hour they were going to stop at a motel. Memories of their lovemaking under the sun swirled through her mind. Heat throbbed in her blood and desire pooled inside her, heavy and aching. The car was far too small. His musky scent filled the air.

What would happen at the motel? Would Michael ask for two rooms? Or a room with two beds? And what if he did? Would she be able to tell him she didn't want to sleep alone?

A combination of nervousness and longing swirled through her, sharp and edgy. Michael didn't look at her, didn't touch her. He just kept driving, his eyes on the road in front of them, his hands on the steering wheel.

An hour later they saw a sign alerting them that Springfield was ten miles away. Her nerves, which had subsided to a jittery hum, started jangling again. She stared into the night, desperate to distract herself.

It was now completely dark. The moon hadn't yet risen and the only light came from a band of stars smeared across the black sky. It was the Milky Way, she realized with awe. She'd never seen it before. It was impossible to see many stars in Midland, and it had been far too long since she'd been out of the city.

"We'll head into town to find a motel," he said, his low voice rasping across her nerve endings. "Give them more places to search."

"Good."

She felt him watching her in the darkness of the car. "Do you want me to leave you in Springfield?" he finally asked. "You'd probably be safe enough if you stayed in your room. They can't search every motel."

"You said I'd be safer if I stayed with you."

He looked back out the windshield. "There are all kinds of danger," he finally answered in a low voice. "You might be better off if I left you behind."

"I don't want to remain here," she said immediately. "I'd rather stay with you."

She could feel him studying her in the darkness. "Why would you want to do that?" he asked, his voice almost too soft to be heard.

She wasn't about to tell him the truth—that she wanted to spend as much time with him as possible, hoarding memories for the day he walked away. "I like to finish what I start," she answered, trying to make her voice casual and breezy. "And I have a grudge against those guys. They shot at me."

"They'll do a lot worse than take a few wild shots at you if they catch us," he said.

"They haven't found us so far, so I'll take my chances. Besides, what would you do without me?" she teased, trying to ease the tension in the car. "Someone has to plan this caper."

"That's what I'm afraid of," he muttered. But the tightness in his shoulders had relaxed. "All right, you're coming with me."

They drove through the outskirts of Springfield until they reached an area full of strip malls, fast-food outlets and budget motels. He finally turned into the parking lot of the inn set the farthest back from the street. "This looks like a possibility," Michael said.

The motel had a seedy, run-down air about it. Michael drove slowly around the building, clearly cataloging everything he saw. The cracked asphalt behind the motel held a handful of vehicles. Only two of the streetlights were lit, leaving the parking lot dim and shadowy.

"This will work." He nodded at two semis parked close together. "They'll provide plenty of camouflage."

He swerved the car into a spot deep in the shadow of one of the trailers, then eased out of the car. "You stay here," he said. "I'll go check in. If they're looking for two people, it would be better if the motel staff don't see you."

"All right."

She watched him walk toward the front of the building. He moved stiffly, as if his back still hurt. And she was sure it did. A person didn't recover from a bullet wound in twenty-four hours.

But not once had he complained. Not once had he even mentioned the wound in his back. He might describe himself as a cop who worked on intuition and luck, but he was as stubborn and iron-willed as anyone she'd known.

Stubborn enough to insist there was nothing between them but captor and victim.

Stubborn enough to walk away from her without looking back.

CHAPTER FOURTEEN

MINUTES DRAGGED BY as she waited for Michael to reappear. Concern grew slowly at first, then mushroomed into panic as she imagined the worst. The police had been waiting for him when he walked into the motel lobby. The Midland cops had seen him from the street and quickly surrounded him. He could be lying on the ground right now in a pool of blood, his life ebbing away in a seedy motel parking lot.

She was just about to leap from the car when he slid into the seat beside her.

"Are you all right?" she asked, grabbing his arm. "What happened?"

"Nothing happened." He gave her an odd look. "I was being careful and took my time."

She let go of him and fell back against the seat. "I imagined the worst."

He gave her a weary grin. "There goes your imagination again, Ellie. Those books of yours are a bad influence."

"I pictured you lying dead on the asphalt of the parking lot with the Midland cops standing around you," she admitted.

He laughed. "You said I'm melodramatic? You're the queen of the dramatic moment."

"I am not a drama queen," she began, her voice indignant. Then she realized he was baiting her, trying to distract her from her fears. And he'd succeeded.

"You're good, Reilly," she said as she reached into the back seat for the bag with the toiletries she'd bought that morning. "You're very good. But you're not going to suck me into an argument again."

"Too bad," he said, watching her with a glint in his eyes. "Fighting with you is always so...stimulating."

Heat shimmered through her at his words. She straightened to face him and stilled. His eyes blazed, suddenly hot with desire. As she stared at him, unable to look away, an answering wave of need rolled through her.

He was the first to look away. "We'd better get inside," he said, his voice gruff.

Neither of them spoke as they walked through the narrow, dimly lit corridor of the motel. The building had a musty smell, as if the rug had gotten wet and not completely dried out. The muffled sounds of television accompanied them down the hall. Clearly, soundproofing the rooms wasn't a priority of the owners.

"Sorry we have to stay in such a dump," Michael muttered. "I figure it will be more anonymous."

"This is fine. I never considered myself a Ritz kind of person, anyway," she answered.

"Maybe not, but I'm damn sure you've never stayed in motels like this before."

"I've never stayed in many motels, period," she

admitted. But that was going to change, she vowed. It would be part of the new, exciting Ellie Perkins. She'd go on vacations to exotic places and stay in luxurious hotels.

He stopped in front of a door and opened it, then stepped aside so she could enter. There was one double bed in the room, plus a shabby dresser that had definitely seen better days. Two chairs sat by the window, their upholstery faded and worn.

"Well, it's cleaner than the place we stayed last night," she said after a moment.

"Now there's a ringing endorsement." He frowned. "We could have stayed in an alley and it would have been cleaner than last night's room."

"This is fine," she said again, her voice firm. Her gaze drifted to the bed, then she made herself look back at Michael. "It's not like we're living here. We're just sleeping here tonight."

Heat rose up her neck. When she looked at the bed, the last thing she thought about was sleeping.

She glanced at it again, then immediately turned her head away. Michael must have noticed.

"I registered as a single. There was no way I could ask for a room with two beds," he said, his voice defensive.

This was the point at which she needed to be bold, needed to tell him that she was glad there was only one bed. She opened her mouth, but the words caught in her throat.

Tension stretched between them as they stood in the center of the room. She couldn't take her eyes off his face, and he seemed equally unable to look away. Just as she was about to take a step toward him he turned and handed her the bag, practically shoving it into her hands.

"Go ahead and use the bathroom first. You must be beat."

I'm not that tired, she wanted to say, but her nerve failed and she slipped into the bathroom. Ten minutes later, wrapped in a towel, she walked back into the room to find Michael peering out the window through a crack in the curtains.

"See anything?" she asked.

"Not a thing. I don't think they'll find us tonight. They can't have any idea where we've gone." He let the curtain drop and turned around. "I'll, uh, take my turn in the bathroom."

He seemed almost as nervous as she was, Ellie thought in amazement as he disappeared into the bathroom. Maybe he was just as unsure as she was about the next move.

She folded her clothes carefully and laid them on one of the chairs. Then she looked over at the bed, shifting from one foot to the other, agonizing over what to do.

"Darn it, Eleanor," she finally fumed. "Decide what you want."

And that didn't take any thinking at all. She wanted Michael. This might be their last night together. If everything went smoothly tomorrow, she'd return to Midland and Michael would...

She wasn't sure what Michael would do, but it was

highly unlikely that he'd return to Midland with her. Tomorrow he would walk away from her, and she was very sure he wouldn't look back.

Unraveling her towel, she tossed it on the chair and slipped into the bed. But her courage failed her when the bathroom door opened. She yanked the covers to her chin.

"All set?" he asked. He was careful not to look at her.

"Yes."

He nodded and tossed his clothes on the other chair. Then he padded over to the bed, wearing his T-shirt and the black boxers she bought at the convenience store. Her heart jumped in her chest and her stomach quivered when he slipped into the bed next to her.

It was now or never, she told herself. In a minute he'd curl up and turn away from her, and then she wouldn't have the nerve to touch him. Swallowing hard, her chest tight with anxiety, she rolled onto her side, facing him.

"Michael," she began, then stopped. Never in her life had she asked a man to make love to her. And she wasn't sure how to do it. The words just would not come out of her mouth.

He looked over at her and she stilled. Passion blazed in his eyes. He tried to conceal it, but desire was etched in every muscle, every plane of his face. His eyes burned the deep blue of a flame as he watched her.

And suddenly her hesitation fell away. This was

the right thing to do. She needed to grab for memories, because their time together was dwindling to a handful of hours. She would not leave him with the memory of a cowardly retreat.

"Michael," she said again. Her voice quavered, and she took a moment to steady herself. "I'm glad you got a room with only one bed." The declaration came out as a husky growl.

He stared at her for a moment, as if he wasn't sure what she'd just said, then closed his eyes with a groan.

"You shouldn't have said that," he whispered. "You're making it impossible for me to do the right thing."

"And what's the right thing?"

"Not touching you. Staying as far away from you as I can."

"That's not the right thing for me," she breathed, reaching out and linking her fingers with his. All her fears fell away as she watched him struggle with himself. "I want you, Michael."

"I want you, too. But I can't make any promises."

"I'm not asking for any."

He slid closer to her and cupped her face with his hands. "Are you sure?"

"As sure as I can be." She lay perfectly still, her heart racing and the pressure in her chest expanding.

He closed his eyes and took her mouth with a groan. "Then God help us both."

She melted into him as he kissed her, but she didn't taste the desperation she'd felt earlier. Instead his mouth was sweeter, softer, slower, as if he had all the time in the world. Unbearably moved by his tender seduction, she wrapped her arms around him and fitted her body to his.

He swept his hand down her back, then stopped as he realized she was naked. "Ellie," he said, lifting his head and gazing down at her, his eyes hot and smoldering. "You're not wearing any clothes."

"I'm not?" she said, the weight of uncertainty falling away when she saw in his eyes that his need was as great as hers. She felt her mouth curl into a grin. "How did that happen?"

His hand lingered on her hip, his fingers caressing her skin. He bent his head and nuzzled her neck. "You know, I'm beginning to like that mouth of yours," he said against her skin.

"I like yours, too," she whispered, deliberately misunderstanding him. "I like the way you taste." She was astonished at her boldness.

Michael groaned and found her lips again. This time his kiss wasn't sweet or slow. He slid his tongue along the seam, urging her to open to him. And when she did, he matched the rhythm of his movements to the thrust of his hips against hers.

Her whole body throbbed with a desperate, aching need. She wanted to feel his skin sliding against hers, to smooth her hands over his body. She struggled to speak. "This isn't fair," she panted. "You still have your clothes on."

He drew back and ripped his T-shirt over his head, then stripped off his boxers. But instead of sliding over her, as she expected, he bent his head and took her breast in his mouth.

The sensation was so overwhelming that she cried out. Gasping, she arched off the bed, her hips seeking his. But instead of filling her, as she so desperately wanted, he reached down and skimmed his finger over her most sensitive flesh.

Shocked, she cried out his name as spasm after spasm ripped through her. She clutched his shoulders and held on while the storm raged.

Finally, when she felt as if she would never move again, he raised his head. "You're incredible," he whispered, brushing a lock of hair off her forehead. He gave her a slow grin that made her quiver. "I think watching you come could turn into my favorite pastime."

She frowned at him through the haze of pleasure that still rippled through her. "That's not what I want. I don't just want you to watch me. I want to watch you, too."

He groaned again and eased away from her. "Don't worry, sweetheart. You'll have all the chances to watch me that you want."

The words "you promise?" were on the tip of her tongue, but she stopped herself in time. He'd made it very clear there would be no promises. She would mourn her loss tomorrow. Tonight she wouldn't say anything to spoil their time together.

He drew away from her slowly, as if he couldn't bear to let her go. Finally he eased out of the bed. She watched him, puzzled, while he grabbed his jeans from the chair. When he pulled a silver packet out of his pocket and held it up, she realized what it was.

''Where did you get that?'' Surely, if he'd had condoms, he would have used one earlier.

''The washroom at the place we stopped for dinner.'' He gave her a cocky grin. ''Hope springs eternal, you know.''

She sat up in bed and drew the sheet to her breasts. ''Then how come you pretended you didn't want anything to do with me earlier?''

The smile faded from his face. ''Because it was the smart thing to do. I was trying to do the right thing.''

''No,'' she whispered. ''That wouldn't have been the right thing to do.'' She held out her arms and the sheet dropped away. ''This is.''

His eyes darkened as he looked at her. Then he dropped his jeans on the floor and slid in next to her, fastening his mouth to hers at the same time.

Her heart quickened and desire surged to life again. She didn't want him to control himself. Need churned through her, and this time she wanted him inside of her. When she pulled him closer, he rose over her and entered her with one powerful thrust.

She moaned his name as passion roared through her. When he began to move inside her, she lifted her hips to meet him, matching thrust for thrust. And when she exploded with release again, she felt him shudder inside her, heard the harsh rasp of his voice whispering her name.

They lay together for a long time, trembling and spent. Finally he lifted his head. ''Ellie,'' he whispered, framing her face with his hands. "Ellie, what are you doing to me?"

"The same thing you're doing to me," she whispered back. She combed her fingers through his thick hair, loving the feel of the coarse strands against her skin. "You're making me feel things I've never felt before."

His eyes darkened as he looked down at her. "You're scaring me," he muttered, bending to kiss her, his eyes drifting shut. "You matter too much. I don't want anything to happen to you."

Her heart soared with sudden hope. "Michael," she began, "I—"

But he put his mouth on hers and swallowed the rest of her words. "Don't worry," he said when he finally lifted his head to draw a breath. "I'll die myself before I let anyone hurt you."

That was nothing more than he'd said all along, she reminded herself sharply. What had happened to her determination to take what he could give and not demand more?

It had evaporated in the heat of their lovemaking. She would never be satisfied to walk away from him. But she wouldn't be given a choice.

So she would have to make the most of this last night they had together. She shifted beneath him and touched his cheek. "We don't have to worry about danger right now. There's no one else around," she murmured. "And we have a long night ahead of us."

His eyes darkened even more. "So we do. And I have a couple of rain checks to cash in." Then he bent to kiss her again.

SUNLIGHT STREAMED WEAKLY through the crack in the curtain as Michael drifted awake. It wasn't early in the morning. The sunlight was too bright, he thought drowsily. He was going to be late for work.

Someone moved against him and he caught his breath. Then he saw Ellie's head nestled against his chest, felt her legs entwined with his, and remembered.

Icy fear trickled through his veins. He'd never spent an entire night with a woman. After the sex, he always got up and left.

But it hadn't even occurred to him to leave Ellie last night.

Their situation was different, he told himself, feeling an edge of desperation. He'd had to stay with her, because of the danger.

But last night he hadn't been thinking about corrupt cops, or Midland, or the information he carried. He hadn't been thinking about the threat to Ellie, or to him.

He'd thought of nothing but her. He'd wanted nothing more than to make love to her one more time, to taste her again. There was no way he'd have gotten out of that bed to leave her.

It scared the hell out of him. Moving slowly so he wouldn't waken her, he tried to untangle their limbs and bodies. When she murmured a sleepy protest and reached for him, his heart thumped in his chest. He wanted nothing more than to burrow into her warmth, to absorb her scent and her touch, to lose himself in her once more.

He forced himself to let her go.

He showered quickly and pulled on his clothes without looking at her. The healing scab on his back pulled painfully, reminding him what was at stake. When he looked at his watch, he swore viciously to himself.

It was almost nine o'clock. He'd intended to be on the road at dawn, to make it to Chicago before midday and have the whole afternoon to arrange to meet an FBI agent. Now that wouldn't be possible.

They'd needed the sleep, he tried to tell himself. The last couple of days had been stressful and exhausting.

But it hadn't been the stress of the previous day that had made them sleep so late. They'd made love almost until dawn, until they were so exhausted they fell asleep in each other's arms. And not once during the night had he thought about what lay ahead.

He pushed the frightening thought away. These were extraordinary circumstances. As soon as he'd turned in the pictures and information to the FBI and Ellie was once again safe, everything would be back to normal.

A part of him knew that nothing would ever be the same, but he refused to acknowledge it. If he pretended hard enough, tried hard enough, he could block Ellie and all the unwelcome emotions she'd aroused completely from his mind.

"Michael?" she said, her voice husky.

"I'm right here," he answered. He couldn't look at her. If he saw her flushed with sleep and rumpled from their lovemaking he would make a huge mistake. If he touched her now, he might never be able to let her go.

"What's going on?" she asked.

"Nothing yet." He struggled to make his voice businesslike. "It's a little later than I'd planned, so I think I'll call the FBI agent before we leave."

She sat up in bed, clutching the sheet against her. He couldn't help the smile that curled his mouth. "Isn't it a little late for that, Ellie?"

She glanced down at the sheet and her cheeks reddened. "I guess I'm not used to this morning-after stuff," she admitted. But she didn't lower it.

"Who is?" he said wryly, but desire shuddered through him again. He wanted to see her in the daylight, to drink in the sight of her soft skin and smooth body. The need to watch her rise from the bed was almost too urgent to be denied. But all he said was, "I'll be a gentleman and turn around so you can get dressed."

"Could you hand me my clothes first?" Her face burned bright red, but she held his gaze.

That was Ellie—more guts than she knew what to do with.

He caught himself and scowled. He didn't want to linger on all her good points. She was merely a woman he'd gotten involved with because of the extraordinary circumstances in which they'd found themselves.

He didn't realize he'd been brooding until she spoke from behind him. "You can turn around now."

Slowly he swiveled to face her. Her cheeks were still flushed, and she didn't quite meet his eyes. But at least she was dressed. He could look at her without seeing the marks he'd left on her body, the whisker burns and the love bites. Without thinking of everything that had happened the night before. He could pretend that nothing had changed between them.

Or he could fool himself into thinking that was the case.

"Go ahead and use the bathroom," he said, his voice gruff. "I'll call the FBI."

"All right." She gave him an uncertain smile and turned to go.

He was a jerk. Of course she was unsure of herself. She wasn't a woman who was used to playing the morning-after role.

He reached out and grabbed her, pulled her to him for a hard, demanding kiss. "Good morning, Ellie."

She melted into him, her body molding perfectly with his. "Good morning," she murmured. Her voice was a husky purr in her throat, and he felt himself growing hard.

His arms tightened around her for a moment, then he let her go and stumbled backward. "I need to make that call."

"I know." She nodded, but there was a faint sadness in her eyes, as if she could look past his skin and see the fears deep inside him. As if she could see him tearing himself away from her.

He watched her close the bathroom door carefully behind her, and wanted to push it open and claim her as his. He wanted to tumble her back onto the rumpled bed and make love with her for another twelve hours.

Instead he picked up his cell phone and deliberately punched in the numbers.

CHAPTER FIFTEEN

THE BATHROOM DOOR OPENED just as he closed his cell phone. Michael looked up at Ellie, and she stopped dead in the doorway.

"What's wrong?" she asked.

"Why do you think something's wrong?"

"I know you." Her voice was flat. "What happened?"

He sighed, tossing his phone onto the bed. "The guy Charles recommended we talk to is on vacation. He's not due back in the office until next week."

"Oh." She sank into a chair, staring at him.

"Yeah," Michael said wearily. "Oh."

"What are we going to do?"

He wanted to tell her that *they* weren't going to do anything. The part of him that needed to be in control screamed that this was his problem and he would figure out a solution. He did things his own way.

But he hadn't done things his own way since the moment he'd snatched Ellie from the library parking lot. And thank God for it.

Ellie grounded him. Her no-nonsense, practical approach seemed to perfectly balance his intuitive, headlong attack on obstacles in their path. Her quick thinking had allowed them to avoid tragedy more than once.

She'd earned the right to have a say in what they did. And she'd earned it the hard way. She hadn't once whined or complained.

"We'll figure it out together," he said, amazed at the words coming out of his mouth.

The demon sitting on his shoulder whispered that there was only one reason why he was willing to include her. He couldn't bear to leave her behind.

That was absolutely not the case, he told himself, terrified that it was completely true. He was concerned for her safety. And he needed to keep her with him to keep her safe.

"I'll call the office back," he said, pushing those thoughts out of his mind. He had to concentrate on their dilemma. "I'll ask for the newest agent. I'll say I'm a reporter who wants to do a story."

"Why the newest agent?" she asked, a puzzled look on her face.

"Because the rookies haven't had time to be corrupted," he said. "They're so green they're still trying to figure out how to wipe their noses."

"Then what?"

"Then I'll tell him what I need and set up a meeting. Somewhere away from the office."

"You don't think the cops from Midland know where we're going, do you?" she asked, a sudden shadow of fear in her eyes.

"They can't know for sure. I didn't know myself until we made that turn yesterday." His mouth tightened. "But I wouldn't put it past them to have some-body watching the office, waiting for us to show up. They have to think I'd head for the FBI. And Chicago or St. Louis are the most logical choices."

"All right." She bent to put her toiletries in the bag. "It doesn't sound like we have much of a choice."

"There's always a choice, Ellie," he said quietly.

She looked up at him. "What do you mean?"

"It's not too late to stay here. You'll be perfectly safe in this motel."

He found himself holding his breath, waiting for her answer.

Ellie didn't disappoint him. "And let you have all the fun?" she replied. "Not a chance, Reilly."

He tried to ignore the relief that rushed through him. He watched her for a moment, looking for signs of fear or hesitation, but saw only resolve in her eyes. "All right."

He held her gaze while he dialed the FBI office. When a cool, professional woman's voice answered, he switched his attention to business and asked for the newest rookie agent in the office.

The woman hesitated. Then she said, "May I ask why?"

"I'm a newspaper reporter," he said easily, giving the name of the Midland local paper. "I'm doing a story on rookies. I thought a rookie FBI agent might be an interesting addition."

"One moment, please," she responded, and moments later a very young-sounding voice came on the line.

"This is Special Agent Kenneth Givens," he said. "How can I help you?"

"Agent Givens, I need your help." Michael was blunt. "I have information about corruption in a city police department that reaches to the highest levels. There's no one I can trust in the department, so I want the FBI to get involved."

"Really?"

Michael pictured the agent sitting up straight in his chair. He could almost hear the kid say, "Wow! Cool!"

Had he ever been that young and enthusiastic? Hell, no. Michael hadn't been young when he was twelve years old.

"Why don't you come into the office and tell me what you've got?"

"That's the problem," Michael answered. "I was followed out of town. I wouldn't be surprised if there was someone watching your office, waiting for me to show up."

"Really?" Givens said again. His voice almost squeaked with excitement. "Then why don't I meet you off-site?"

"Exactly what I had in mind."

"Could I get your name, please?" the agent asked.

"I don't think so. The less you know, the better for me. And for you."

There was a pause. Finally he said, his voice uncertain, "But I have to enter you into my phone log."

Good. A straight arrow, just as he'd hoped. "Put down 'anonymous tip,'" he suggested dryly.

Michael could almost hear the kid thinking. "I suppose I could do that," he said slowly. "I really don't know who you are."

"Good. Now where and when can we meet?"

"Why don't we meet at one of our satellite offices in the Chicago area?"

"I won't go near any of your offices." Michael's voice was flat. "Pick someplace else."

"I live in Wicker Park. There's a park in my neighborhood. Let's meet there."

Michael scribbled down directions, then looked at his watch. "How about tomorrow morning at nine?" he said.

"Tomorrow?" Michael heard disappointment in the rookie agent's voice. "I thought this was urgent."

"It is, but it's going to have to be tomorrow."

"All right," he finally said. "Tomorrow at nine in the park."

Michael hung up the phone and turned to Ellie, who was watching him with worried eyes. "We're all set. We just have to hold on until tomorrow morning."

"Why didn't you want to meet with him today?"

"I want to check out the park before we meet this guy, and we still have to figure out some kind of disguise. By the time we get to Chicago and make sure the park is safe, it'll be close to dusk. And that's too late. Darkness gives them the advantage."

"What do we do in the meantime?"

Unbidden, memories of the night before rushed through him. Desire stirred immediately and he struggled to push it away. This was not good. He needed to focus on making sure Ellie didn't get killed, not on making love with her.

"We head for Chicago. I want to watch the FBI office for a while and see if anyone is hanging around."

"Let's go, then."

He studied her as she grabbed the bag and headed for the door. She acted as if going to Chicago and walking into a dangerous situation was the most natural thing in the world, as if she didn't give a damn that they both might die.

Eleanor Perkins was a hell of a woman.

"Ellie, wait."

She turned to look at him, her hand already on the doorknob. "What's wrong?"

"I don't want you to get hurt," he said, his heart contracting with fear as he thought about what the Midland cops could do to her. "Maybe you *should* stay here."

She watched him steadily. "I trust you to keep me safe, Michael. And you need someone to help you. I'm not staying behind."

He hoped God would forgive him for the relief that flooded him. And he didn't even want to think about the sense of rightness that filled him at the thought of Ellie by his side. "This is your last chance to be safe."

"You're wasting time, Reilly." Her eyes sparked at him. "I thought we had a lot to do today."

"That's my Ellie. Nag, nag, nag," he said, but his spirits lifted. He knew it was wrong, knew it was dangerous, but he couldn't bear the thought of leaving her behind. "Okay, let's go."

As they drove toward Chicago, Michael outlined a plan. "We'll stop somewhere on the outskirts of the city and change the way we look. Then we'll head toward the Loop and watch the FBI office for a while." He smiled grimly. "If any trash from Midland is floating around Chicago, that's where it will land."

More than three hours later they approached the Windy City. At first new clusters of houses appeared scattered among the farms. Then the farms disappeared completely, replaced by strip malls and office buildings. When he saw a large shopping center, he pulled the car into the parking lot.

"I think we can get everything we need to disguise ourselves here," he said, pulling into a parking spot.

"What do you have in mind?"

"Nothing yet." He gave her a cocky grin. "I'm going to go with my intuition."

To his surprise, she didn't give him a smart answer. With a grin that didn't quite reach her eyes, she said, "I'll have to trust you. You're the one who's done this before."

He frowned and looked at her more closely. "Are you scared?"

She wouldn't meet his gaze. "A little, I guess."

"This from the woman who was willing to take on a bunch of cops with guns in Pinckney?" He took her chin in his hand and turned her face toward his as an unexpected wave of tenderness swept over him.

She didn't look away, but she didn't come back with a quick answer. After a moment she nodded slowly. "I guess I am. Now that we're in Chicago anything can happen. And I don't want you to get hurt."

"Let me get this straight," he said, incredulous. "You're afraid *I'm* going to get hurt? What about yourself? Aren't you at least a little worried about your own safety?"

She managed a wan smile. "I know you too well, Reilly. You'll think of some way to keep me tucked away, safe and sound out of the action, while you meet with the FBI agent and hand over your information. The closest I'm going to come to any danger is the sound of Chicago traffic outside a window somewhere."

"And there's something wrong with that?"

"You'll be on your own. There won't be anyone to help you."

"I'm used to being on my own," he said.

She gave him a steady look laced with sadness and resignation. "I know. Believe me, I realize that."

He wasn't sure why her eyes filled with pain. But he leaned forward and gave her a quick kiss. "I need all the help I can get here, Ellie. And I won't be shy about asking for it.''

''All right,'' she said, but the expression on her face said she didn't believe him.

That was too bad. His first priority was keeping her safe.

He froze, still holding on to her, and looked at her as panic raced through his veins. *It was more important to him to keep Ellie safe than to bring the Midland cops to justice.*

''Let's go,'' he said, his voice brusque. ''We need to find a Chicago newspaper and see if the story ran here.''

They hurried into the mall and he steered them toward a coffee shop. Sitting in a corner with cups of coffee and sandwiches in front of them, he pulled out the newspapers they'd bought.

''There are pictures, but they're small.''

He glanced from the photo to Ellie, then back again. Finally he set the newspaper aside. ''If we change my look, and your face and hair, the average Joe won't recognize us.''

Self-consciously she touched the knot of hair she'd twisted up on her head that morning. ''Should I undo it?'' She pushed her glasses up her nose, a habit that seemed to be unconscious. ''And there's not much I can do about my face. I'm not willing to have plastic surgery, even for you.''

He grinned. ''Plastic surgery won't be necessary.'' He leaned across the table and ran a finger down her nose. "It would be a crime to tamper with this face. No, what I have in mind is much simpler."

FOUR HOURS LATER Ellie stood in front of a mirror in one of the department stores, struck dumb by the appearance of the woman who looked back at her. She'd had no idea what had been hidden beneath her long hair, glasses and frumpy clothes.

Their first stop had been the one-hour optometrist's office in the mall, where she'd been fitted with contact lenses. Then they'd gone to the salon.

An hour later she'd emerged with a short, shaggy haircut that feathered around her face. Subtle highlights made her hair glow with a golden sheen. The haircut had somehow made her eyes look enormous and her cheekbones high and mysterious.

Now, wearing the clothes Michael had picked out for her, she hardly recognized herself. She wore her usual brand of jeans, but a size smaller than normal. Red sneakers and a tight red T-shirt stood out like beacons in the night. Bright red lipstick made her mouth look sexy and pouty, and she wore a flashy set of fake diamond earrings and a rock on a chain around her neck that would have looked gaudy on a streetwalker.

Michael grinned at her in the mirror. "What do you think?"

"I think…" She couldn't drag her gaze away from her image. "I think I don't know this woman."

"Sure you do, Ellie. She's the woman I've gotten to know the last few days. Now she just looks the part."

"You think I'm a—a high-priced tart who's one step above standing on a street corner?" she sputtered.

His laugh rumbled from his throat and curled around her heart. "Hell, no. I'm not talking about the makeup and the jewelry and the tight clothes. That's just the flash, what we want people to remember."

He touched one finger to her cheek. "I'm talking about the sexy, beautiful woman I see in the mirror. The woman who should realize how gorgeous she is."

He was completely sincere. Tears prickled in her eyes, and this time she didn't worry that he would see her cry.

"No one's ever called me sexy or beautiful before."

His smile faded. "Then you've known only idiots. I can't believe no one ever told you how lovely you are. All they had to do was look."

No one had ever taken the time to look.

She glanced down at herself, her gaze lingering on the red sneakers. "I think it's the shoes," she said, trying to lighten the mood. "I never thought of myself as a red-shoe kind of person."

"That's where you were wrong," he said, his eyes crinkling in a grin. "Ellie Perkins is definitely a red-shoe kind of woman."

She raised her head to give him a watery grin. "Then let's go kick some butt with my new red shoes."

Laughing, he leaned forward and pressed a quick, hard kiss on her mouth. "That's my Ellie."

As they headed out of the mall she looked at the three small bags he carried. "I can't wait to see the new Michael Reilly."

He draped an arm over her shoulder. "Honey, he will be the perfect match for the new Ellie Perkins."

By four o'clock, they were safely registered in another anonymous motel and she was waiting for the new Michael to emerge from the bathroom.

When the door opened, she actually felt her jaw drop. Michael came out wearing baggy jeans and flashy leather sneakers with the laces left untied. It was the uniform of hip young men in any large city. His T-shirt was large and loose, but the most startling transformation was his hair.

Instead of black and wavy, he'd cut it short and gelled it into spikes. It was also now bright yellow, the artificial blond she'd seen on rap stars on television and teenagers in Midland. It made him look at least ten years younger.

He grinned at her reaction, then reached up and settled a baseball cap backward over his hair. The transformation to street punk was complete.

"What do you think? We make a good pair, don't we?"

"The hooker and the gangster," she said dryly. "I feel like I've just stepped out of a music video."

He pulled the hat off and tossed it on the bed, then ran his hand through his short, stiff hair. "That's the point. Trust me, honey, a hooker and a gangster are the last two people the Midland cops will be looking for. No one is going to mistake us for a librarian and a cop.''

A reckless excitement hummed through her. ''Then let's go and stake out the joint.''

At six o'clock they sat in a window booth in a small coffee shop down the street from the federal building in Chicago. They had a good view of the foot traffic in and out of the place, as well as a view down Dearborn Street in both directions. Tension hummed through Michael, the same edgy energy she'd felt when he'd confronted his partner in Midland.

''Do you see anything?'' she asked.

''Not a thing.''

She watched his gaze sweep up and down the street, cataloging everything he saw. He ate as he watched, but she was sure he didn't taste a thing.

Suddenly he sat up and dropped his sandwich. ''There they are.''

''Where?'' She leaned forward, peering out the window.

''Walking into the building.''

She saw the backs of three men entering the building. ''Are you sure? You couldn't have gotten a very good look at them.''

''I'm sure.'' His voice was grim and he pushed his plate away. ''I know all three of them.''

''What do we do now?''

''We sit here and wait for them to come back out.''

A half hour later the three officers emerged from the building. Michael waited long enough to see which way they were heading, then he threw some money on the table and hurried out the door with Ellie. The cops were half a block in front of them.

The uniforms made it easy to follow them. The trio bobbed and weaved through the evening rush-hour crowd until they turned a corner and headed for a parking garage. Once they disappeared, she and Michael crossed the street and made sure there was only one exit from the structure.

"Come over here," he said, taking her arm and leading her to a recessed doorway. "Now pretend we're having a disagreement."

She stood facing him, her mind completely blank. How did a person fake an argument? "I can't think of a thing to say," she finally admitted.

He gave her one of his lopsided grins. "I guess I can understand that. It's hard for most people to find any flaws in me."

Although she saw exactly what he was doing, she responded, anyway. "Now there's a remark I could argue with."

He laughed under his breath. "That's one of the things I like about you, Ellie. You're so predictable."

He froze as they heard the sound of a car leaving the parking garage. He immediately scowled and leaned forward in a threatening pose. The sudden transformation was startling. "Tell me I'm a complete loser. And don't hold back. Use that vivid imagination of yours. Pretend that I've cheated on you and stolen from you and smacked you around. And you've suddenly gotten the strength to walk away from me.''

She took a deep breath and tried to imagine what she would say in that situation. ''You're more disgusting than something a dog would leave on the sidewalk,'' she said, leaning toward him and allowing the words to flow out of her mouth. ''Don't you dare come near me again. If I see you I'll kick your rear end into the middle of next week.''

As Michael leaned toward her, snarling, a car zoomed out of the parking structure. His eyes followed it until it rounded the corner.

When the vehicle was out of sight he drew in a deep breath and stepped back, taking her hand. ''Well done,'' he said, smiling. ''And remind me never to get on the wrong side of you.'' He glanced down at her red shoes. ''I don't want to be on the receiving end of those things.''

Ellie realized she was shaking. ''Do you think they noticed us?''

''Nope,'' he said, taking her hand as they walked back toward the elevated train. Michael had parked the car at a station close to their motel and they'd taken the L in case someone knew what they were driving. ''They didn't give us a second look. Stupid bastards.''

''Why stupid?''

''They should have been watching everything, noticing everyone around them. But I guess they've gotten too arrogant to think they could be taken down.''

He smiled grimly. "That's why they're stupid bastards."

Suddenly he tensed and stared straight ahead. After a moment he grabbed her hand and yanked her into an alley. Then he pressed her up against the wall, fastened his mouth to hers and shoved his hand up her T-shirt.

CHAPTER SIXTEEN

THERE WAS NO PASSION in the kiss, no feeling. She tasted only tension and strain and knew the kiss was for show. But desire still fluttered inside her and she wrapped her arms around him and curled one leg around his thigh. She felt her touch jolt through his system, and his hand trembled on her belly. Finally, after what seemed like forever, he lifted his head.

"Let's go," he muttered, pulling her down the alley away from the street.

Garbage littered the cracked asphalt, and the smell of rotting food saturated the air. Out of the corner of her eye she saw small animals scurry beneath the dumpsters, and she tightened her grip on Michael's hand.

Watching her feet, she darted around the broken bottles, crushed cans and scraps of cardboard that littered the alley. When Michael stopped suddenly, she bumped into the solid wall of his back.

"Stay here," he whispered, pushing her into a narrow seam between two buildings. "And make sure you're hidden."

The space was barely wide enough to hold her, but she edged her way into it. Michael disappeared from view and she strained to listen.

She heard nothing beyond the normal sounds of traffic—the roar of engines, horns honking and brakes squealing. Five minutes passed, then ten.

She was just about to burst from the crack and go look for him when he reappeared in front of her. "Let's go," he said, his voice normal.

"What happened?"

"Not now."

He hurried them to the elevated train platform, then stood at the back of the crowd, watching everyone around them. His face was hard and set, his eyes cold and penetrating. There was no trace of the easygoing Michael. He was a hunter, she realized uneasily. And he was waiting for his prey.

When the train pulled into the station, he led her to the door and paused for a few moments as he scanned the passengers. Apparently satisfied, he pulled her along behind him as he wove his way through the people crowding the aisles of the train.

As they pulled out of the station the train swayed from side to side, and she leaned into Michael. "What happened back there at the parking garage? Why did we duck into that alley?" she murmured into his ear. The clatter of the wheels on the tracks was so loud that she wasn't afraid of being overheard.

"I saw two more of them. Apparently they'd stayed behind the first three to make sure they weren't followed." His mouth tightened. "Maybe they're not as stupid as I thought."

"Did they see us?" she asked, clutching his hand more tightly.

"Oh yeah, they saw us all right." His voice was dry. "They could hardly miss us. I had my hand up your shirt and my tongue down your throat. But I don't think they recognized us. They didn't give us a second glance."

"So they don't know we're here?"

His face tightened. "I didn't say that. We have to assume they know we're in Chicago. Or at least that we're heading in this direction. Why else would they be afraid of being followed?"

She gnawed at her lower lip. "Are we going to go ahead with the meeting tomorrow?"

"We don't have a choice. The longer we wait, the more chances they have to catch up with us. You're not going to be safe until that information is in the hands of the FBI."

"And you won't be safe until then, either."

"I still won't be safe," he said, his voice flat. "Without me as a witness, a lot of that information is worthless. And I'm the only eyewitness to the murder of Rueben. They're going to need to get rid of me, too."

"What will you do?" she asked. She braced herself for his answer.

"The FBI has a lot of safe houses. I'll stay in one of those."

The pain in her heart was so swift and so intense that she pressed her hand to her chest. He would disappear after tomorrow and she'd never see him again.

Of course he would disappear tomorrow, she told

herself sharply. She'd known it all along. What was the matter with her?

She knew perfectly well what had happened to her.

The last two days with him and the night of passion they'd shared had changed her forever. It had opened up a whole new world for her, showing her what love-making could be when two people cared about one another.

At least be honest with yourself, she told herself brutally. *You're in love with Michael and you know it.*

The problem was, he wasn't in love with her. She knew it and still she'd woven daydreams about happily ever after. Well, that fantasy ended tomorrow. And then it was back to Eleanor Perkins, frumpy children's librarian.

No, she corrected herself. Not frumpy. Never again. She'd vowed to change her life, and that's exactly what she would do. She might not have Michael in her life, but she'd survive.

"What are you thinking about?" Michael's breath tickled her ear. "You look so solemn."

"I hope the crooked cops get what they deserve," she said, her voice hot with anger. "And after they do, I hope they rot in hell."

"You're so fierce," Michael whispered, pulling her closer to him. "I'd be shaking in my shoes if I didn't know what a marshmallow you really are."

She turned on him. "I'm not a marshmallow, Reilly. I'm as tough as you."

He leaned over and pressed a kiss to the top of her

head. "No, you're not," he murmured. "You're a lot tougher."

Her anger withered and died. She didn't want to waste any of their precious hours together in hard words and anger. She wanted to create memories that would last a lifetime.

"I'm sorry," she said, pressing closer to his side. "I get angry every time I think about what they're doing to you."

He curled his arm around her and gave her a fierce, tight hug. "You never cease to amaze me, Eleanor Perkins."

They stood together hip to hip for the rest of the trip, not speaking. There was no need for words. Michael knew as well as she that this would be their last night together.

When the train reached the stop where they'd left the car, they merged with the crowd of people exiting the train and making their way down the stairs. Once on the street, she and Michael hurried to the car.

He motioned for her to stay back as he examined the vehicle carefully. Finally he nodded. "Nobody's touched it. Let's go."

They'd bought a map, and she used it to navigate to the park the FBI agent had named as a meeting place. The neighborhood was an odd mixture of run-down buildings, some clearly abandoned, and brightly painted ones, obviously remodeled houses and two-flats.

A few minutes later they stood surveying the small park. Michael's face hardened as he looked around.

"This won't work," he said, his voice flat.

"Why not?"

"It's too open. There's nowhere to hide."

"Isn't that good? If there's nowhere for us to hide, it means there's nowhere for the Midland cops to hide, either."

"There are too many abandoned buildings close by." He nodded at one across the street from the park. "They could hide in any one of those and ambush us." He compressed his lips. "Hell, they could have a sniper waiting in that building and we'd never know what hit us."

"What are we going to do?" She glanced at the backpack slung over his shoulders, then looked away. She wanted to fling it away from him, so far that no one would ever find it. She wanted to free him of the burden of the information, so he wouldn't have to worry about snipers and being killed.

But one of the reasons she loved him was because he was so determined to do the right thing. So she took his hand instead of clawing at the pack.

"We pick a new spot," he said, turning to look at the park from all angles. Then his eyes came back to the vacant building across the street. "Like that building."

IT HAD BEEN DARK for a while when Michael hung up the pay phone and scanned the street behind him. There was no way the Midland cops could know where he was. Logic told him that. But tension hummed through his nerves and the back of his neck itched. There was trouble ahead. Nothing had gone right since he'd stood between those buildings and watched Rueben Montero die.

He took a roundabout route back to the motel where he'd left Ellie, but his foot pressed a little harder on the accelerator as he got closer. She would be anxious, he told himself. He wanted to let her know that everything was settled.

Ellie. He felt his mouth curl at the corners, in spite of the mounting tension. If he was honest with himself, he'd admit that Ellie herself was the reason he was hurrying back to the motel. He didn't want to be away from her any longer than necessary.

Only so he could protect her, his mind immediately protested. He grasped at that straw, skittering away from the rest of the truth. He couldn't bear to take it out and examine it. In spite of everything they'd been through together, in spite of the fact that he would trust her with his life, he insisted to himself he would handle everything better alone.

That included their rendezvous tomorrow with Givens.

Somehow Michael had to convince her to stay in the motel while he dealt with the FBI agent.

It wouldn't be easy.

"I DIDN'T KNOW you were a fan," he said, entering the motel room and nodding at the screen.

She snatched up the remote control and turned off the soap opera. "It was the first channel that came on."

"Yeah, yeah, yeah," he drawled. "I've heard all the excuses. Admit it, Ellie. You just have a taste for the dramatic."

But instead of rising to the bait, as he had hoped, she scooted closer to him. "What happened? Did you get hold of Givens?"

"Yeah, I did." He snorted. "He thought my objection to the park was 'brilliant.' We're meeting in that abandoned building across the street. And we're meeting earlier than we'd planned. I made it for 5:30 a.m., just in case."

She frowned, her eyebrows puckering. "Isn't an empty building even more dangerous? There must be all kinds of corners to hide there."

"There are. I went through the place before I made the call to Givens. But if I arrive early enough, I can make sure there aren't any unpleasant surprises waiting for me. And if there are, I have a better chance of avoiding them than I would out in the open."

"What is this 'I' stuff, Reilly?" She'd picked up on the thing he'd hoped she'd miss. "Shouldn't it be 'we'?"

"It will certainly be 'we' tonight," he murmured, allowing himself to do what he'd ached to do from the moment he'd walked in the door. Gathering her in his arms, he pressed a kiss to the soft, fragrant spot beneath her ear. "Believe me, Ellie, I won't be thinking of anything but you tonight."

He felt her gathering herself to protest, but he cut off her words by pressing his mouth to hers. Her taste swept all other thoughts from his head. There was only Ellie and the hours they had together. He intended to make every minute count.

LATE IN THE NIGHT he opened his eyes to peer at the clock on the night table. Two o'clock. Time to go.

But before he disentangled himself from Ellie he allowed himself one more taste of her mouth. He skimmed his hand down her side one more time, memorizing the shape of her hip and the silky texture of her skin. When she murmured in her sleep and tried to get closer to him, he felt desire stirring again.

They'd made love several times already. He'd held her and kissed her and caressed her each time as if it was the last. And he'd gloried in her response, losing himself hopelessly in her embrace until he wasn't sure where Ellie ended and he began.

It had been the most soul-shattering experience of his life.

But it was time to go. Time to put his need for Ellie away, to hide it so deep inside that it would be lost forever.

He eased out of bed and moved silently to the bathroom, picking up his clothes from the floor on the way. It took him a few minutes to find everything. He'd been so frantic to be inside her, so desperate to hold her, that he'd torn off his clothes and tossed them aside without thinking.

Now he had to collect them in the dark without waking Ellie.

He was almost at the bathroom door when she said sleepily, "Michael?"

"I'm right here, Ellie." He cursed himself for lying to her. "I'm just going to the bathroom."

"All right."

But when he came out of the bathroom, dressed in his dark clothes, she was sitting up in bed, lamplight from the night table pooled around her, the sheet clutched to her breasts. "I thought you said you were just going to the bathroom," she said quietly.

He couldn't bear the disappointment in her voice. "It's too dangerous for you to come with me," he answered softly.

"So you were just going to abandon me here?" Her wide eyes were full of anguish. "Just walk away and never come back?"

That had been his plan, God help him. "I thought it would be easier," he muttered.

"Easier than what? Telling me to my face that you didn't want me with you?"

"Ellie, you know I don't want to drag you into my mess."

"I'm already in your mess all the way up to my neck. Admit it, Michael. After everything that's happened, you still don't trust me."

"That's not true," he protested, but even to him his denial sounded weak. "It has nothing to do with trust. I'm trying to protect you."

"Maybe you just don't trust me enough to let me make my own decision. Either way it boils down to the same thing. You aren't about to let anyone get close to you." She held his gaze with hers. There was no anger on her face, just hurt resignation.

"I thought we'd been pretty damn close for the last few hours," he said, trying to lighten the mood.

She merely continued to stare at him. Finally he sighed.

"I do trust you, Ellie," he said, sitting down on the bed next to her but refusing to look at her. "And it scares me to death. I'm not sure how to handle it. I thought it would be easier for both of us if I just disappeared."

"That's the coward's way out. And I never thought you were a coward, Michael."

"I'm a coward when it comes to you," he said. "I couldn't bear it if anything happened to you."

"Don't you think I feel the same way about you?" she said, her voice softening. "If there's a chance I can help you, I want to be there."

"It'll be a lot safer for you to stay right here."

"I don't care about safe," she said, leaning toward him. "I already told you I'm not interested in safety as much as in doing the right thing. And the right thing is making sure the backpack and your evidence get delivered to the FBI."

He was losing control of the situation. He knew it. But had he been in control of anything since the moment he'd kidnapped her?

"It's going to be dark in that building," he said, desperate to find a way to convince her to stay behind. "Completely black. And we won't be able to turn on any lights."

Even in the dim room he saw her face pale. Then she straightened her shoulders, still clutching the sheet to her chest. "I don't care. As long as I'm with you, I can deal with it."

"All right," he heard himself say. "You can come with me. But you have to promise to do everything I tell you. Exactly the way I tell you."

He was horrified that he'd agreed. But an enormous weight lifted off his shoulders. He wouldn't have to leave her for a few more hours.

She scrambled out of bed, a mischievous grin flickering across her face. "Don't I always do exactly what you tell me?"

"Yeah," he muttered, "that's what I'm afraid of."

CHAPTER SEVENTEEN

THE DOOR OF THE ABANDONED building squealed on rusty hinges as Michael pulled it open. He froze, looking for any movement in the surrounding blackness. But all the houses remained silent, and nothing moved on the street.

"Let's go," he whispered.

Ellie clutched his hand tightly, clamping her fingers around his. As she hesitated at the entrance, her fear throbbed like a living thing. Then she squared her shoulders and stepped through the door.

The darkness wasn't complete. Streetlights cast a dim glow on the floor and created distorted shadows on the wooden boxes and shelves that filled the room.

"I think it was a warehouse," he whispered, hoping to distract her. "There's an office on the second floor that looks down onto this room. It'll be the perfect place to watch for Givens and make sure he's alone."

"How do we get up there?"

There was a slight quaver to her voice, but she straightened her shoulder and looked him in the eye. Awed at her courage, he paused long enough to give her a reassuring squeeze. "You're something else, Ellie," he whispered.

He touched her face, his fingers lingering on her cheek. Then he drew away, disturbed by her ability to distract him from what he had to do. "The stairs are over here," he said, his voice harsher than he intended. "I checked them out while it was light. They're in good shape."

He led her silently up the wooden staircase, holding tight to her hand. He brushed his lips over their joined fingers just before they reached the second floor.

The office he'd checked out earlier was dusty and depressing. An old steel desk sat against one wall, listing to one side. There were two office chairs next to it, both of them equally unappealing. But there was a wide window that looked down over the open area below. He'd be able to watch Givens come into the building. And he could make sure the FBI agent was alone before he approached him.

"There are a couple of chairs here," Michael whispered. "Sit down in one of them. We're going to be here for a while."

He heard her fumbling in the darkness, then she said, "How do you know Givens didn't have the same idea as you? Maybe he's here already, too."

She was trying hard to sound helpful and professional, but he could hear the fear beneath her words.

"When we walked around the building before we came in, I was checking little things I'd left behind yesterday afternoon. None of them were disturbed."

"Okay." He heard a tiny sigh in the darkness. "So now we just wait."

"That's it. With any luck at all, by 6:00 a.m. you'll be heading for home."

Instead of answering, she reached for his hand again and held on tight. Hers felt cold and clammy, and he prayed that he was right. He wanted her out of this situation as soon as possible. His neck still itched and his gut was jumping up and down with a warning. Something was wrong. He just didn't know what it was.

He went over every minute of yesterday, examining everything they'd done and everything that had happened. He couldn't find any flaws in their plans. His reluctant conclusion was that he couldn't change the arrangements now. They wouldn't find a better spot to hand over the evidence to the FBI. And the longer they waited, the closer the Midland cops would get.

So he moved the other chair close to Ellie and sat down in it. Picking up her hand, trying to reassure her with his touch, he asked her about her work. She answered his questions and asked him about his job as a detective. And as they talked in whispers, he felt her gradually relaxing.

Incredibly, he found some of his own tension easing. It would be all right, he told himself. They would get through this.

It wouldn't be long before the first hint of light would penetrate the inky blackness of the warehouse. Knowing it was time to get ready, he touched his finger to her lips and stood up. It was still too dark to see to the first floor, but soon they would be visible to anyone who walked in the door.

He moved their chairs to the other side of the room, out of sight, then pulled Ellie to the floor, squatting next to her.

"You need to stay here," he said, his words barely a breath in the still, heavy air. "In fact, I'm going to pull the desk out from the wall and I want you to get behind it. Stay there and don't say a thing. Don't come out until I tell you to."

He felt her nodding, then eased the chairs away from the wall. She scooted into the space he'd created and sat silently. Not even a rustle came from her hiding place.

"Good," he said, reaching out blindly to touch her one more time. "Stay right where you are. With any luck at all, this will be over in an hour."

"Okay."

Her voice trembled in the darkness, and he leaned closer. "It'll be light soon," he said. "Can you hold out for a little longer?"

Her hesitation was just a moment too long. "Of course," she said. "I'm fine." He knew she was lying. "You don't have time to worry about me. Concentrate on what you have to do."

He groped in the darkness until he found her hand. "Do you want to tell me why you're afraid of the dark?" he asked quietly. "It might help to talk about it."

He was sure she would refuse. But to his surprise, her breath came out in a ragged sigh. "I'm not sure anything will help. I know I'm being silly, but being wedged behind this desk is making it worse."

"I'm sorry, Ellie, but you have to stay there," he said, squeezing her hand. "The desk isn't much, but it's your only protection."

"I know."

After a long pause, she began speaking again. Her voice was so low that he had to lean close to hear her.

"My mother used to lock me in the closet as a punishment when I was young. Usually it was only for an hour or so, but a few times she forgot about me and I was in there all night." She cleared her throat and gripped his hand more tightly. "I'm an adult now and I know it's silly, but then I guess most fears are, aren't they?"

"It's not silly at all." Rage rolled through him in huge, scalding waves as he pictured Ellie as a terrified child, forced into a tiny space and enveloped in smothering darkness. "Your mother was a child abuser. I'd like to lock her up in the deepest, darkest hole on the planet and throw away the key."

He felt her fingers skimming lightly over his face. "It sounds as though you have some personal experience with child abuse."

He'd never told his secrets to anyone. Not even Charles, although he was sure his friend suspected. But the darkness made Michael feel oddly free, the intimacy less threatening. And Ellie wouldn't judge him or pity him. It was the one thing he was sure of.

"My mom died when I was twelve, and it was just me and my old man. He was a Midland cop." He paused as the memories skittered away like bugs, afraid of the light of exposure. He worked to gather them back to him.

"He'd hit my mother when she was alive, mostly when he came home late at night after he'd been drinking. After she died, he went a little crazy." The remembered pain tore at Michael's heart. "Not because he missed her. But because he'd lost his punching bag."

"Did he…did he kill her?"

"No. The doc said she had a heart attack. I think she just got tired of living."

"I'm sorry, Michael." Eleanor gripped his hand and held on tightly.

"It was a long time ago." But he shifted his hand so their fingers entwined. "After she was gone, my father changed. He got even meaner." Michael's mouth hardened. "Pretty soon I figured out that the best way to deal with him was to avoid him and his fists. So I made sure I wasn't around when he got home from work."

"Who took care of you?" she whispered.

"I took care of myself." And a piss-poor job of it he'd done, he thought bitterly.

"A twelve-year-old child can't take care of himself."

The horror in her voice made his heart twist in his chest. "I managed just fine."

"Until?"

"How do you know there's an 'until'?"

He heard her scoot forward from behind the desk. She fumbled in the darkness until she found his face and cupped it with her hands. "You're a good man, Michael. Someone had to help you turn out that way."

"It was Charles," he said gruffly after a moment. He should have been scared to death that Ellie knew his secrets. But he knew she would never betray him, never try to use her knowledge against him. "He was the police chief of Midland. He picked me up one day while I was trying to break into a car." His mouth twisted. "There was a bunch of change in the ashtray, and I guess I was hungry."

"And then what?" Her voice was infinitely gentle.

"He hauled me into the station, and I was sure he was going to arrest me. But when he found out who I was, he let loose with a string of words I hadn't heard from anyone but my father. I thought he was swearing at me, and I tried to run. But he caught me before I could get out of the building."

The memories came bursting through the door Michael had closed on them. But they weren't as painful as he'd expected. "When he dragged me back into the interview room, he told me he wasn't mad at me. Then he took me to his house and turned me over to Betty. She made me take a bath, and gave me a decent meal. And I never really left after that."

"What happened to your father?"

Even though he knew she couldn't see his eyes, he looked away. He was afraid she'd see the fire of his hatred and his shame even in the dark. "Internal Affairs had been investigating him for a while before Charles caught me. They suspected he was on the take, and of course Charles knew about the investigation. He never told me exactly what happened, but my father confessed to extortion and shakedowns, and went to prison. He died in a fight there five years later.''

"I'm so sorry," she said, leaning closer. "Being stuck in a closet seems like nothing compared to what you went through."

"You can't change your past. You can only change your future. I swore that I would never be like my father." He felt stripped naked, exposed to the world.

"No wonder you're so determined to stop the corruption in Midland, even if you have to do it alone."

"Yeah, that's me. I'm a real Lone Ranger."

"I'm serious," she said, her voice passionate. "You're risking your life to do what's right. I don't know anyone else who would go this far."

"There are plenty of cops who do it every day."

"Then how come none of them are helping you?"

"You don't pull your punches, do you, Ellie?"

"I'm just pointing out the facts," she said, her voice prim again.

He reached out and pulled her close, pressing one last kiss to her lips. When her mouth softened he let her go and moved away. It was one of the hardest things he'd ever done.

"Get back in there and don't come out until I come for you," he said, his voice rough with emotion. "I don't care what you think might be happening." He pressed something into her palm. "Take my phone. And if something goes wrong, call Charles."

"Nothing's going to go wrong," she murmured, squeezing his hand once more before she let him go.

"I hope to God you're right," he muttered under his breath as he moved away.

Sidling up to the window in the office, he looked down at the deserted warehouse below. No one had come into the building yet. So far, so good.

A slice of weak daylight seeped into the building and he glanced at his watch. Fifteen minutes before Givens was supposed to be here. The only thing left to do was wait.

ELLIE STRAINED TO SEE Michael across the dark office, but the only thing she noticed was a darker shadow near the window. If she held her breath she could hear the soft whisper of his breathing on the other side of the room. The faint sound comforted her. She wasn't alone. Michael was with her.

Knowing he was in the room with her made it easier to fend off the monsters that lurked in the darkness. They hovered on the fringes of her consciousness, but she held a picture of Michael in her mind and dared them to come closer.

She hoped the FBI agent was on time because she wasn't sure how long her bravado would last.

She heard a tiny scrabbling sound and her heart leaped in her throat. She closed her eyes and drew in a shaky breath when she realized it was Michael, positioning himself on the other side of the room.

This fear of the darkness was inconvenient and silly, and she'd have to deal with it, she told herself firmly. Right now she was useless to Michael. If something went wrong she wouldn't be able to help him.

And he might need her help. Closing her eyes so she wouldn't actually see the darkness, she took deep breaths until her heart rate leveled. The thought of helping Michael steadied her. His mission was far more important than her dreary, mundane phobia.

"Quiet," he whispered in the darkness, his voice urgent and intense.

She curled into an even tighter ball and concentrated on listening. The door on the ground floor squealed and a shaft of light stabbed the darkness.

She waited for what seemed like an eternity, her heart hammering in her chest. Then Michael said, "It's Givens. And it looks like he's alone."

But he didn't move. Minutes stretched out unbearably as she waited for Michael to make a move. Finally he scooted over to her. She could just make out his face in the lifting darkness.

"Givens is alone and there's no sign he's been followed. He's getting nervous, so I'd better go down." He hesitated for a moment, then shoved the backpack into her arms. "Hold on to this for me."

"Aren't you giving it to him?"

"I want to make sure everything is on the level." He gave her a grim look. "Something doesn't smell right."

"Then don't go down there," she said, her voice urgent. She grabbed his arm. It was a steel bar beneath the fabric of his shirt. "Stay here until he leaves. We'll think of another plan."

He shook his head. "Too risky. The longer we wait, the closer the Midland cops will get. I don't have a choice. But I'm not handing over the information until I'm sure it's safe."

She stared at his face, only an outline in the darkness. But even so she could read his resolve. She wasn't going to stop him from going down those stairs. "You're nothing like your father," she said quietly. "You're the most honorable man I know, Michael Reilly."

He shook his head. "I'm just a cop, doing my job," he said. "That's all."

He leaned forward to kiss her, a brief meeting of their lips. Then he settled back on his heels. "Thanks for the vote of confidence, Ellie." His voice was barely a whisper. "You don't know how much it means to me."

He brushed a finger over her cheek and down her neck. "Stay here no matter what happens. Don't come out until I get you. If you have to call Charles, wait for him here. He'll come and get you."

"Be careful, Michael." The words *I love you* hovered on her lips, but she hesitated and then it was too late. He was gone, vanishing into the darkness like a wraith, silent and invisible.

Apparently, in spite of her vow to the contrary, she still didn't have the guts to reach for what she wanted. She should have told Michael she loved him before he went down to face the FBI agent. But she'd lost her courage, and now she might not have another chance. Clearly Michael had been worried about something.

Alone in the darkness, feeling completely isolated, she strained to listen. She didn't hear a sound. Time stretched out unbearably as the darkness pressed in on her, heavy and smothering. Surely Michael had reached the FBI agent by now.

Suddenly bright lights cut into the blackness and the sound of feet pounding on the concrete floor echoed in the tiny room. Angry voices spoke in harsh tones and the sound of a fist hitting flesh was shockingly loud.

Fear paralyzed Ellie, but her fear for Michael quickly overcame her reluctance to move. She scrambled out of her secure hiding place and crawled over to the window that looked down on the space below.

Her stomach dropped and she slapped a hand to her mouth to stifle a gasp. Michael and another man, their arms raised in surrender, stood in the center of a circle of armed men. And standing near the door, a gun at her back, her eyes wide and terrified, stood a young woman holding a small baby.

CHAPTER EIGHTEEN

ELLIE SHOVED HER FIST into her mouth to muffle her cry of horror. Something had gone terribly wrong. Somehow the Midland cops had found out where they were. She recognized the officer who had stopped her car in Midland, and the three cops she and Michael had followed from the federal building yesterday. Another looked vaguely familiar, but she couldn't place him.

But all of them had an identical look on their face—cold, implacable hatred. And it was all directed at Michael.

"Where's your 'evidence,' Reilly?" the cop who had stopped their car growled.

Michael raised one eyebrow. "Screw you, Ruiz."

The cop who'd spoken punched him in the face. But Michael merely wiped away the blood that welled from his lip and kept his steady, contemptuous gaze on the officer's face.

"Search the place," Ruiz said, turning to look at the other cops.

Michael gave a short, sharp laugh. "You think I would bring it here? I'm not that stupid."

"He seemed to think you would." Another cop nodded at the man standing next to Michael.

"He doesn't know squat. I've never met him before. How would he know what I'd do?" Michael's gaze flickered over the other man, whom Ellie assumed was Givens, the FBI agent, then dismissed him.

The cops shuffled their feet and looked at each other, clearly uneasy.

"Let Gloria and her kid go and we might be able to come to an agreement," Michael said after a moment.

The officer holding the gun on Gloria pushed her closer to the ring of men. "Now why would we want to let her go? She's our ace in the hole," another man said. "We didn't drag her all the way from Midland just so we could let her walk away. We thought we might need some bargaining chips with you, Reilly."

"I don't bargain with the lives of women and children. I won't even talk to you until I see Gloria walk out the door."

The man who seemed to be in charge gave Michael a long look, then nodded. "All right." He walked over to Gloria and plucked the baby from her arms. "Get out of here," he said to her. "But just to make sure you behave yourself, we'll hold on to Rueben, Jr."

"No!" Gloria screamed, reaching for her baby. The police officer held the child with one arm and shoved at her with the other. She stumbled backward, then fell heavily to the floor. The baby started wailing.

Michael leaped toward the man holding the child,

but Ruiz punched him in the face again. Another man grabbed his arms from behind and wrestled him to the floor. The other officers tightened their grips on their guns and looked from Gloria, sobbing and scrambling to get to her son, to the screaming baby. The uncertainty, alarm and panic on their faces was obvious, even from Ellie's vantage point above them.

Clearly if something didn't happen soon, there would be a tragedy.

Without thinking, Ellie scurried toward the door, stopping only to shove the backpack into an ancient file cabinet. She ran down the stairs, halting a few steps from the bottom.

"Stop," she yelled. "I know where the information is. Give Gloria back her baby."

"Who the hell are you?" Ruiz, the cop who seemed to be in charge, pointed his gun toward her and scowled.

"She must be the broad that Reilly kidnapped," another of the men said.

"She doesn't look anything like that librarian," Ruiz said, frowning as he studied her face. His expression hardened. "But who the hell cares who she is? Give me the information or I'll blow out his brains." He pointed the gun at Michael's head and held it steady.

Oh, God, what had she done? She'd made the situation far worse. "Michael already told you the information isn't here," she said, trembling. She straightened, determined not to show fear. "But I know where he left it. If you let us all go, I'll tell you.''

''You got it backward,'' the man in charge said, releasing the safety on his gun. ''Tell us where it is or we'll splatter his brains on the wall.''

Without warning, Michael rolled into one of the officer's legs, taking him down. When the other officers jumped in to help, Michael pulled a couple of them down on top of the pile.

''Run, Ellie,'' he yelled. ''Get out of here!''

She froze for a moment as she watched the deadly struggle in front of her. The officer who held the baby had circled the child's body with one arm, and with the other was trying to pull one of the officers off the pile.

Without thinking, she raced forward and plucked the boy from him. Before she could take a breath, Gloria snatched the child away from her.

''Rueben,'' she sobbed, pressing kisses onto his head. ''Oh, Rueben.''

''Come on.'' Ellie grabbed Gloria's arm. ''We have to get you out of here.''

But Gloria stumbled over one of the combatants on the floor and by the time she'd regained her balance, an officer had her by the arm again. Another cop grabbed Ellie roughly around the wrist and yanked her toward him.

Incensed, she kicked his knee as hard as she could. When the officer yelped and let her go, she kicked him again, in the other knee.

"Run, Ellie," she heard Michael yell. "Get out of here."

But there were two officers standing in front of the door. Without hesitating she ran the other way, back up the stairs and into the darkness. One of the officers lunged for her, but he tripped over Gloria and fell heavily to the floor, swearing viciously.

"Let her go," she heard another one say. "She won't get far. We've got men watching every exit. Even if she manages to find a door, she won't be going anywhere."

Ellie raced up the stairs and ran blindly across the floor, weaving her way among the huge boxes and piles of pallets that littered the floor. When she'd run as far as she could she squeezed between two boxes and wriggled into the corner.

Her heart hammering in her chest, her breath coming in ragged gasps, she listened to the noise below. She braced herself for the explosion of a gun, but it never came.

Instead she heard the men talking and arguing, and eventually some climbed up the stairs. The glow of their flashlights preceded them, and she shrank farther back into her patch of darkness.

But they didn't stop on her floor. Instead they kept going, climbing the stairs to the next floor, then to the floor above that.

She tried to picture the building in her mind. She wasn't sure, but thought there were at least four stories. Maybe five. They could be anywhere above her, she realized with despair.

And now the building was dark again. Her heart thundered in her chest with the rhythm of panic and her breath came in short, wrenching gasps. Hysteria hovered at the edge of her consciousness.

The growing daylight barely penetrated the layers of grime and dirt on the windows, but she fastened her gaze to the thin ribbon of light and kept it there while she tried to slow her ragged breathing. As long as she was looking at the weak beam, she could pretend she wasn't trapped in the dark.

Her fingers skimmed over the cell phone she'd shoved into her pocket. Her hand trembled with the need to push the buttons and summon help. But she didn't dare use it. One of the Midland officers could be inches away, just waiting for her to make a mistake. One sound would be all it took to betray her location.

Keeping her eyes fixed on the slowly enlarging band of light that danced on the wall, she concentrated on steadying her breathing. When she could finally hear over the pounding of her heart, she sucked in a gulp of air, then held her breath.

The murmur of men's voices drifted down from far above. Suddenly one voice raised in anger, then she heard a hard thump on the floor.

Panic fluttered through her again, but this time it wasn't because of the dark. Was Michael all right? Had they hurt him? Or worse?

No, she told herself firmly. Michael was all right. He was smart enough and clever enough to survive.

But he needed some help. And there was no one but her to do it.

She pushed away the tiny voice that told her to run, to get away at any cost. Even Michael had told her to get away.

But she wasn't going to leave him at the mercy of the men who'd tried to kill him, she vowed fiercely. No one else knew where he was. There would be no cavalry rushing to the rescue. It was up to her to save Michael and the others.

But first she had to move out of her cramped hiding place between the boxes and move farther into the blackness.

For a moment her courage failed her. She buried her head in her hands and tried to block out the dark. But as she sat there silently, seconds and minutes ticked inexorably away in her head. Anything could be happening to Michael.

Slowly she removed her hands from her eyes. It was time to grow up, she told herself harshly. It was time to get past the phobias from childhood and deal with her fears like an adult.

But as she moved out from the protection of the boxes she started to tremble. Fear gripped her in its unflinching grasp and shook her roughly. She stopped at the edge of her hiding place, shaking and weak. She couldn't move a step forward.

''...have to kill him.''

The voice floated down the stairs, cold and matter-of-fact. They were talking about Michael. Her heart plunged in her chest.

This is it, she told herself grimly. *Either you walk through the darkness and up those stairs, or you can listen to those men shoot Michael and the FBI agent and Gloria and her baby.*

She hadn't heard any noises coming from this floor of the warehouse. Chances were none of the cops had waited on this level to search for her. Why would they bother? They'd said the warehouse was surrounded. She wasn't going anywhere.

She forced herself to take one step toward the stairs, then another. She kept her eyes fixed on a distant window as she placed one foot in front of the other.

Her toe collided with something heavy and she almost cried out. Biting her lip to keep the sounds in, she looked down and saw a heavy box lying at an angle on the floor. She moved around it carefully, then continued moving toward the stairs.

As she reached the steps, the darkness became more complete. Very little light penetrated this far into the building. That was good, she told herself. They wouldn't be able to see her as she got closer to them.

A vise seemed to close around her chest as she moved away from the last bit of light. She was sure the men above her would hear her heart thundering and know she was coming.

It was an excruciatingly slow process. On each stair she had to stop to breathe, then force herself to take another step. When she finally reached the next floor and turned the corner, there was another comforting beam of light striping the floor from tiny, narrow windows high in the wall. Saying a silent prayer of thanks, she used the glow to find the staircase to the next floor.

It took almost as long to navigate that staircase. As she reached the top, the men's voices became clearer. They were on the floor above her. She was almost there.

She froze when she heard one that sounded as if it were right next to her. "We'll draw straws," the man said. "Short straw pulls the trigger."

He wasn't next to her, she realized, growing limp with relief. He was at the top of the stairway. But she would have to get past him to find Michael and the others.

As she rounded the corner and faced the last set of steps, another wave of relief poured over her. There were lights above her. She wouldn't be climbing into total darkness.

Edging up the stairs, one at a time, she moved painfully slowly, waiting for a telltale squeak of the wood to reveal her presence. But God was watching out for her, because the stairs didn't make a sound.

When she reached the top, she plastered herself against the wall, trying to gather courage to peer around the corner. When she finally got up the nerve to look, she saw several bare light bulbs in a room down the hall. Were all the cops in the same room as Michael?

She had just started to edge down the corridor toward the light when she heard a thumping sound coming from behind her. She spun around, expecting to see a Midland cop looming over her. But no one was there.

The thumping sound came again and she slipped into the room it seemed to be coming from. She saw three vague lumps on the floor.

"Ellie?"

Michael's incredulous voice came from the first lump, and she dropped to her knees beside him.

"Are you all right?" she asked in an urgent whisper.

"I'm fine. What are you doing here?"

"You didn't think I'd leave you, did you?"

"Yeah, I thought you'd leave! That's what I told you to do."

"Well, I guess I didn't listen again." As she was talking she ran her hands over his body, discovering that his feet and hands were tied.

"This rope is so tight," she said, struggling to undo the knots.

"Slow down and concentrate," Michael said, moving his fingers to brush her hand with a featherlight touch.

"I think it's getting looser," she said, her heart thumping and her hands clammy. "Hold still."

He obediently kept perfectly still while she tugged the last knot free from his hands. He shook off the ropes and bent to undo his ankles. "Get started on Givens."

She moved to the next person and felt the FBI agent staring at her. "Who are you?" he whispered.

She didn't bother to answer. Tugging on the ropes, she felt the first knot give. Thank God the cops had been rushed and done a sloppy job.

Leaving Givens to finish untying his feet, she moved over to Gloria. The woman's hands and feet were tied, as well. But they hadn't tied up the child. He clung to Gloria, his face buried in her neck.

"Don't worry about me," the woman said, her voice urgent. "Leave me and take Rueben. Get him out of here! Keep my baby safe!"

"We'll get both of you out of here," Ellie whispered as she struggled with the knots.

Before she could finish untying the woman, footsteps echoed in the hall outside the door.

There was no way she could get out of the room. Looking around frantically, she realized they were in a bare room, with no place to hide.

"Corner," Michael hissed to Ellie.

No light penetrated the corners of the room. Without hesitating, she slipped into the corner and hid her face against her knees. Thank God Michael had insisted she wear dark clothes.

Peeking between her knees, she saw that he and the FBI agent had draped the ropes over their ankles and wrists to make it appear they were still tied up. They had retreated into the shadows, but it was horribly obvious to Ellie that the ropes no longer bound them.

A man appeared at the door and hesitated before he came in. He held a gun in his left hand, pointed at the floor.

She heard Michael suck in a breath. "Hobart?" he said, clearly shocked.

"Yeah, it's me."

Ellie realized why the young man looked familiar. He was the rookie Michael and his partner had been training. Beneath the bravado in the young man's voice, Ellie could hear the fear.

"What the hell are you doing mixed up with those losers?" Michael asked.

"I see only one loser, and you're it," the other man said with a sneer. "You're busting your rear end for chump change. Do you know how much money they're pulling in every week?"

"Do you know what they have to do to get it?" Michael's voice was relentless.

"The drugs are going to get sold anyway," Hobart answered, his voice calm. "We're just getting our share."

"And does getting your share include killing innocent men?"

"You're not so innocent, Reilly. You killed your own informant."

"Is that what they told you?" Michael's voice dripped with scorn.

"That's what happened." But Hobart didn't sound as sure.

"I was there, Hobart. Ruiz pulled the trigger. I saw the whole thing go down."

"You're lying." The young man raised the gun and aimed it at Michael. "They told me you'd give me some bullshit story."

"Why would I lie? I've got nothing to lose. I'm going to die, anyway." Michael nodded his head toward Gloria. "Why would I lie to her before she dies? She deserves to know the truth about what they did to the father of her son, before you shoot her." He paused for a moment. "You are going to shoot her, aren't you, Hobart? And the child, too?"

"Shut up, Reilly. Just shut up." Ellie could see the kid's hand shaking.

"All right, I'll shut up. Why don't you do the talking before you kill us? I'm guessing it's going to take a little time for you to work up the nerve to shoot a baby. How did you find us?"

"Sam and I watched you leave in that piece of garbage car you stole." He gave Michael a disgusted look. "You should have picked something better for your last ride."

"Sam was in this, too?"

Ellie heard the despair in Michael's voice and wanted to strike out at the man who was causing it.

"Nah," Hobart said. "He didn't know a thing. I told him I was sick and he took me back to the station. That's when I contacted Ruiz. We called all the police departments between Midland and St. Louis and Chicago and asked them to watch for the car. As soon as someone called us and told us they'd spotted it, we knew where you were heading."

"You're a very obedient puppy dog, Hobart. Do you listen to every scumbag who gives you orders?"

"Shut up, Reilly." The young man glared at Michael and raised the gun again.

"So how did you get the information out of Givens here about our meeting this morning?"

"That was easy." Hobart smirked and lowered the gun again. "We talked to the receptionist at the FBI office and told her that someone might be trying to lure one of their agents into an ambush. When we said that he might be posing as a police officer, she got up and went to talk to someone. It was real easy to look at her log and see who you'd talked to. The Boy Scout here—" he waved his gun in Givens's direction "—played it by the book all the way. He logged in the phone call and his intention to meet with the subject. All we had to do was find out what he looked like and wait for him to leave the building. We've been following him ever since."

"You're a smart guy, Hobart. Too bad you picked the wrong side."

"I don't think I did, loser," he answered, cool again. "I'm the one holding the gun."

He raised the weapon, aimed it at Michael and released the safety.

CHAPTER NINETEEN

MICHAEL HEARD THE CLICK of the safety being released, and lunged for Hobart's legs. He felt Givens leap up beside him and grab the arm holding the gun.

Hobart grunted once as Michael punched him in the gut. But even as the rookie cop doubled over, he tried to wrestle free of Givens.

The FBI agent grabbed his arm and slammed it against his knee, as if it were a piece of kindling he was preparing for a campfire. The cracking sound of a bone shattering filled the room, and Hobart fell to the floor.

Michael looked over at Givens. "Nice move."

"Thanks." He gave Michael an apologetic glance. "I figured I needed to do something to stop him, since it was my fault these guys found you."

"Consider yourself redeemed." Michael turned toward Gloria and saw that she was struggling to free her hands from the partially untied ropes. "Stuff something in Hobart's mouth so he doesn't call for help. I'm going to untie Gloria. We need to get out of here."

Michael heard the sound of cloth ripping as he freed Gloria, then hurried to the corner and drew Ellie away from the wall. Her skin was clammy and cold and she shook violently beneath his hand.

How in the hell had she managed to get all the way up here in the dark? He wanted to crush her against him, to reassure her that she wasn't alone in the enveloping blackness. Instead he drew her closer to the others. Gloria stood holding the baby, swaying slightly. Givens held the gun, his expression icy and determined.

Michael couldn't stop himself from giving Ellie a quick, hard squeeze. Then he took her hand. "Let's go. We don't have time for you to fall apart."

She glared at him and opened her mouth to answer. It would be something blistering, he was sure. But he laid his hand against her mouth.

"No noise," he warned.

She nodded and he took his hand away. Then he bent down to Hobart, who was curled into a ball on the floor, cradling his broken arm.

"What were you supposed to do to us?" Michael demanded after he'd loosened the gag.

"Screw you, Reilly."

Michael calmly retied the gag, then kicked Hobart's broken arm. Muffled by the gag, his scream was no more than a gurgle in his throat. He writhed in pain as Michael stood over him and watched.

Michael bent and removed the gag again. Hobart's face was pale and shiny with sweat in the faint light from the other room. "One more time, Hobart. What were you going to do in here?"

Hobart gave him a sullen look. "I was supposed to shoot all of you."

"Even the baby?"

The other man nodded as he looked away, shame on his face. "I was going to put the gun in your hand afterward. You already killed Montero. We'd say you were cornered and killed everyone, then committed suicide."

"Tidy." Michael stood up and took the gun from Givens. Then he jerked his head in the direction of Ellie and Gloria. "Get them out of here," he told the FBI agent. "And move fast. Once they hear shots from this room, they're going to expect Hobart to come back."

The FBI agent nodded and herded the two women toward the door. Gloria whispered into the baby's ear, and miraculously, the child was quiet. Just before they stepped out the door, Michael stopped Givens with a hand on his arm.

"Ellie's afraid of the dark," he said in a whisper. "Hold on to her."

The agent nodded, then they disappeared.

Michael didn't hear a thing. Had they found the stairs? Had they managed to descend to the next floor? Or had Ellie freaked out?

She wasn't going to freak out now, he thought, pride humming through him. In spite of her fear she'd managed to make her way up three stories in the dark. And done it in time to save all of them.

What was he going to do without her?

He pushed the thought from his head. He didn't have a choice.

Bending down next to Hobart, he put his mouth close to the other man's ear.

"I want you in the corner," he said. "You can either move there on your own, or I'll do it for you." He looked deliberately at the broken arm Hobart cradled with his other hand.

The rookie understood the message and scrabbled painfully across the floor to the farthest corner of the room. Then he curled into himself again.

The kid wouldn't be going anywhere. Satisfied, Michael looked around and saw the pieces of rope that had bound them. Picking them up, he quickly tied Hobart's ankles together.

Then he pulled out Hobart's gun and pointed it deliberately at the floor. He fired three shots into the wood, then paused. Finally he fired the fourth shot.

Shoving the gun into the waistband of his jeans at the small of his back, he slipped across the hall and stood at the top of the stairs. Then he made what he hoped were convincing retching sounds, as if Hobart was tossing his cookies.

He heard a crude laugh coming from the other room. "It sounds as if the rookie didn't much care for his assignment."

Ruiz. Michael's mouth tightened. Instinctively he turned toward the room where the other cops waited for Hobart. His hand hovered over the gun at the small of his back. It would save everyone a lot of trouble, time and money if he just took care of these guys right now. Animals who would kill an innocent woman and child didn't deserve to live.

But after a moment he let his hand drop to his side. If he killed those men he'd be no better than they were. He forced himself to start down the stairs before he could change his mind.

When he reached the first floor there was no sign of Givens, Ellie or Gloria. Dread crept up his spine. Had Ruiz left someone downstairs to make sure no one escaped? Givens didn't have a weapon. He'd be helpless if he came face-to-face with an armed man.

"Ellie!" His sharp whisper echoed off the walls, but there was no answer.

Maybe they were already outside. He moved to the door and peered through the tiny opening left when the door hadn't been latched. No Ellie or Givens or Gloria. But he recognized the man lounging against a Midland unmarked police vehicle across the street, and his mouth tightened. Ruiz hadn't been bluffing. He'd left men outside the warehouse.

Michael moved swiftly to search the remainder of the first floor, sweat dripping down his sides and his heart pounding with fear. Givens wouldn't have stopped on an upper floor. He knew as well as Michael that they had to get out of the building before Ruiz and the others realized they'd escaped.

Had they been caught? Was someone pointing a gun at Ellie right now, waiting for Michael to show up?

Moving toward the back of the building, he glanced into one dark and dingy room after another, checked behind all the stacks of pallets and abandoned boxes. There was no sign of them.

As he approached the end of a corridor, he saw a cluster of darker shadows against the wall. His heart rate rocketed and he slipped into a tiny room. When he peered around the corner, he counted only three silhouettes and closed his eyes in relief.

He heard whispers from the group and stopped immediately. What was going on?

"…nothing's going to happen to you," he heard Givens saying.

"You don't know that." The voice belonged to Gloria. It was surprisingly dignified and composed. "This is an answer I must have before we walk out that door. Will you do this for me, Ellie?" she asked.

"Of course," Ellie answered. Michael saw her reach out and take Gloria's hand. "You must have relatives who could raise him. Why ask me? You don't know me at all."

"I know all I need to know about you." Gloria took a step closer to her. "When you first appeared and Detective Reilly knocked over the man with the gun, you could have run out the door and saved yourself. But instead you saved Rueben. You grabbed him out of the arms of that man who was threatening to kill him." She paused, and Michael saw her search Ellie's face. "Any woman who is willing to save a child instead of herself has goodness inside of her, and much love to give. If I am dead, I want Rueben to have that kind of love."

Michael wanted that kind of love, too, he realized,

his heart aching as he gazed at the two women. But he wouldn't do that to Ellie. She deserved far better than he could give her.

"You're not going to be dead, Gloria," Ellie said gently. "Michael and Agent Givens won't allow that to happen. But if the worst occurs, I promise I'll raise Rueben for you. And I'll try to be half as good a mother as you are."

"Thank you." Gloria bent her head to her son's head. She whispered something in Spanish, then looked up and nodded. "I am ready."

Givens was reaching for the door when Michael hurried up behind them. "Wait," he whispered, his voice an urgent rasp in the darkness. "What's going on?"

Ellie and Givens turned around, their faces pale in the watery light. Ellie took an instinctive step toward him, then stopped. "Where have you been? Are you all right?" she asked, her voice quavering.

"I'm fine," he said, peering at her. "What's wrong?"

"Nothing." She looked away and surreptitiously wiped her face. "We were just worried about you."

She'd been crying over him? He reached for her, but Givens broke in, his voice brusque.

"Put it on hold, Reilly. We don't have time for this. We've got to get out of here."

Michael dropped his hand, ashamed and horrified that he'd been distracted by his need for Ellie. "You're right." He refused to look at her, afraid she'd distract him again. "What's going on? Is there someone out there?"

"I haven't seen a thing. And that worries me. There's someone at the front door."

"I saw him. Let me take a look out here."

He took Givens's place at the tiny crack in the door and peered out into the watery dawn light. Nothing moved. The air was still and heavy, as if the particles of oxygen were suspended in a thick soup.

He watched and waited, his heart racing. Suddenly he heard a faint shout from the upper floor of the warehouse. He turned to Givens.

"We don't have a choice now. They've found Hobart," he said, his voice hard. "We can't wait. We have to get out of here."

The FBI agent nodded, then before Michael could move, he opened the door and stepped outside.

The guy had guts, Michael thought, impressed. If someone had been waiting for them, the agent would have made a perfect target. Michael pulled the gun from his waistband and stepped out beside him, bracing himself for a volley of bullets. But the dawn remained silent.

Michael reached back inside and drew out Ellie and Gloria. "Stay behind us," he said in an urgent whisper. "And for God's sake, do exactly what we tell you."

Gloria had her face buried in her son's hair, but she nodded. Ellie took a deep, shuddering breath and wrapped her arm around the other woman's waist.

They hadn't taken three steps forward when a Chicago police officer stood up from behind a Dumpster. "Stop right there. Drop the gun and put your hands in the air."

Michael slowly laid his weapon on the ground, then raised his hands. Givens did the same. Michael didn't dare look behind him to see what Ellie and Gloria were doing. He hoped like hell they were staying behind him and the FBI agent as he'd instructed them.

"We're law enforcement officers," he called, careful not to make any sudden moves.

"Yeah, that's what we heard."

Michael noted the disgust in the Chicago officer's voice and closed his eyes. How ironic. They'd been rescued, but their rescuers thought he and Givens were the bad guys.

"We're not the ones you want," he called. "They're still inside the warehouse."

"Thanks for the tip, pal." The Chicago officer's voice dripped with sarcasm. "We'll be sure and check it out." The man moved closer, his weapon steady in his hands, nothing but scorn in his eyes.

Michael stood completely still. From the look on the Chicago cop's face, it wouldn't take much for him to start shooting.

"He's right," a familiar voice said from behind the Chicago cops. "They're not the ones you want."

"Charles," Michael said, staring at his friend but careful to keep his hands above his head. "What are you doing here?"

"When I found out that Gorman was on vacation,

I figured I'd better head up here. There was too much potential for a screw-up.''

"You know this guy?" The Chicago cop glanced at Charles, his face full of suspicion.

"I do. And if I'm not mistaken, the other one is an FBI agent." Charles nodded at Givens.

"That right?" The cop looked over at him.

"ID's in my pocket." Givens spoke without moving his hands.

The cop grunted, then motioned for them to lower their arms. Pulling a radio out of his pocket, he spoke a few terse words. Moments later, three men came running around the building wearing black jackets with FBI stenciled in large yellow letters. All of them held guns in their hands.

"Meet the cavalry," Givens muttered. He stepped forward. "About time you guys showed up."

Michael hurried over to the agents. "The information you need is in a room on the second floor. The one with the window overlooking the main floor." His mouth tightened. "If the Midland cops inside haven't already found it."

"They haven't." He heard Ellie's voice as she moved up behind him.

He turned and watched her approach. She slipped the backpack off her shoulders as she did so. "This is what you want."

CHAPTER TWENTY

"I CAN'T BELIEVE you went back to get that back-pack," Michael raged at her as they walked out of police headquarters after hours of answering questions.

"You risked your life, more than once, to get that information this far. And Rueben died for it. How could I leave it behind for the Midland cops to find?"

Michael stopped and ran his fingers through his hair, his movements jerky and agitated. Judging by the way it looked, he'd done the same thing more than once during the long hours they'd been kept separate and questioned.

"What was Givens thinking? Jeez! I started to have some respect for the guy after the way he acted back there. Now I'm going to have to revise my opinion of him."

"He tried to stop me, but I didn't pay any attention to him."

"Now there's a surprise."

Ignoring his growl, she stopped and turned to face him. "Going back for the information was the right thing to do, Michael," she said gently. "It's what you would have done."

"Everybody knows I'm a damn fool," he snapped. "I'd hoped you were smarter than that."

"Fine," she said, feeling the edges of her temper starting to fray. She'd been frantic, wondering what was happening to him. And now, when they were finally reunited, when all she wanted was for him to wrap his arms around her and never let go, all he could do was yell at her. "I'm a damn fool, too. All right? Is that what you wanted to hear?"

He shoved his hand through his hair again, leaving it sticking straight up. She wanted to reach up and smooth it back into place, but curled her fingers into a fist instead. If she touched him, she was afraid she would start to cry. And she would never forgive herself if she broke down in front of him now. She didn't want him reaching for her out of pity. She couldn't bear it.

"You could have gotten hurt, Ellie. Or worse." His voice was almost a whisper. "I couldn't bear that."

"But I didn't." She turned to face him again, hope suddenly rekindled. "I'm fine and so are you. And I'd really rather not fight with you."

"Now there's a first," he said, and his expression changed into the teasing mask he'd worn so often. The mask he used to disguise his real feelings, she realized with a spasm of pain.

She needed a signal from him, some kind of clue about what he wanted. She knew exactly what *she* wanted. She wanted Michael. And she wasn't interested in settling for a superficial affair. She wanted it all—the husband, the family with two point nine children, the house and the white picket fence. She wanted happily ever after.

She had no idea what Michael wanted. Finally, afraid to ask but desperate to know, she said, "What happens next?"

He shoved his hands into his pockets and started walking down the street. "It's going to take time to round up everyone in Midland who was part of the corruption. Apparently Ruiz is singing like a canary, but they have to verify his information and interrogate the others they caught at the warehouse. The FBI wants me to keep a low profile for a few weeks."

That wasn't what she'd meant. "In Midland?"

"No. They're keeping me in a safe house up here."

"What about me? Do I go back to Midland?"

"No. It's too dangerous right now."

Her heart began to soar. Now was when he was supposed to tell her that he wanted her in the safe house with him.

He walked on, not looking at her. "I've arranged with Charles for you to stay with him and Betty. He can protect you until it's safe for you to go back to Midland."

Her hopes crashed to the ground at his carefully neutral words. "Maybe I should stay with you in the safe house."

God, she was pathetic. She was practically throwing herself at him.

"No!" He swallowed and shook his head. "That's not a good idea. Both witnesses shouldn't be in the same place. Too dangerous."

Her heart shriveled in her chest as she stopped and faced him. Pain and anger raced through her, tumbling over each other and swelling to fill her until there was no room left for anything else.

"So you're walking away." She turned her head so he wouldn't see the devastation in her eyes. "At least be honest about it."

"Hey, I would have given you a call when I got back to Midland. We would have gotten together sometime."

She glanced at him and saw the truth on his face. "No, you wouldn't have, Michael. You wouldn't have come within a mile of me."

"I'm no good for you," he said, and she saw the desperation on his face. "You don't need someone like me in your life. You need someone who'll be there for you. Someone who can give you those kids you want. Someone who can build a life with you."

"Who said I wanted kids?"

"You didn't have to say it. I saw your face when Gloria asked you to take Rueben. You'll make a great mother," he said gruffly.

"But you won't make a great father?"

"No." His voice was flat and final. "I don't know a thing about raising kids."

"You know a lot about raising kids. You know exactly what not to do."

"That's not the same as knowing how to do it right."

The ache was throbbing and growing inside her, and suddenly all she wanted was to be alone. She didn't want to face Michael, to let him see the pain of loss in her eyes. She didn't want anyone to see her, not when she was so naked with grief and despair.

She stumbled as she turned around, and Michael caught her elbow to steady her. Wrenching away from him, she tried to hurry off.

"Ellie, wait."

She turned slowly to face him. He spread his hands in a helpless gesture. "How about if I give you a call when I get back to Midland? We'll get together and see how it goes."

She studied his face and felt ice harden around her heart. She saw his request with perfect clarity. He was trying to put some distance between them while he regained his emotional balance. When he'd recovered enough to be certain he could keep her at a distance, he'd call her.

Slowly she shook her head. "No, Michael. You can't call me. I'm not going to sit and wait for you to make up your mind. I let my mother take my life away from me for over twenty years, and I'm not going to let anyone else do it." She drew in a deep, shaking breath. "Good luck with your case against the Midland cops. But I know you won't need it. You're a good detective."

She didn't want to look away. It was the last sight of Michael she'd have, and she wanted to drink it in. Because she was studying him so carefully, she saw the first tiny flare of panic in his eyes.

"You're leaving me?"

She swallowed the taste of pain and regret. "No, you're leaving me, Michael."   •

"I said I'd call you. You're the one who's walking away."

She shook her head. Then she drew in another deep breath. If she meant what she said about changing her life, about taking chances and taking risks, now was the time to begin.

"I love you, Michael. I would do almost anything for you. But I won't let you wander in and out of my life whenever you like. I deserve better than that. If you want to see me again, you have to choose. Love me like I love you. Commit to making a life with me, to sharing children with me. And if you can't do that, turn around and walk away."

She waited endless moments, watched fear and need war with each other on his face. His eyes were haunted as he said, "Ellie, I'm all wrong for you."

"I think you're exactly right for me. But if you don't see that, then I guess we don't belong together."

He didn't answer, and despair engulfed her. Turning again, she began walking blindly down the street. She had taken a chance, risked rejection, and she had lost.

"Ellie, wait."

She stopped, hope struggling to raise its head as she heard the desperation in his voice. He hurried after her, but stopped just out of reach. Swiveling her head, she saw the fear on his face, but there was resolve there also. She held her breath.

"Ellie, I—I…"

She waited, forcing herself not to go to him.

He shut his eyes and said in a rush, "I love you, Ellie." He opened them again and took a step closer, but still didn't touch her. "I think I fell in love with you when you ran away from me in the warehouse and fell into that hole." He drew in a deep, trembling breath.

"But I'm not good enough for you," he continued. "You deserve someone who can give you everything you need. And that's not me. I'm no good at this emotional stuff. I'll never be able to tell you how I feel, to do all that touchy-feely crap."

A laugh tore through her pain, scattering it to the winds. "You're exactly who I need, Michael. We fit together perfectly. And I don't just mean in bed. I can't imagine spending my life with anyone else but you." She reached out and touched his face. "You're my mate, Michael," she whispered. "The one person in the world who was created for me."

She drew her hand back. She needed to touch him too badly, needed to feel his arms around her too much. And she needed to get the words out. "You said you didn't know how to tell me how you feel, but you just did." A small grin curved her mouth. "And as for that touchy-feely stuff, I've never been too good at it, either. We can learn together."

"Ellie," he whispered, and finally reached out and swept her into his arms. He buried his face in her neck and she felt moisture on her skin. "You'd better be very sure that this is what you want. Because I'll never let you go. You're everything I thought I could never have. And everything I've ever dreamed about.''

He lifted his head and all the shadows were gone from his eyes. She saw only love shining there, hot and pure. ''When will you marry me, Ellie?''

''Don't you think you should ask *if* I'll marry you first?'' Her heart was ready to explode with happiness.

His arms tightened around her. ''Hey, it's okay with me if you just want to live in sin. But our kids might be embarrassed.''

He bent his head to kiss her. The fear and stress of the last few days, the despair she'd been feeling just moments ago, all fell away. Nothing existed but Michael, kissing her with all the passion and love she'd known was hiding inside him. Nothing mattered but the miracle of loving him, a miracle brought to life from the ugliness of the last few days.

Finally he lifted his head and looked down at her, all the shadows gone from his eyes, replaced by the promise of a bright future. ''I guess you knew what you were talking about all along, Ms. Librarian.'' He nuzzled her neck, then grinned down at her. ''Maybe I should start reading those books of yours. It looks like I believe in happy endings, after all.''

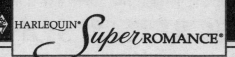

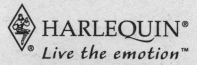

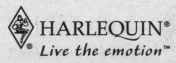

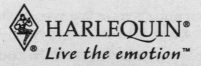

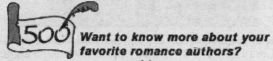

If you enjoyed what you just read,
then we've got an offer you can't resist!

Take 2 bestselling love stories FREE!

Plus get a FREE surprise gift!

Clip this page and mail it to Harlequin Reader Service®

IN U.S.A.	IN CANADA
3010 Walden Ave.	P.O. Box 609
P.O. Box 1867	Fort Erie, Ontario
Buffalo, N.Y. 14240-1867	L2A 5X3

YES! Please send me 2 free Harlequin Superromance® novels and my free surprise gift. After receiving them, if I don't wish to receive anymore, I can return the shipping statement marked cancel. If I don't cancel, I will receive 6 brand-new novels every month, before they're available in stores. In the U.S.A., bill me at the bargain price of $4.47 plus 25¢ shipping and handling per book and applicable sales tax, if any*. In Canada, bill me at the bargain price of $4.99 plus 25¢ shipping and handling per book and applicable taxes**. That's the complete price, and a savings of at least 10% off the cover prices—what a great deal! I understand that accepting the 2 free books and gift places me under no obligation ever to buy any books. I can always return a shipment and cancel at any time. Even if I never buy another book from Harlequin, the 2 free books and gift are mine to keep forever.

135 HDN DNT3
336 HDN DNT4

Name	(PLEASE PRINT)	
Address	Apt.#	
City	State/Prov.	Zip/Postal Code

* Terms and prices subject to change without notice. Sales tax applicable in N.Y.
** Canadian residents will be charged applicable provincial taxes and GST.
   All orders subject to approval. Offer limited to one per household and not valid to
   current Harlequin Superromance® subscribers.
® is a registered trademark of Harlequin Enterprises Limited.

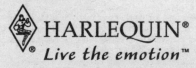